Coyote Cowgirl

Coyote Cowgirl

Kim Antieau

A Tom Doherty Associates Book
New York

COYOTE COWGIRL

Copyright © 2003 by Kim Antieau

This book is printed on acid-free paper.

Book design by Michael Collica

A Forge Book
Published by Tom Doherty Associates, LLC
175 Fifth Avenue
New York, NY 10010

www.tor.com

Forge® is a registered trademark of Tom Doherty Associates, LLC.

Library of Congress Cataloging-in-Publication Data

Antieau, Kim.
    Coyote cowgirl / Kim Antieau.—1st ed.
        p. cm.
    "A Tom Doherty Associates book."
    ISBN: 0-765-30267-5
    1. Women detectives—West (U.S.)—Fiction. 2. Restaurateurs—Fiction.
3. Art thefts—Fiction. I. Title.

PS3551.N745C69 2003
813'.54—dc21

                                                            2002045497

First Edition: June 2003

Printed in the United States of America

0 9 8 7 6 5 4 3 2 1

For my parents,
Lloyd and Mary Antieau,
with love,

and

For *Coyote Cowgirl*'s midwives,
Charles de Lint and MaryAnn Harris.
You are incarnations of ineffable *cariño*.
À *mes chers amis, merci de tout mon coeur.*

Acknowledgments

Thanks to Irene Gallo, Patrick Nielsen Hayden, and everyone at Tor/Forge who worked on *Coyote Cowgirl*. *Merci*, Nancy Milosevic (*et amies*), for help with Crane's language of love—French (although any liberties taken are my own). Thanks also to Agica Milosevic, for your loving support throughout the years, and to Lloyd Antieau, Pam Chillemi-Yeager, Jeanne Hardy, Mario Milosevic, and Charles de Lint, for being the first to read and cheer on *Coyote Cowgirl*. *Gracias*, Patricia T. Pearlman, priestess at the real Goddess Temple in Cactus Springs, Nevada, and Genevieve Vaughan, who built the Temple in honor of Sekhmet as a place of refuge and reflection for peace activists and others who respect and honor the Earth. Thanks to the board and staff of the Fort Vancouver Regional Library and the boards and staffs of public libraries throughout the country who courageously defend the Bill of Rights and protect our intellectual freedoms daily. Thank you to Gary Kelley, for the gorgeous cover art. Many thanks and much gratitude to Charles de Lint and MaryAnn Harris for their determination and efforts in getting *Coyote Cowgirl* out into the world. You always kept the faith, Charles. Love to my other coyote cowboy, Mario. Thanks for the dance, sweetheart. May the members of the Coyote Clan always find wild places in this world to call home.

Coyote Cowgirl

One

El Día de los Muertos

The skull did not speak to me right away.

As I remember it, the evening started out like any other Day of the Dead celebration. The open-air courtyard was filled with our relatives and esteemed customers of the Oui & Sí, Scottsdale's famous French and Mexican restaurant, owned and run by my parents, Jacques and Alita Les Flambeaux, beloved by all who knew them.

Food abounded, all prepared by my parents, my brother, Antoine, and sister, Belinda. Tables and plates overflowed with glazed salmon steaks and green mayonnaise, scallops and mushrooms in wine sauce, tarragon chicken, cheese-stuffed chiles, enchiladas with green sauce, Mexican rice, green rice, tortilla soup, all kinds of breads and appetizers, and endless rounds of margaritas and French wines.

Golden light from table candles and an occasional torch made the courtyard look otherworldly. I stood with one foot on the ground and one on the tile floor, which was part of the corridor leading back to the indoor section of the restaurant and the kitchen. I leaned against a pillar and watched my father and mother at the head table looking as though they were bride and groom at their wedding, robust and rotund, with the crystal skull on its ruby scepter between them.

If it weren't for my grandmother, Nana, who now sat next to my father at the head table, I would have grown up believing I was a changeling in this family of the big and Amazonian. She and I were the only small ones, except for Cousin Michael, who did not attend this year, forcing me to don the ceremonial dead-skeletal-ancestor costume which was all black except for the glow-in-the-dark green bones. No one had wanted to ask me to do it, because no one wanted to draw attention to my skinny body or to the fact that no one had seen me eat in the almost twenty years that had elapsed since the skull had last spoken to me. I had been five or six when it happened, and my parents feared I was a few acorns short of a real tree, like my mother's mother, Winema, whose name was rarely invoked.

"You're all skin and bones," Antoine said, startling me as he grabbed me from behind.

"You scared me," I said.

"Girl, you are always a WIJ." He was dressed as a French aristocrat.

"A witch?"

"A WIJ. Woman in jeopardy."

I rolled my eyes. "You're going to be a brother in jeopardy if you don't get away from me."

He grinned. "Don't screw up. Dad will kill you." He leaned closer. "And if the skull talks to you, Jeanne d'Arc," he whispered, "just pretend you didn't hear a thing." He laughed and strode away.

Too cute to kill, I thought, too close a relation to screw.

My father rose from the table and slowly made his way over to my hiding spot, stopping to whisper to this or that lady or clasp this or that hand. I wanted to slink away before he got to me. Instead, I grabbed a glass of wine from a passing waiter, gulped it down, and then set the glass on the bus cart behind me.

"Hello, Father," I said when he reached me.

"Hello, Jeanne," he said. His size often surprised and intimidated me. Although he was not particularly tall, he was big. He could easily crush me under his thumb. Not that he had ever struck me. Ever.

"It's a nice party, Dad. I'm sure everyone is having a great time."

He nodded as he looked around the courtyard. "Twice a year, once for the dead and once for the living. I do enjoy these gatherings. Perhaps I am not as French as I would like to believe!"

"You do like wine, Poppa," I reminded him.

"Ah yes. Water is for fish to piss in. Now, you understand that you'll come into the courtyard as a representative of our ancestors, taking the skull back to the otherworld."

"Yes, Dad." I had only witnessed this ceremonial rite every year for the past twenty years. The skull and ruby scepter were my parents' most prized possessions. Everything they had ever achieved had been done with the help of the skull and scepter, or so my father often reminded us. The rubies on the scepter were nearly priceless, and the skull was not exactly a trinket. My father allowed the skull and scepter out of their specially made safe twice a year.

"I want them put directly into the safe after your performance," he said. "The rest of us are going back to the house since Momma and I are leaving for vacation tomorrow. *D'accord?*"

"*Sí,* Poppa. I'll make certain they go right into the safe. You can count on me."

"Your cousin Johnny is here," he said.

"Oh?" I tried to hide my delight.

"Don't let him near the skull. Or you. He's not one of us,

you know. He's gotten himself in quite a lot of trouble. Your uncle James is always bailing him out of jail."

"Don't worry, Dad."

He squeezed my arm. "You know, Jeanne, you take things so seriously. You really should go out and have some fun." He nodded, turned, and walked away.

I sighed, glad he was gone. He meant well, but I knew he was worried I was going to freak out and start hearing voices or something. I was the baby of the family: the one without any innate ability, the one who had not excelled in college, the one who had no avocation or vocation. I could not even cook.

I felt hands on my hipbones and heard whispered breath in my hair. "I've always wanted to fuck skin and bones."

"Johnny." I turned to Cousin Johnny, his long blond hair nearly white in the semidarkness. He pulled me completely into the darkness.

I heard my father begin to address his guests. "This is a fiesta of my wife's ancestors," he said. "My ancestors, the French, don't party much. We merely eat, drink, and make love!" The crowd applauded appreciatively. Johnny kissed my breasts through my costume.

"Someone will see," I whispered. He stuck his tongue in my mouth while my father said, "On this day when the veil between the worlds is the thinnest, I thank all those who have gone before us." I heard my father pick up the scepter with the skull on the end of it. "As you all know, this skull was made perhaps thousands of years ago by the Maya or Aztecs— we don't really know. My great-great-great-grandfather was a chef for one of the missions in South America. They were so grateful for the healing work he did, via his culinary skills, that they gifted him with the skull. The scepter has been in my wife's family for generations, too. When we met, we discovered the skull and scepter fit together like two pieces of a puzzle, joining our two families as they were always meant to be joined. I thank all those who went before us. Thank you for our lives. *Viva les ancêtres!*"

That was my cue. I pushed Johnny away and slipped the hood over my head.

Now I was one of the undead.

The music began, a kind of guitar dirge. I knew the musicians were near, but I did not see them. I could barely see anything as I stepped off the tile and onto the ground. I felt momentarily disoriented. Dizzy. Then people began clapping steadily, along with the music. I was not a performer, I did not want to do this, but something about being totally covered and almost anonymous—except for the fact that everyone knew me—helped me loosen up. I crouched a little, trying in my own stiff way to be theatrical. I watched my parents' faces as they smiled and clapped for me, their befuddled living descendant impersonating their revered dead ancestors.

And then I saw the skull, now reclining, like a gleaming crystal half-person with a jeweled spine.

"Back to the other world we go!" I croaked my line.

So far the skull hadn't uttered a word.

I grabbed the scepter and lifted both. I had to touch the skull. That was part of it. It had to be broken from the scepter. So I tucked the scepter under my arm and against my body and popped off the skull, then held it aloft for everyone to see.

The crowd roared.

Really, it did.

Jubilant, I raced away, silent skull and scepter in hand.

I ducked under the overhang and ran down the corridor, into the huge kitchen full of shiny stainless steel, and up the stairs to the apartment. I ran to the office and set the scepter and skull inside the open safe.

"Hello, cousin."

I turned around. Johnny.

"Hello, cousin," I answered, out of breath. Johnny grinned and closed the office door. He wasn't really my cousin. His mother had married my uncle James five years ago. Since then, Johnny and I had ruffled the sheets together on more than a few occasions.

I peeled off my skeleton.

"Sorry, no more skin and bones," I said.

"No, but a lot more skin," he said.

Then we did it on the couch.

I tripped the light fantastic. Johnny-be-good for *moi*.

Later, we made love on my bed and talked over old times.

"It wasn't even a felony," he told me. "All charges were dropped. Just a little dispute over a gambling debt."

He smelled of cheap cologne and my sweat.

The open window brought in a fragrant breeze and no more sounds of a party breaking up.

"Do you owe money again, Johnny?"

"He cheated. The dice were loaded."

I laughed. "You're so full of shit," I said. "You and I are the losers of the family."

He snorted. "In your family being a loser means you haven't lived up to your royal name or you've burnt the crêpes suzette or something. In my family being a loser means doing a dime in the big house."

I laughed. "What big house? The one your mother got my uncle to buy for her in Tucson?"

He grinned. "I never could get any shit past you. Got any money?"

I shook my head. "Just my good looks."

"That's enough for me."

We fell asleep singing, "My Bonnie Lies over the Ocean."

In the morning when I got up, Johnny was gone. He left a Post-it on the television. The note read, "Love, J." I switched on the television.

I took a shower. Got dressed.

Went to the office. Glanced at the safe.

I had forgotten to close it last night.

I blamed Johnny's wandering hands.

I walked to the safe and started to swing the door shut.

And noticed the scepter was not next to the skull.

I leaned my head inside, moving the skull back and forth in the tiny enclosure.

The scepter was disappeared.

I tossed the room, like a real pro.

Did not find it.

Went back to the open safe door.

Only the skull inside.

All my hopes were dashed. No, they had flown the coop, too.

"Well, now you've really done it," the skull finally said.

I slowly sank down onto the couch.

I could only concur.

The television droned on in the background. ". . . other news, police report that the latest disappearance, this time of a Tucson woman, has positively been linked to the other so-called WIJ disappearances. The initials were left in lipstick on the bathroom mirror. If you have seen this woman, police—"

Voices downstairs.

Johnny? He'd decided he did not have the heart to steal from me after all?

Footsteps on the stairs.

"Jeanne!" Belinda.

"Jeanne d'Arc!" Antoine.

"*Ma fille!*" Dad.

I jumped up and slapped the safe door shut.

"Wait!" the skull shouted as the safe door closed. "I can help you find the scepter." The door slammed shut.

"Too much TV watching is going to drive you crazy!" my father called from the other room.

"Already been driven there. Have parked the car and lost the keys," I mumbled as I hurried into the living room where my family awaited.

"Good morning, sweetheart." My mother opened her arms, and we embraced. When I pulled away, she smiled at me and was not in her eyes. Had I ever really seen her?

"Momma?" I asked.

"Yes, sweetheart? Have you eaten? We're on our way to the airport, then off to see your cousin Lavinie, and on to Hawaii. I wish you'd come. Even as far as Lavinie's. She would love to see you, and you love San Francisco."

I smiled. How did she know if Lavinie would be glad to see me or if I loved San Francisco? I didn't even know these things.

"Pop really came to see if the family jewels were safe." Antoine sat on the couch and put his feet up on the coffee table. My mother gently tapped his shoes, and he dropped his feet to the floor again.

"If he's worried about family jewels," Belinda said, "he should look no further than your trousers—eh, brother? Or have they been damaged from overuse?"

"Don't be vulgar," my mother said.

My father put his arm across my shoulder. "I want you to take it easy, Jeanne. The restaurant is closed for two weeks, sugar. Use one of our cars if you like. Visit friends."

"But, Dad," Belinda said, adjusting the collar of her yellow silk blouse, "how can we manage without Jeanne?"

My mother gave Belinda a look.

My father dropped his arm from my shoulders and walked out of the room, toward the office. I bit my thumb.

Please don't open the safe, please don't open the safe.

"Antoine's going on a road trip," Belinda said. "Mom and Dad are going to Hawaii. And now you're suggesting little Jeanne leave home. Gee, I'll be left out in the cold again."

"Belinda, you live in the desert," Antoine said. "It's never cold. Come on, evil, wicked sister." He stood. "We must leave Cinderella to the ashes whilst we plan more chores for her." He rolled his eyes at me and took Belinda by the elbow.

Please don't open the safe. I will never be trusted again if you do. I will be banned from la familia *forever.*

"Ta!" Antoine called, winking at me and waving to my mother.

"Jacques, come on, darling," my mother called. "We are finished with business." My mother's hand pressed down on her black hair, which was pulled back and tied with a pretty red bow that matched her lipstick. She looked like the Spanish princess my father said she was.

She turned to me and smiled. "Don't bite your fingers, darling. It is not very becoming."

Becoming?

What am I becoming? Too young to die, too old to be new at anything.

"Here I am," my father said, coming into the room and smiling at us.

He had not discovered his loss.

"We'll see you in a couple of weeks," my father said, kissing my cheek. "You did good last night."

"Don't worry so much," my mother said. "You'll find your place in the world."

"She has her place, Alita," my father said, taking my

mother's hand and turning her toward the stairs. "She has a place in this family."

"Bon voyage," I called, knowing my father was always impressed by my French, no matter how meager it was in comparison with my siblings, who spoke nearly flawless French, Spanish, and English.

As soon as I heard the downstairs door shut, I pounced on the telephone and called our house.

Uncle James answered.

"Hello, Uncle James. Do you know where Johnny is?"

"No, I don't. I guess he was out all night with friends. You know Johnny."

"Yeah, I know Johnny," I said.

"I'm supposed to pick him up at the restaurant at noon. He's hitching a ride with me back to Tucson. At least that was the plan last time I spoke to him."

"Which was when?"

"At the party last night."

"Noon?" I glanced at the VCR clock. Two hours. Could I wait that long to see if life as I knew it was over? "OK. Thanks, Uncle James. I'll see you in two hours. Bye."

I dropped the phone on the couch, then hurried downstairs. I looked around the empty kitchen in case Johnny had "accidentally" left the scepter behind. Then the dining area. Finally into the courtyard.

I usually enjoyed the restaurant when it was closed. Something about being in a place where so much had been going on and now wasn't was magical. Or something. It vibrated with what had been and would be. Today I felt no magic.

I sighed and walked along the open corridor, near where I had stood during most of the previous evening. Antoine called it the Corridor of Fame: on the wall hung several portraits of my ancestors. First was Jean Les Flambeaux, our great-great-great-grandfather, whose right hand rested on the crystal skull. Next to him, Princess Anna Franceso who held the scepter in both hands. Then Great-grandfather Antoine, his fingers curled around a platter of dead duck *à l'orange.* Great-grandmother Maria Anna Marquez, dressed to the nines squared, leaning on the scepter, its stones spraying bejeweled light back at the spectator, which was me at the moment. Then Alita and Jacques Les Flambeaux, my parentals, holding the two puzzled pieces—the skull and scepter—between them.

The final portrait was a photograph of our family taken ten years earlier when I was fifteen, me standing next to Nana, surrounded by the rest of the family, all of them grinning and comfortable in the world. My father's right hand gripped the skull and scepter. When my parents opened the restaurant twenty years ago, they had almost called it Skull and Scepter, but Nana said, "I say it in Spanish, *no,* and in French, *non!*" and my father said, "I say *oui* and *sí!*" And the name stuck.

I turned from my family portraits and stepped out into the courtyard sunshine. I had to find the scepter.

It was no secret that I was the idiot savant in the family— if you dropped the *savant* part. OK. I wasn't stupid, but I was not gifted. I could not remember a moment of "Ah-ha, I am not like the rest of the family." Except maybe for the incident with the skull. I still remembered that day. My mother had dressed me in white tights and a tutu, given me a wand, and—voilà—I was a fairy, *une fée, una hada.* It was the Day of the Dead, and *mon père* wanted a photograph with me holding the skull. When they left me alone for a moment with the crystal skull, he—and it was a male voice—said, "Turn me to the left, please. My right profile is my best side."

It puzzled me that in my memory, I was not surprised. All seemed ordinary, and I did as the skull requested.

My parents returned, and my father said, "Face me, Jeanne. The skull, too."

"But he says this is his good side."

"The skull spoke to you, darling?" my mother asked, bending at the waist to lean down to me.

"Yes, Momma," I replied.

She straightened and looked at my father. "Perhaps she has an imaginary playmate," my mother suggested.

"No," I corrected, "the skull talks to me."

"Just like *mi madre,*" my mother said, putting her fist in her mouth. She ran out of the room, crying. "I'm calling the doctor."

For once, my father said nothing. He glanced at me, then went after my mother.

I looked at the skull. "Why is she so upset that I might be like Grandma Winema?" I asked.

"They believe she had a few screws loose, not that I'm one to talk. I haven't any screws at all."

I could hear my mother sobbing in the other room. My father returned, his face flushed, and took the skull from my tiny hands.

"Go to your room, honey," he said.

As I hurried away, I heard the skull say, "No imagination."

After medical tests revealed nothing was wrong with me, Nana suggested they leave me alone. My father had the safe built, and I gladly stayed out of earshot of the talking crystal skull.

Until last night.

Now I stepped out of the sunlight and sat in a chair at the base of the statue of Saint Brigid. From her feet, a concrete spring sprang. I lay my cheek against it.

"Hello, *petite-fille,*" my grandmother said.

"Hello, Nana," I said, sitting up as my grandmother walked out of the restaurant proper. I had not heard her come in; I was going to have to be more observant, I thought, especially if some psycho was running around abducting women.

I stood and kissed my grandmother. Then I followed her back into the cool, gleaming kitchen.

"Have you eaten?" she asked.

I shrugged. "I'm not hungry."

She retrieved a broom from the long cabinet in the corner. "You worry too much," she said.

"So I've heard," I said.

She shook her head. "You've always taken everything so seriously, *nieta*. All is not always what it seems."

"I know," I said. "But I am tired of being the family screwup."

"You have done nothing terrible."

I remembered Johnny's remark about burning crêpes suzette.

"You are a good girl," my grandmother said. "Listen to your bones, and all will be well."

"My bones? Nana, aren't grandmothers supposed to tell granddaughters to listen to their hearts?"

Nana raised her eyebrows. "I've seen the boys you like. I think your bones would have more sense."

I smiled. What could I say? Gee, you're wrong, Nana; it's only my latest who has stolen the family jewels.

"Now, go. I must sweep away any spirits left over from last night. I don't want to accidentally sweep you away."

I left Nana to her broom and incantations and went outdoors. I walked to the Civic Center Mall—or The Park as we called it—a short distance from the restaurant. I wandered aimlessly, stopping to stare at the giant feather and inkwell in front of the library, trying to imagine as I always did what kind of bird that feather could have come from and what kind of writer could tell a big enough story to soak up all that ink. Would it be the autobiography of a really *big* person? Or a tall tale?

I giggled. I was getting slaphappy.

Nana said feathers awakened us to messages from the ancestors: this was why she would not allow us to sleep on feather pillows. "Too many messages, too much wakefulness."

I stared at the giant feather one last time.

I was awakened. What was the message?

I walked back to the Oui & Sí. Nana still mumbled and swept. It was 11:45 A.M.

At noon, Uncle James drove up. He came inside for a cup of coffee with Nana. I paced outside in front of the restaurant.

Johnny did not show.

Nana made the three of us lunch from Day of the Dead leftovers. Uncle James sat at the island, noisily sucking down enchiladas, while I moved my food from one side of the plate to the other. When he finished, he kissed Nana good-bye.

I walked him to his car. "What about Johnny?"

He shrugged. "He must have decided to go to Las Vegas. He said he might go there and look for work, thought maybe Cousin Miller could find him something. Don't worry about Johnny. He can get into and out of trouble all by himself."

Uncle James gave me a hug, got in his car, and drove away.

Nana came outside, carrying her purse and sunglasses. "I've got errands to run, sugar. You want to come?"

I shook my head. She gave me a bear hug.

"Eat something," she advised as she released me. She lightly slapped my face, then walked to her car.

I hurried inside and went up to my room. I pulled my suitcase from the closet and quickly filled it with clothes. I grabbed my purse and keys, then went into the office to get my paycheck. Tomorrow was payday, and my father had left the checks neatly lined up in alphabetical order in his top left-hand drawer for Belinda to distribute. I reached for my check and then started to leave.

I heard muffled screams.

Coming from the safe.

"Shut up," I said, and began to leave again.

The screaming continued.

Disgusted, I went to the safe and flung open the door, which was not locked since I hadn't spun the dial.

"What?" I said.

"Take me with," the skull said.

"Not on your life," I said.

"No pun intended?" the skull asked. "I can help you find the scepter. We have been living together for decades. I'm attuned to its vibrations."

"Last time you talked to me, I almost ended up in a funny farm. To this day, my brother calls me Jeanne d'Arc because she heard voices, too."

"Yes, I remember her well. You know, if she had only listened to me, she might never have—"

"If you were so concerned about the scepter, why didn't you scream when Johnny was in the process of stealing it?"

"I thought he would take me, too. My life—such as it is— is rather dull. Johnny seems the adventurous sort. At least you two seemed to be having a wonderful romp—"

"I'm leaving."

"But I can help! Please take me out of this den of safety."

I stared at the clear stone visage of the skull. I was either absolutely insane.

Or I wasn't.

I grabbed the skull and stuffed it into my suitcase. Ignoring its muffled cries, I walked down the stairs, locked the apartment, went out through the restaurant, and locked its doors. I threw the suitcase in the backseat and drove away from the Oui & Sí. As I traveled down Scottsdale Road on my way to the expressway, the skull's cries grew louder and louder.

Finally, I pulled into a gas station parking lot, reached back, and unzipped the suitcase.

"What!" I cried.

The skull lay on top of my apricot-colored camisole.

"You'll barely make the city limits in this old junk heap. Your father said you could use his car."

"You heard that?"

"I have excellent hearing. One of my many attributes. Now, about the car?"

The piece of crystalline had a point. I got back on Scottsdale, then drove to Pima Road and out to our house, a short distance from town. We had moved away from the restaurant and into this house when I was about ten, and it had seemed way out in the desert then. Urban sprawl had extended so far that soon our desert house would become a city dwelling. Today, three cars stood in our circle drive. I zipped up the suitcase again, got out of my car, and went to the black sedan, a kind of company car not really belonging to any one person. I put the suitcase in the backseat, then went into the house.

"Hello?"

No one home. I breathed deeply. I wished I didn't have to go after Johnny. I would love to stay right here in this empty house. I could swim naked in the pool, eat anytime and anything (or nothing) without worrying about anyone watching or commenting on my movements.

I walked back to the kitchen. It smelled of cinnamon today. The wooden cupboards and ceramic tile countertops made the room feel warm and cozy, cool and comfortable. Except I was rarely comfortable in a kitchen, despite the fact that I had spent a good deal of my life in one or another.

I took the sedan keys from their hook near the kitchen door. Below the hooks, the light was flashing on the answering machine on my mother's desk. I pressed the PLAY button.

"Jeanne, sorry. I was in trouble. I hope your dad didn't get too mad at you. Um. See you around. This is Johnny."

I screamed. He had known I wouldn't call the police. "I'll find you, Johnny."

I erased the message, then wrote out one of my own on my mother's notepad: "I'll be gone a few days. Don't worry. Love, Jeanne."

I left my parents' house, got into the car, and drove away. I had never driven by myself farther than Tucson. I flipped a switch and locked all the doors. Too bad I didn't have tinted windows. Now everyone could see I was a woman alone. A woman in jeopardy, like my brother said. I hoped I didn't run across the WIJ psycho. Maybe if people saw the skull, they would think I was a psychopath and leave me alone. Weirdness was the best defense.

I pulled the car to the side of the road, opened the suitcase, and took out the skull.

"Don't be obnoxious or I'm putting you right back," I said as I set the skull, face forward, on the flat part of the dash.

I pulled the car back on the road and headed for 17.

"And away we go!" the skull said.

Life, as I had known it, was never going to be the same.

Two

Sur la Route de Las Vegas

The skull did not say much until we were past Flagstaff, driving west on 40.

"Let's stop at the Grand Canyon," the skull said. "I am sensing the scepter's vibrations."

"I don't believe you."

"You believe everyone else. Why not *moi?*"

"Because you're just a piece of rock."

"Who has the wisdom of the ages within."

"Uh-huh," I said. "If you start lying to me, I'm going to toss you out on your crystalline butt."

"No, you won't."

"I will put you in the trunk."

The skull said nothing.

I turned on the radio. The skull hummed to the tunes. I pushed the buttons until I found news.

". . . flash flood warnings are up for central Mohave and Yavapai Counties. This unusual weather system is moving . . ."

"Flash floods? It's November." The sky was clear, but we were heading toward clouds.

"I remember the flash flood of—what would the year have been in your calendar, 1202? Nearly took out half the Mexican interior . . . or was that earlier on the coast? Oh, the brain cells are fast fading."

"Hush. I'm listening to the news."

"It'll rot your brain, and you'll end up like me."

". . . the Yuma City native has been missing since Sunday. As in the other disappearances, the initials 'WIJ' were discovered, this time on a notepad by the phone. Although authorities speculate WIJ may be the killer or kidnapper's initials, others have wondered if he—or she—is in the movie business. Hollywood insiders tell Channel 2 News that *WIJ* is movie business parlance for 'women in jeopardy' films."

"I could have told them that," I said. Because Antoine had told me.

As we—and I use the term *we* loosely—got closer to Kingman, black clouds covered the sky. Dusk became full-blown night. A torrential downpour began, the rain coming down in sheets, preventing me from seeing even a few feet in front of me. As I glanced off to the side, everything appeared silver. Concerned that flooding had already begun, I did not pull off the road, and instead slowed the car and hoped no one would rear-end me.

"I hate this, hate this, hate this," I murmured.

"That's just your attitude," the skull said. "Look at me. I'm still smiling."

"That's because you have no face."

"But does that keep me from being cheerful? I think not."

"If you don't shut up, I'm going to have an accident, be killed, and you will end up in a million pieces!"

"*Au contraire, moi* dear, it would take more than a simple car accident to—"

"Shut up!"

"I always thought you were the sweet one in the family,

docile and polite. How wrong I have been. Good. I like a little fire. Oh, *ma petite,* look at that. I've made a pun. You're little and you're a Flambeaux: a little fire! How clever—"

I picked up the skull and tossed it into the backseat, then turned up the radio; between it and the rain, I could not hear a thing—not even a skull thing.

Somehow I saw the Kingman exit sign and slowly got off the expressway, following the blurry red taillights of the semitruck ahead of me. I stayed behind it as it turned in to the truck stop. The world was silver and black. I stopped under the brightly lit overhang near the gasoline pumps. The parking lot was filled with semitrucks, campers, and a few cars. I glanced at my gas gauge: half full. I opened my purse and took out my wallet. Inside was a twenty-dollar bill and my paycheck.

"Shoot." I had forgotten to cash my check. I sighed. I had a credit card with a minuscule credit line: I used it only in emergencies. The gasoline could wait. I pulled the car up into the restaurant parking places along the front of the building. I turned around in my seat and looked for the skull. It was upside down with its nonexistent nose in the seat crack. I leaned over and turned it around.

"That was uncalled for," the skull said, "after all I've done for your family."

"I'm sorry. I'm just under a lot of pressure. I'm not usually this rude. And crystal skulls aren't usually talking to me and getting their feelings hurt. I didn't even know skulls had feelings. I'm babbling."

"Yes."

"I'm going inside," I said. "Scream if anyone tries to steal the car."

"Oui, oui, ma chère."

I got out, locked the car, and ran to the restaurant door, where a life-size skeleton plastered against the glass waved to me. I went inside. Everyone stopped to look at me. I shook the rain off myself and my purse. The fluorescent lights shaded the faces of the truckers and waitress into that funeral-parlor glare. As soon as I sat on a gold stool at the counter, the waitress handed me a menu. I glanced at it: standard greasy food fare. My family would be appalled. I tried to find the least offensive item on the menu, finally asking for one of those little boxes of raisin bran and a cup of tea. After the waitress brought it, I dipped my spoon into the cereal and froze. I glanced around. No one watched. What was wrong with me? I had eaten in front of people before—just not my own family. These people were definitely not family.

I forced myself to eat the too-sweet cereal, glancing around once or twice, careful not to catch anyone's eye. Apparently I was one of the few women on the road tonight, unless they were all in the rest room. I was going to kill Johnny. I did not want to be out alone in the dark driving through a monsoon. For all I knew, this place could be filled with stalkers, psychos, rapists, and murderers.

A woman's fears were never done. Or overdone.

I paid my bill and went back outside. The rain had not let up, and the parking lot was flooded. I quickly got in the car and locked it. A man stepped out of the restaurant, his features blurring with the rain; with his shoulders hunched, he lumbered away toward the semitrucks, lurching back and forth like an extra on the movie set *Night of the Living Dead.*

I picked up the skull and put it on the dash.

Another trucker stumbled out of the restaurant.

"Oooooweeee! I like this place!" the skull cried.

"I guess being locked up in a safe for the past twenty years makes anywhere look swell," I said. "It gives me the creeps, as if any second some maniac is going to pop up and say boo."

"*Boo!*" the skull screamed.

I screamed.

Someone rapped on the window.

I screamed again and tried to start the car.

Another rap.

"Miss?"

I turned. A police officer stood melting in the rain next to my car.

I quickly opened the widow.

"Yes?" I asked.

"We're experiencing some flooding," she said. "Which way you headed?"

"Up 93 to Las Vegas."

She nodded. "For safety's sake, just wait a little while longer. North is pretty clear. Drive carefully." She touched her hat and turned away.

I rolled up the window.

"I'm going to call home," I said. "I'll be right back."

I sighed. I was talking to glass.

I jumped into the rain and ran to the outside phone under the restaurant overhang. A moldy jack-o'-lantern grinned at me from its perch on top of the phone. I picked up the receiver. No dial tone. I dropped the receiver and went into the restaurant. The waitress nodded to me.

"The phone outdoors is—"

"There's one by the little girl's room." She pointed to the other side of the restaurant.

"Thanks."

I hurried back to the rest rooms. The truckers were quiet, staring into their coffee cups. In an alcove between the men's and women's rest rooms was the phone. I took a piece of paper with my parents' calling card number from a hidden pocket in my wallet and phoned home. The machine answered. I checked messages in case Johnny had called again. He hadn't. I hung up. On impulse, I phoned Lavinie.

"Sing to me," Lavinie answered.

"Hiya, Vinnie," I said, trying to keep my voice low.

"Jeanne?"

"Did my mom and dad get there all right?"

"Sure. Why? Were you worried? They're down in the shop, making fun of my herbs and things. Do you want me to call them?"

"No. I just—" What did I want? I was feeling scared and lonely so I called my mom and dad? "Has anyone called from home?"

"No. Johnny Jackson called and left a message on the machine that he needed to talk to your dad. He didn't leave a number."

"Talk to Dad. Why?"

"Maybe he needs bail money."

Or he couldn't hock the scepter and he's holding it for ransom and asking my father for money.

"That sonofacarp. Do me a favor. If he calls again, don't let him talk to Mom or Dad."

Lavinie was silent for a moment, then said, "OK. Are you all right?"

"I'll let you know. Give my love to my units. I missed you last night. The Day of the Dead isn't the same without you."

She laughed. "Why don't you come for a visit?"

"Maybe later. Love you. Bye."

I hung up and turned around. The restaurant looked normal again. Just a dark rainy night a couple of days after Halloween at a truck stop in northwest Arizona. I was a gal on my way to Las Vegas. To castrate a thieving, lying ex-ex-ex-lover. I hurried to the entrance and nodded to the waitress.

"*Joyeuses fêtes des sorcières et des fantômes,*" she said to my back.

I stopped. She had said "happy Halloween" in French.

I turned around. "Pardon me?"

"I said drive carefully, sugar." She smiled, and coffeepot in hand, she walked away.

Now I was hearing things from live people. Bad enough dead people were talking to me, now live people were speaking in French.

What the hell was going on?

I went outside. The parking lot was no longer flooded, and the downpour had become a light shower.

How becoming.

I unlocked the car and got inside. Moments later, I drove the car away from the parking lot.

I thought I heard someone call my name.

"Did you say something?" I asked the skull as we turned onto the road.

"Not *moi*. My lips are sealed. Well, actually, I don't have any lips, but you get the idea."

I turned onto the freeway entrance ramp and glanced in my rearview mirror. Someone was tailgating me.

"Get off my ass, buddy," I said, accelerating onto 93. The other car stayed close. I pressed the pedal to the metal. The other driver did the same, then flashed his car lights.

I glanced at the dash, in case someone was trying to tell me something about my car. My lights were on. No warning lights pulsed. Didn't feel like I had a flat.

The car flashed its lights again. And honked its horn.

Had I accidentally cut someone off and now they were after me?

Or had one of the truckers decided he liked the looks of me?

I glanced in the mirror again.

No. Not a truck, a car.

Maybe it was my imagination or the driver was flashing someone on the other side of the expressway.

Suddenly the other car accelerated again, put on its left turn signal, and got into the left-hand lane.

He was going to pass me.

My heart pounded in my throat.

Maybe he was going to run me off the road.

Or shoot me.

I stared straight ahead.

I could hear water splashing against his tires as he drew alongside me.

"Pass, pass, pass," I said through gritted teeth.

His horn blared.

I had to look.

Inside a small red car, a shadowy man gestured wildly.

"Ohmigod."

I pushed the accelerator to the floor, and my car shot forward.

Faster and faster.

Until the lights of the man's car were no longer visible.

"I would have protected you," the skull said.

"How? By annoying him to death?"

I breathed deeply. I wanted to get off at the next exit and just go home. I would explain everything to my father, and he would take care of it. He could find Johnny and the scepter with a snap of his fingers.

Except then I would still be the lamebrain youngest child who could not do anything right.

But I would be safe. Alive.

I shook my head and glanced in the rearview mirror. The red car was far behind me, if there at all. I was safe. I had taken this drive a dozen times, at least, with my mother when she visited cousin Hortense, who was not a real relative either, and I had gone a few times with my father in the last couple of years while he helped Cousin Miller get his restaurant up and going. I could do this.

"Do you want me to tell you about the time I gave Hernán

Cortés the wrong directions? He was lost in the jungle for days. Got rot in all the appropriate places."

"Do you have a name?" I interrupted.

"I have had a *nom d'emprunt* or two."

"What?"

"I have assumed many names."

"Would you like me to call you by any of them?"

"*D'accord.* You can call me Crane. Or Cráneo."

"Old family names?"

"A rose by any other name smells as sweet."

I frowned. What was he talking about? Crane. Cráneo.

"Ooh. *Crane* is French for 'skull'; *cráneo* is Spanish. Very clever. Crane it is."

We left the rainy zone and sped along 93 until the road switchbacked down to the Hoover Dam. I wanted to stop and gaze at the two art deco angels whose enormous arms stretched into wings reaching elegantly for the desert sky. My mother had taken my picture next to the angels one day, before the visitors' center had been built, when only she and I walked barefoot on the astrological wheel set in brass and stone near the angels until our feet got too hot and we slipped on our flip-flops and ran giggling back to the car. Had she been in her eyes then?

I drove slowly across the dam, thinking, as I often did, that I could feel the turbines humming beneath tons of concrete. I waved to the angels, then continued on up the narrow windy road, dark walls of rock rising up on either side of the car.

The car behind me flashed his lights.

I looked in the mirror.

The little red car.

He honked his horn.

My stomach lurched. My heart raced.

I sped up but could not go too fast. Cars came toward me

on the other side, and the road curved too sharply and had no shoulder.

The red car lights flashed.

The road began to straighten. I floored my accelerator and left the red car in the dust.

I slowed down to go through Boulder City. Once I was up over the hill, I turned down a side street, then another, pulling the car under a tree that blocked out the streetlight. I breathed deeply and waited.

Five minutes.

Ten minutes.

"Are we there yet?" the skull asked.

I slowly drove back to the main road and headed for Las Vegas, which soon appeared in the distance, shimmering in the desert night like some long lost oasis in the *Arabian Nights*. No red car followed us.

"Mom, I have to pee," the skull said.

I glanced at it.

"Just trying to improvise some family intercourse here."

"Well, stop it."

We drove into Las Vegas, and I somehow managed to turn onto the Strip, which no local would ever do in her right mind. I tried to get my bearings as cars rushed past me on either side and mobs of pedestrians stepped across intersections long after the lights had changed. The Strip had the longest lights in the world. I unrolled my window and listened to the honking cars and breathed in gasoline fumes. From here, the entire city appeared to be lit in a kind of blue light, and everyone was in a hurry, except me. I squinted at each cross street, trying to recall Miller's address. I passed Caesar's and the Flamingo, with its synchronized lights creating an ever-flowing cascade of light and color enveloping the Flamingo sign. Johnny once remarked that the sign was orgasmic; I had laughed and fondled his—

"Oops, sorry." I slammed on my brakes and waved to the stray pedestrian.

It seemed forever later that I came up to the New York–New York, MGM, and Excalibur Casinos—none of which had been around when I was growing up. Across from them was the Tropicana, a kind of fixture in my childhood memories. I had spent more than a few mornings and afternoons near the pools watching pink flamingos lift their legs delicately as they moved from one lush patch of grass to another. They appeared so graceful and sad. When I was a teenager, I decided that if Blanche du Bois had ever been a bird, she would have been a flamingo.

Now I waved to the Statue of Liberty at the front of the New York–New York Casino, turned the car left, dodged a couple dozen peds, drove a bit, then turned right into the Tropicana parking lot. From here, I could call Cousin Miller and get directions to his place.

I turned off the car and picked up the crystal skull. "Alas, poor Horatio."

"Wasn't it Yorick?" the skull said.

"Whatever. I'll catch you later." I stuffed the skull into the suitcase. I looked around. A few people got into and out of their automobiles. No weirdo lurking about. I got out of my car, closed the door, and stretched. I opened the back door, pulled out the suitcase, then unlocked the trunk, and heaved my suitcase inside. I slammed the trunk shut, stretched again, and yawned.

And saw a man getting out of his little red car.

He looked up and saw me.

"Hey!" he called, reaching into his car.

"Shit." I raced toward the closest entrance to the Tropicana, ran up the steps, and pulled on the door.

It was locked.

I glanced behind me.

The man waved. "Wait!"

Suddenly someone pushed open the door. I ran inside—inside a long empty hallway of hotel rooms.

I hurried to the end of the hallway.

And found another hallway.

Completely confused, I spun around, looking for the elevators.

I saw another door to the outside.

I ran out it. Hurried down the sidewalk. A dark alley. Then I was at the empty pools. No one around. Lots of foliage and shadows for psychos to hide in. I hurried. Hurried. There. There was the entrance to the casino. People. Safety.

I ran up the stairs and went inside.

Silence disappeared. That unmistakable *ching, ching, ching* of the slot machines. Smell of perfume and cigarettes. A line of people waiting to get into the buffet. And a security officer.

I was safe.

I turned around. The man from the red car was right behind me, his face contorted in rage or pain.

I ran to the security officer.

"This man has been following me," I said, pointing to the red car man.

The security officer stepped between us.

"Sir, this young lady says you've—"

"I'm trying to return her purse!" He held out my purse. "She left it at a restaurant in Kingman."

The security man looked at me, then stepped back a ways.

I took the proffered bag.

"What are you, some kind of nut following me seventy-plus miles to give me my purse?" I said.

"What's wrong with *me*? What's wrong with you! You see a brown man and you run screaming?"

"You got half that right."

"What?"

I stared at him and tapped my foot.

"Oh. You mean I'm a strange man in the night chasing a woman down a lonesome highway."

I raised my eyebrows.

"I hadn't thought of that."

"You should have. You scared me half to death!"

The security officer cleared his throat. "Is everything copacetic?"

"I'm fine," I said. "Thank you." The officer returned to his post near the far wall.

I opened my purse and checked the contents.

"You think I'm going to chase you through two states to give you back your purse after I've pilfered it!"

"Someone could have gotten it before you did," I said through clenched teeth.

He rubbed his knee.

"What's wrong?" I asked.

"I tripped trying to catch up with you back there. It's an old track injury." He limped over to a chair and sat in it.

"Miss," I said to a passing cocktail waitress. "Could you bring this man some ice? He just fell on your steps."

"Sure thing," she said.

The man smiled. "What? You a lawyer or something? 'He fell on your steps.' "

I shook my head. "I don't know what I am. I was one of the dead and now my life is . . . No. I'm not a lawyer."

"I'm Miguel Madero," he said, holding out his right hand.

"I'm Jeanne Les Flambeaux," I said, gripping his hand, then quickly letting go.

"Yes, I know. I looked at your license, figuring if I called your name you'd stop. That just made you go faster."

"Yeah, well, I've kind of been hearing strange things lately. Can't really trust my senses."

"Shouldn't you always trust your own senses?"

"I bet this is the last time you do a good deed," I said.

The waitress returned with an ice pack and a doctor. I excused myself, went to a nearby row of phones, and called Miller's restaurant; he and his wife, Molly, were not there. I phoned their house and got their voice mail.

I returned to Miguel and the doctor who told me, "He needs to stay off his feet. The hotel will, of course, extend hospitality to you both tonight. Can you register for him so he can go straight to his room?"

Miguel stood. "I'm fine. And I already have a room reserved under Paul Gurare."

"I thought your name was Miguel Madero."

"I am meeting a client here tomorrow. He reserved the room. See, I didn't actually follow you to the Tropicana. We just happened to end up here at the same time."

"How coincidental."

Just then a woman in uniform came up to us. "I'm Wendy for the Tropicana. I'll help you get settled. Dr. Reynolds will check on Mr. Madero later."

The doctor nodded and left.

"I don't need all this fuss," Miguel said.

"If you'll come with me," Wendy said to me.

"But we're not together together," I said.

The woman looked from me to Miguel. "Two rooms are no problem." She smiled. I was tired.

"I'll be right back," I said to Miguel.

He shook his head. I followed Wendy down a long wide hallway, past glass cages of snakes and birds, down the stairs into the casino and beyond to the registration counter. Wendy found the Paul Gurare registration, informed me she was crediting his account—like I cared—and then took my information. When she finished inputting, she gave me two key cards and asked if I could get back to Miguel on my own.

"Yes, I've been here before," I said.

When I found Miguel again, he said, "This is foolish."

I handed him a key card. "Yeah, well, you saved our client some dough, and I don't have to drive all over Las Vegas looking for my cousin's house."

We silently walked to the elevator and got on when the door opened. I remembered playing on these elevators while I waited for my mother when I was a child. Now the elevator talked to us, announcing each floor before it opened. Miguel and I looked out the glass into a Las Vegas night, ignoring the other people on the elevator. A spot lit up the green Statue of Liberty. I smiled. Miguel glanced at me.

"I like looking at her," I said. "I know she's not the real Statue of Liberty. Still, she's so big. She looks like the embodiment of freedom."

"Las Vegas represents freedom to you?"

"I used to come here with my mom," I said, "while she visited a sick cousin. I liked being away from my sibs, with just the two of us. I liked being out of the kitchen."

The elevator announced the eighteenth floor. Miguel flinched as we stepped out into a soft welcome silence after the cacophony of the casino.

"Do you want to lean on me?" I asked.

"No. The painkiller is starting to kick in."

"You took a pill from that doctor? You are some kind of nut. You don't even know if he was a real doctor."

"You are paranoid," he said as we walked to our rooms.

"I may be paranoid, but you were chasing me."

We stopped. Our rooms were beside each other.

Miguel unlocked his door and opened it. I had forgotten my suitcase, and Miguel had obviously not had time to get any of his things because he had been chasing me. I sighed. The guy had returned my purse to the detriment of his knee.

"I can get anything you need from your car if you like," I said. "I need to go get my suitcase anyway."

He pulled keys out of his trouser pockets. "That's mighty neighborly, sister," he drawled as I took his keys.

I laughed. "I just want to rifle through your things and see if you're some mad killer."

"It's the little red—"

"Yeah, I know, the little red car."

I made my way through the noise and chaos of the casino to the parking lot. I was exhausted, and it was not even midnight. In the city that never sleeps, I was ready for some shut-eye. I retrieved my suitcase, then went to the little red car. No wonder Miguel had not been able to keep up with me; this car looked as though it were on its last ball bearing. I grabbed his briefcase and a small bag and lugged them all back into the hotel, my suitcase and the skull bouncing up and down on my shin.

"Crane, you're hurting me. Can't you move?"

"Oh, *ma petite,* think of the realities of that question," the muffled response came.

A couple passed by, looking askance at me. I laughed. Now I was talking to my luggage.

Miguel's door was slightly open.

"Hello?" I called, dropping my suitcase at the threshold.

"Ouch," the suitcase said.

I walked by the bathroom and closet. Miguel lay on the king-size bed, his eyes closed, apparently asleep. I set his bag and briefcase on a chair, put his keys on the dresser, and tip-toed out.

My room was a mirror image of Miguel's. I put the suitcase on the bed, opened it, and took out the skull.

"Can I have a window view?"

Skull in hand, I opened the curtains. I waved to the Statue of Liberty.

"She's not bad for a green broad," the skull said.

"I'm sure you've seen your share of those," I said. "Being dead and all."

I set the skull on the windowsill, facing out. Then I called Miller's house. Still no one answered. I left another message on their voice mail.

"The scepter is near," the skull said.

"Good. Then Johnny's still in Las Vegas."

"No, I mean *near* near."

I put the suitcase on the chair and stretched out on the bed. I picked up the remote and switched on the TV.

"What do you mean?" I asked as the channels flashed by.

"I told you I sense its vibrations."

"Whatever that means."

"It means I believe the scepter is in this hotel."

I leaned over and picked up the phone and called the hotel operator.

"Do you have a Johnny Jackson registered?"

"Checking. No, I'm sorry," he said.

"Thanks." I hung up. "Maybe he's in the casino."

I was hungry, couldn't afford room service, and was too tired to move.

"So what should I do?" I asked. "Carry you up and down the bizillion hallways of this hotel until you sense the good vibrations of the scepter?"

"Darling, it is you who cares about the scepter. I agreed to help. I'm telling you, it is nearby."

"Don't get cranky. I'll go looking in just a minute. I want to rest my eyes."

"If you ate better, you'd have more stamina."

"You should talk. You're pretty bony yourself." I giggled and closed my eyes.

Three

A Quien Madruga, Dios le Ayuda, or The Worm Turns on the Early Bird

I opened my eyes and sat upright. The television blathered, "A Flagstaff man has apparently joined the ranks of the missing WIJ women. . . ." The television clock read 3:00 A.M.

"Did you have a nice nap?" the skull asked.

"I feel like shit," I said. I missed my bed, I missed my family, I even missed the restaurant. Just about now I could sneak downstairs for a snack.

I thought I heard laughter coming from the hallway. No, the walls were more soundproof than that. I turned off the television. I heard laughter again. Something about that sound.

I went to the door, opened it, and looked down the hallway. First to the right. Then to the left.

Laughter. A group of men.

Johnny.

I screamed.

Or roared.

I ran and leaped onto Johnny's back before he could turn around.

"What the—?"

We fell to the ground with me on top.

The other men disappeared like mist in the wind.

Johnny squirmed around until I was sitting on his stomach.

"You yellow-bellied mucous-draining thieving lying felonious stupid sack of shit! Where is my scepter!" I leaned on his shoulders and stared into his face. He smelled of liquor.

"Well, what a coincidence, baby. I was just—"

"Don't tell me any lies, you creep. Just take me to my property or I'm calling the police. And don't think I won't."

"I can explain everything."

I punched his shoulder.

"Where is it!"

"I pawned it."

"You sack of shit. Where?"

"I don't remember.

I stood up. "Well, then, let's just drive around Las Vegas all night until we find it."

"Who said it was in Las Vegas?"

"Johnny, don't play games with me. This is my life, my parents' livelihood. You know that. How could you have done it?"

I was suddenly exhausted, sad, and hungry.

Johnny sat up and leaned against the wall. "All right. My mom found out what I did, and she took it. She has it. She was going to give it to James to give to Alita or Jacques."

"Your mother? How'd you have time to go to Tucson?"

"I didn't. Mom is here, at a spa up past Indian Springs. She paid for my ticket to fly from Phoenix to here."

I shook my head. Something was not right about this story. "Why didn't she just tell you to give it back to me in Scottsdale? Why fly you here?"

"I don't know. Wait. She flew me here first; then I told her about the scepter."

"I want to talk to her now."

"Jeanne, it's three A.M."

I pulled on his shirt until he got up. "Come on."

Reluctantly, he followed me into my room. "You brought the skull?" he said. "Why?"

"So you could steal it, too," I said, shutting the door. I came into the room and pointed to the phone. "Where is she?"

"Can't this wait?"

I stared at him.

"Crystal Springs Spa." He pulled a card out of his pocket and handed it to me. "Suite six."

I pushed him out of the way and called the number on the card. The receptionist did not want to put me through, but I insisted.

Sharon's sleepy voice came on the line. "Hello?"

"Sharon, this is Jeanne Les Flambeaux, your husband's niece."

"Yes, dear. What is it?" She cleared her throat.

"Johnny tells me you have the scepter he stole from me."

Johnny chewed his fingers and looked away from me.

"Yes," she said, yawning. "It's right here with me."

"I'm coming to get it."

"Well, darling. I'll bring it home with me. You don't have to come all this way."

"I'm in Las Vegas, and I'm calling the police if I don't get it back immediately."

"We don't need the police," Sharon said. "I've got it. I'm *family*. It is a *family* heirloom."

"I'm leaving now."

"Why don't you get some sleep? I promise the scepter is safe. Meet me for breakfast at nine at the spa. Johnny knows the way."

"Seven."

"Honey, they don't serve breakfast until seven-thirty."

"Then seven-thirty. Make sure you bring the scepter with you."

"Of course."

I hung up the phone. Son and mother were both a couple of sleazebags.

Johnny slouched in a chair. "What time are we going?"

"Weren't you listening? Seven-thirty."

"That should work," he said.

"I'm glad it meets with your approval," I said. "How long does it take to get there from here?"

"About an hour."

"OK. We'll leave at six o'clock. Much as I loathe the sight of you, you aren't leaving my side until I get the scepter back."

"I just want to get some sleep."

"I don't care what you want." I went to the window, picked up the skull, and brought it back to bed with me. I lay down with the skull on my stomach.

"Scream if he moves," I whispered.

"Comprendez, bonne amie," the skull said.

I closed my eyes.

Began drifting.

"Ahhhh!" the skull screamed.

I bolted upright.

Johnny was still slumped in the chair, his eyes closed.

"What did you do that for?" I asked.

"He moved his head," the skull said.

I sighed. "Scream if he tries to leave the room," I said. "Wake me at six A.M."

"I'm reduced to being an alarm clock?" the skull asked.

"Be all that you can be," I said, and closed my eyes.

I gradually awakened to the sound of Crane singing, *"Frère Jacques, Frère Jacques, dormez vous? Dormez vous?"*

I pushed the skull away and sat up. I was sticky, hungry, and annoyed, but I was not going to risk taking a shower. I kicked Johnny's feet.

"Come on."

He groaned and opened his eyes.

"Can't I have a cup of coffee or a shot?"

I put the skull in the hotel's plastic laundry bag, got my purse and keys, and nudged Johnny out the door.

It was still dark, dawn approaching, when we stepped into the parking lot. I couldn't yet see the red haze that accompanied nearly every day in Las Vegas now. When I was a child here with my mother, it had been as clear as any desert day had been for probably thousands of years. Of course, Las Vegas had been radioactive long before the red haze arrived, but I couldn't see radioactivity.

We got into the car. I put Crane on the dash, and he hummed quietly as I pulled the car onto Tropicana Avenue and then out on to Highway 95, heading northwest.

"So this man is your heart's amour?" Crane asked.

"Not even close," I said.

"What'd you say?" Johnny asked.

"I wasn't talking to you."

"Then to who?"

"Myself. Now shut up."

"What happened to you?" Johnny asked. "Less than two days ago we were making love."

"You have to ask?" I said. "I trusted you, and you stole from me."

"You left the safe open. I thought that was an invitation."

"Oh, fuck you, you lowlife. I can't begin to tell you how angry I am with you."

"Well, the name-calling is a rather poetic clue," the skull said.

"You should have closed the safe," Johnny said.

"If I had a gun I'd shoot you dead," I said.

"No, you wouldn't," Crane said.

"OK. I'd shoot him in the groin."

"That would kill him," Crane said.

"I couldn't shoot him in the brain. That would be an exercise in futility since he's brainless!"

"Hey, I'm right here," Johnny said. "Have some respect."

"I did, J.J.," I said. "In fact, I was the only one anywhere who thought you were worth more than two plugged nickels.

"What does that mean, anyway?" Crane asked. "Two plugged nickels?"

"I don't know!" I said. "Call the library. I'm trying to have a meaningful conversation."

"With him?"

I glanced at Johnny. "Good point."

We traveled the rest of the way to Indian Springs in silence. The freeway quickly turned into a two-lane road as the city disappeared behind us. Dawn spread across the desert, changing the gray to pink and gold, making it all look like a panoramic oil painting of a desert dawn, only we were a part of it, the car making a shadow on the side of the road, smaller then bigger, smaller then bigger.

"Ain't life grand?" Crane said.

I glanced at Johnny. He slept, his head against the window. We passed the sign for Indian Springs.

"It is beautiful," I said, looking out across the desert. In the distance, under blue black clouds, lightning flashed. "When I went to the University of Arizona, Johnny would take me up the foothills of the Catalinas at night. From there, you could see Tucson stretched below, just wavering dots of light, like some kind of mirage, with heat lightning slicing and splicing above it, almost like white fireworks. It was so beautiful. And Johnny would sit next to me on the hot hood of someone else's car, oohing and aahing, and pointing to the streaks of lightning. I felt so comfortable. No one expected anything of either of us. So it was fun being together. Now he does this. Sometimes when I was with him, I almost felt OK."

"What do you mean?"

"It's hard to explain, but I never feel quite right, like I'm not whole, or I'm missing something, or someone. I keep thinking that someone will hold me in their arms, and they will be it. They'll be the person who will make me feel as though I belong here on this Earth now."

"Well, I hate to rain on your party, *ma petite,* but I feel as though we are getting farther and farther away from *le sceptre,* not closer."

"Now you tell me. Johnny!"

"What?" He sat up and looked around. "Just past that sign. Turn right."

"I see the sign," I said, slowing the car. I turned at the CRYSTAL SPRING SPA sign onto a dirt road. "What I want to know, you sack of shit, are you lying to me about the scepter? Because I'm just tired enough to call my father and tell him I was stupid enough to let you near me and that you stole the scepter. He knows people who know people who can make you disappear, and you know it." None of this was true, at least at far as I knew.

"I swear on my father's grave that Mom has the scepter."

"Your father is still alive, nimrod," I said.

"Quit calling me names," Johnny said.

"Quit calling you *names?* OK. I'll just choose one, you lying thieving sack of shit. Is that better?"

Ahead of us lay Crystal Springs Spa, one of those typical desert habitats built low to the ground, deep in the Earth, a kind of New Age bomb shelter, only now it was used as shelter from everyday life rather than some Soviet A-bomb. It all looked vaguely familiar.

I parked the car, put the skull under the seat, and got out.

Johnny shuffled across the kitty-litter-like dirt which was ground cover for much of Arizona and Nevada.

"She's probably still sleeping," Johnny said. "She hates to have her beauty sleep interrupted, Jeanne."

I made a noise. We followed the path around the building and down onto a patio golden with the sun that sat on the horizon, big and red, bleeding rose-colored light across the desert until it reached us.

Dearest Auntie Sharon was checking her makeup in her compact mirror. She smiled and stood when she saw us.

"Good morning, children," she said, her voice dripping sweetness. "Sit, sit."

She motioned to the white metal chairs opposite her. A waiter dressed all in white brought us water. Something about this place was so familiar.

"I'd like the scepter now," I said.

"It's in my room," Sharon said. "I'll get it after breakfast. I must have my coffee first." The waiter brought her a cup of coffee, a croissant, and half a grapefruit. "Darlings, would you like something?"

I was not going to break bread with these two.

"I don't mean to be rude, Sharon," I said quietly. "But I want the scepter in my hands now. I want to get it home."

"Bring my son some eggs, toast, and sausage," Sharon said to the waiting waiter.

"Your parents aren't due home for two weeks," Sharon said to me. "You've got all the time in the world. Relax." She smiled, buttered the top of her croissant, and then bit into it. "I think your mother knows the owner of this place from back in her rebel days."

I wanted to say, "How would you know?" or "My mother was never a rebel, idiot."

Instead, I breathed deeply.

I had to be calm.

She was still Uncle James's wife. I wanted to shake her and make her get the scepter. *Now.* But I waited. No sense completely blowing my family reputation in one sitting. They all thought I was a sweet nothing, so I would play the sweet nothing. I looked out across the desert. They assumed I was sweet and gentle because I was quiet, I supposed. For all they knew, I had a running monologue going on in my head about how stupid they all were. I didn't. Usually. But they couldn't know that. Mostly I watched and tried to figure out how things came so easily to most people: carrying on a conversation, knowing what they wanted, eating. Being perfect.

The waiter brought Johnny's breakfast. Johnny picked up the link sausage with his fingers and broke the yolk of his egg with it, then put the dead thing in his mouth and sucked on it.

I had just about had enough.

"Aunt Sharon, you've had your coffee and breakfast. Please get me the scepter. Or give me your key, and I'll go get it."

Sharon glanced over her coffee cup at Johnny. "Can you go and get the scepter for your cousin, Jonathan?"

Johnny put down his fork, then glanced at his watch.

"Ahhh, actually. Mom doesn't have it. I lost it in a poker game last night."

"What?" I looked at Sharon. "How could you let me come all the way out here?"

"He's family, dear," Sharon said.

"Why did you bring me here, then, Johnny Jackass? Why this stupid pretense?"

Johnny hung his head. How could I have been so stupid?

"I owed a bundle, Jeanne. He could have hurt me."

"I wish he had," I said.

"Now don't get on your high horse, missy," Sharon said. "Everyone makes mistakes. Your family isn't all that perfect either."

"At least we don't steal from each other."

"Don't be so sure," Sharon said, all her fake sweetness gone.

I pushed away from the table.

"I can't believe I ever let you get your penis anywhere near me!" I cried. "You will pay for this, Johnny." I picked up my glass of water and threw it in his face.

Then I hurried away.

"You and her?" Johnny's mother said.

"Hey, how am I going to get back to Vegas!" Johnny called.

When I got to the car, I took the skull from beneath the seat and tossed it into the backseat. Then I drove out of the parking lot, throwing up gravel as I went.

"The scepter isn't here," the skull said.

"No shit, Sherlock."

I peeled out onto the road. Tears nearly blinded me. All was lost now. Johnny wasn't going to tell me who had the scepter. But he would have to tell the police. First I had to let my family know what had happened.

Suddenly the car hiccoughed. Chugged. Sputtered.

I glanced at the gas gauge. More than a quarter tank.

I gave it more gas.

The car jerked again.

I pulled off to the side of the road. I looked around. The top of a building was just visible over the desert foliage to my right. I turned into the drive.

The car burped and lurched, and I stopped it under the only tree.

"So much for your idea of not taking my car," I said.

"At least it's not hot out," Crane said.

"I'll see if I can find help," I said. "If I don't return, some psycho got me."

"Take me with!"

"No."

"Puh-lease."

I groaned. "I didn't know the undead could whine."

"We prefer to call it *haunting*."

I picked up the skull and put it in the laundry bag again. Then I got out of the car and started down the road, my feet crunching over the desert floor. I passed a cardboard sign with an arrow and the handwritten message: TEMPLE. In the far distance, lightning lit up storm clouds and the mountains beneath them. The dirt road curved, and I saw a round white one-story building on a slight hill. I walked up the path to a small female figurine on a red stone slab. Pennies lay strewn at her feet.

"Hello!" someone called.

I turned around. A tall disheveled man strode toward me, his right hand outstretched.

"Hello," I said, taking his hand.

His hair was greasy and thinning, his smile lopsided.

"My car broke down," I said, setting the bagged skull on the ground. "May I use your phone?"

"I don't have one out here," he said, "but I'm pretty handy with cars if you want me to take a look-see." He glanced at the bag. "Is that a crystal skull in there?"

Startled, I laughed. "Yes. A family heirloom. I didn't want to leave it in the car."

The man squinted at me. "What's your name?"

I hesitated, then said, "Jeanne Les Flambeaux."

"Little Jeanne? My goodness! I haven't see you in fifteen years, give or take. What are you doing out here? Did your momma send you?"

"I'm sorry," I said. "Who are you?"

"You don't remember me?" He looked crushed. "I'm Bear Morrison. Your mother and I used to demonstrate together.

Then we used to do a little gambling. That's when I met you. You and your momma even came out here a few times."

"Out here?"

"Not right in this spot. This temple has been up for only a few years. I helped built it out of mud and straw."

"What is it?"

"It's a temple dedicated to peace and the Egyptian goddess Sekhmet. She can be a slayer of humankind or a healer. She represents the sun's rays at noon. Genevieve Vaughan visited Egypt when she was a young woman and asked the goddess to help her conceive a child. Years later, after she had her children, she bought about twenty acres from the government—it had been stolen from the Indians and used for nuclear testing. Genevieve gave the land back to the Shoshone, and they allowed her to build this temple dedicated to Sekhmet. Go on inside. Give me your keys, and I'll look at your car."

I dug my keys out of my pocket and gave them to Bear.

"You're not a maniac or anything, are you?" I asked.

Bear laughed. It was a bearlike rumble, deep and growly. For a moment, I thought I did recognize him.

"That depends upon who you ask." He smiled and loped away.

I picked up the skull and walked into the temple. It was cool inside, with four entrances, no doors, and an open circular ceiling with interlocking iron cords making shadows on the slate and gravel floor. Most of the light came in through the ceiling and the east entrance. A fire pit adorned the center of the temple. To the left of where I entered, a life-size statue of Sekhmet sat on her black throne. The ebony-colored goddess had the head of a cat and the body of a woman, complete with one breast slightly larger than the other. She stared at me serenely, her black arms resting on her black skirted legs. Offerings of flowers, walking sticks, and candles encircled her. Across from Sekhmet, a painting of the Virgin of Guadalupe leaned against the wall, sheltered by the white arch of a partially recessed alcove. The flames of several votive candles back lit photographs resting against the Virgin's feet. On the walls near her, a variety of goddess figures crowded the shelves.

To my right, in a tiny alcove in the wall above a table covered with candles and decorated with a pentagram, a small naked alabaster woman lounged on a pink seashell. Perhaps Aphrodite. Then another entrance, and next to it, a life-size seated figure who was the color of the Earth, slightly red and brown. The woman gazed at the planet Earth in her lap. A sign near her read MADRE DEL MUNDO, ARTIST: MARSHA A. GOMEZ.

I walked over to *Madre del Mundo.* She was perhaps the most powerful-looking woman I had ever seen, just as the mother of the world should be, I supposed. Tentatively, I reached out and touched her forehead. It was cool. Then I touched my forehead. Warm.

I sat cross-legged on the floor and pulled Crane out of the laundry bag. He said nothing. I leaned back against *Madre del Mundo.*

This place was so unexpected, a goddess temple popping up in the middle of the desert. Through each entrance, I glimpsed a different world. Outside to my right was a bowl of water on a rock table surrounded by desert brush. To my left, the path curved into a wooded area. Between Sekhmet and the Virgin of Guadalupe, the distant sky was dark with clouds that seemed to melt down into the mountains. Above, the sky was morning colored, like blue turquoise.

I picked up Crane and put him in my lap.

"Have you ever seen a place like this?" I asked.

"Oh yes, *ma petite.* A long while ago."

"I like it," I said.

"Moi, aussi."

A short time later, Bear returned, wiping his hands on a kerchief.

"The good news is it was a clogged fuel line which I blew out. You can get to Las Vegas just fine, but I wouldn't drive it much farther than that. Your car needs some serious fixing. I left the keys in it." Bear smiled. "I was just about to have breakfast. Would you do me the honor of sharing it with me?"

"Sure. Can I help?"

He shook his head. "You hang here. I'll bring it out. I've got to wash up, anyway."

Bear left. I leaned over to look outside and watched him walk down to a tiny building a short distance from the temple. I leaned back again.

Everything was still and quiet. I had lived in the desert all my life, but I did not pay much attention to it, except to fantasize about living someplace cooler in the summer. Sometimes, especially in the middle of the day at our house, the world got so quiet that I grew nervous and had to turn on music or jump in the pool and make lots of noise. I couldn't remember ever liking silence, or being alone, or being with other people.

"A peso for your thoughts," Crane said.

"Just thinking about my life," I said. "I really have no idea what I've been doing for so long. You know, I can't ever remember wanting to do or be anything, except maybe someone else who had ambition. I've got no drive, no fire. I've just been a lump of nothing all my life."

"I would have to disagree, *ma chère.*"

"What do you know?"

"I have been with you all your life," Crane said. "Despite my unfortunate incarceration. I know more than you realize."

"Here we are." Bear stepped into the temple carrying a tray. He set it on the slate floor near me and *Madre del Mundo*. Then he sat next to the entrance between Virgin of Guadalupe and *Madre*.

"This is ginger tea," Bear said, handing me a cup of steaming liquid. "It'll give a little bite to your morning."

I took a sip. When the sweet warm liquid hit my belly, I immediately felt a jolt of something. Maybe strength.

"You haven't eaten in a while," Bear said.

"A long while," I agreed.

"Consider this a gift from Sekhmet and the *Madre del Mundo*," Bear said.

Bear handed me a dark green plate upon which was a kind of mandala of fruit. Pear slices overlapped each other to encircle the center of the plate, which contained a mixture of fresh strawberries, blueberries, and kiwifruit. Bear put a plate of scones, croissants, and marmalade jam on the ground by my feet.

"This is lovely," I said.

"Your mother always said, 'Presentation, Bear, presentation!'"

I laughed. "She still says that at the restaurant."

I picked up a strawberry and bit into it.

"Your mom and I met in the late sixties or early seventies when I came out here to protest nuclear testing. We went to some of the same rallies. I thought she was cool because she had kids and a husband and still did peace work. And she was great to have around because she could make a great meal out of almost anything. She had long black hair that flew every which way."

I picked up the fork and began eating the fruit. It all tasted wonderful and new, as if I had never eaten any fruit before this moment.

"And she was always so there," Bear said. "When you talked to her, she looked right at you and listened completely. I met your grandmother then, too."

"Nana? Dad's mom?"

I opened the croissant with my fingers, then smeared marmalade on the inside.

"No. Winema, your mother's mom."

I shook my head. "I never met her," I said. "They don't talk about her except to say she was crazy." Like they thought I was because a certain crystal skull talked to me.

"She wasn't crazy," Bear said, picking up a piece of kiwi and putting it in his mouth. "She was eccentric. She was put in a mental institution once against her will. It left quite a mark on her." He laughed. "Weird Winnie. She was an explorer, studied archeology and went on expeditions to Mexico, Central and South America. Then she'd come back here with tales of ancient UFO sightings, or lost Atlantis-like places."

"She sounds fun," I said.

He nodded. "She was, but she and your mom didn't get along. Then there was that thing with the land and Winnie kind of disappeared for a while."

"What thing with the land?"

He shrugged. "I don't remember. I think Winema had land in Scottsdale that she bought when your grandpa died, and she sold it to your parents. Or something. You'd have to ask them."

I bit into a scone, then sipped the ginger tea. Exquisite combination plate.

"You didn't know any of this?" Bear asked.

I shook my head. "The only relatives my parents talk about are the dead illustrious ones. I had trouble enough living up to all that. I never asked about anyone else. Besides, for a while my parents thought I was crazy like her. I had to get all these tests. It was awful."

"I remember," he said. "That's when you stopped eating, wasn't it? It was as if you couldn't stomach things anymore."

I looked at him. Odd that he knew all of this, yet I was not uncomfortable with him.

"No. Everything started tasting weird," I said, realizing this for the first time. "I often got sick or worried or sad or angry after I ate. I'd get all these feelings I didn't understand and I'd act them out. I stopped eating around people, so they wouldn't know what I was feeling."

"Maybe you weren't feeling your own feelings," Bear said.

"He may be on to something," Crane said.

"Your mother always worried too much about you," Bear said, "more than the rest."

"I never noticed. Why? Because she thought I was crazy?" I glanced at Sekhmet. She watched me.

"It happened before that. It's what made her stop going to the protests. She was pregnant with you, and she came up here to protest a nuclear test. It was supposed to be a secret, but everyone knew. It's hard to keep movement in the desert completely hidden. So Alita came up, even though she didn't usually go to rallies when she was pregnant. She was pretty big! Anyway, we went out to protest in a safe place, but they changed the scheduled time, and the test went off sooner than we expected and the wind shifted. We were outdoors, and we got exposed."

I stared at him.

"The doctors said we were all fine," Bear said, "but your mother was really upset. She thought she had done some awful thing. 'I was just trying to save the world,' she said, 'and now I've harmed my family.' We all tried to comfort her."

How could she have put me in that kind of danger?

"She was grateful that you were born healthy," Bear said, "and she never went to another rally. I bought land out here. She started coming to Las Vegas when you were a little older. She liked the roulette wheel."

"My mother gambled?"

Bear nodded. "We all do, don't we? I don't know, she was different after the accident. She came back to Nevada almost compulsively. To the scene of the crime, like. You visited me a couple of times, down the road, before I turned it into the Crystal Springs Spa. It was my home. Still is."

"That's why it seemed familiar," I said. "I came out to the spa to get something from my aunt Sharon."

"Ah yes," Bear said. "She's a handful. I came out here to the temple to get away from the Aunt Sharons of the world."

I laughed. My plates and cup were empty.

"That was great," I said. "Thanks for the family history. I didn't know any of that."

"I hope it helps," he said. "See, I don't think they ever really thought you were crazy. I don't think they really thought Winema was, either. Your mom had the doctors run all those tests out of fear and guilt. She didn't know what the bomb had done to you. Or to her. She was so happy that you were all right."

I nodded. Actually daughter dearest was not really "all right."

"Just because you can hear me," Crane said, "does not make you insane. Maybe the rest of the world is loony because they can't hear me."

"I'm glad I saw this place," I said to Bear. "Thanks for everything. Can I help you clean up?"

Bear shook his head and piled the plates onto the tray.

"Would you like to leave an offering?" Bear asked.

I slipped Crane into the plastic bag and then stood.

"Like money?"

Bear laughed. "No. Just anything from your heart."

"Like an old boyfriend. I'd like that. Actually, I don't have anything."

"I'll stay," Crane said.

Bear smiled. "That's all right. Tell your parents I said hey."

We walked out of the temple into the autumn sunshine.

"If I hear from Weird Winnie, I'll tell her I saw you," Bear said.

I stopped. "Hear from her? She's dead."

Bear frowned. "No, she's not. She lives in Mexico. She came up just a couple of years ago. She's really into the Internet, got her own Web site, spreading messages of love and joy, with a smattering of UFOs and Atlantis sightings, I think. I've never actually seen it, just heard of it. I'm more of a book person."

I just stood there with my mouth open.

"Catching flies, *ma petite?*" Crane asked.

"Did your mom tell you your grandma was dead?" Bear asked.

"I can't remember," I said. "I just assumed. We don't really talk about her. We don't talk about anything. They cook. I don't eat. It's what has worked for us all these years." I laughed weakly.

Bear held out his hand. I gripped it, then stood on my toes to kiss his cheek.

"Bye."

I hurried down the road. Suddenly, a tiny red rock caught my attention. I bent over and picked it up. It was perfectly round, about the size of my thumbnail. I turned and ran back to the temple. Bear was gone.

I stepped inside.

Cool and quiet.

I walked to Sekhmet, bent down, and put the red stone at her feet.

"Thanks for this place," I whispered. "And the meal."

I waved to *Madre del Mundo* and all the rest, then glanced out the entrance that faced the mountains and approaching storm. A black bear lumbered away from the temple. I blinked, and the bear went behind a shrub.

I walked to the car. I'd have to hurry to make checkout. It was time to go home and face the music. I could do it. After all, I had survived a nuclear blast, hadn't I?

Four

On the Synchronicity Trail

Crane was unusually quiet on the trip back to Las Vegas. I rehearsed how I would tell my father about Johnny stealing the scepter. If he got angry, I would just shout back, "Well, Mom exposed me to radiation, and Grandma Juarez isn't dead! So there."

Very mature.

The car got me to the Tropicana. I went upstairs to my room, took a quick shower, and changed my clothes. As I packed my suitcase, someone knocked on the door.

"Who is is?" I called.

"Miguel Madero."

I opened the door. "Good morning, road warrior."

"Good morning, woman in jeopardy."

I stared at him. "Is that some kind of joke?" Today he wore shorts and a shirt and carried a white paper bag. His hair was combed back into a short ponytail.

He frowned. "Did I say something wrong?"

"Haven't you heard about that psycho who is kidnapping women—and a man—and leaving behind the initials *WIJ*?"

"I still don't get it," Miguel said.

"Woman in jeopardy. *W-I-J*."

"Oh. Sorry. No, I don't watch the news." He held out the bag to me. "A peace offering."

"Coffee. Great." I snatched the bag from him and went back into the main part of the room. Miguel followed.

"Actually, it's fresh squeezed orange juice."

I took out two paper cups and handed one to Miguel. I sat on the bed and sipped my juice. Miguel sat in a chair opposite me. My orange juice tasted sweet, cold, and slightly bitter. I remembered Bear had suggested that the feelings I got when eating weren't mine. Maybe he was right. I had assumed food triggered emotions in me that lay dormant most of the time. When I ate with Bear this morning, I hadn't felt anything except wonder at the stories he told.

"Did you sleep well?" Miguel asked.

"Actually, no. I had some family business. What about you? Hey, you're not limping. I'd forgotten! How's the leg?"

"All better," he said. "Thanks."

"Did you meet with your client?"

He nodded. "Yep."

"What do you do?" I swallowed the last of the orange juice.

"I'm an attorney."

I laughed. "And you don't watch the news? What kind of attorney is that?"

"A well-adjusted one."

"You practice law here?"

"My client Paul Gurare had business here, and he convinced me to come out and combine business and pleasure. We both live in Sosegado, Arizona."

"That's south of Tucson?"

"Yes, in the middle of the desert, no question about it. It's become a kind of artists' and writers' mecca. Paul has a restaurant there called La Magia. I mentioned your name to him. He said he'd heard of Alita and Jacques Les Flambeaux. Great restaurateurs, he said."

"Those are my parents," I said. "They have a restaurant in Scottsdale, and they've helped start a few others for relatives and friends."

"Small world," Miguel said. "Paul was going to show me around town, but he had to go back to Sosegado. His chef suddenly quit. So he took his loot and left. So now I'm here in a place I didn't really want to be in in the first place."

"His loot? He's a gambler?"

"Yes. He goes on these gambling junkets to win money and collectibles for his restaurant. He likes magical things. This time he won an ancient ruby-studded scepter. He said it could be worth a fortune."

I jumped up. "Where is he! Take me to him!"

Miguel stood. "What's wrong?"

"That scepter belongs to my family. It's stolen. That's why I'm here, chasing down my low-life cousin who stole it!" I was at the door. "Come on."

"Jeanne, I told you. He's gone. He took a plane home around nine o'clock A.M."

I stopped. That was why Johnny had me go out into the desert with him, to stall for time until this Paul Gurare got out of town. Gee, I hadn't realized Johnny had enough brains to concoct an actual scheme.

"I've got to get to him," I said. "Miguel, will you call your friend? Tell him the scepter is stolen. Ask him to keep a hold of it until I get there. Use my phone."

My heart thumped in my chest as Miguel punched in the numbers.

"Paul? Hey, it's Miguel. Uh-huh. I've got some strange news. Remember that woman I told you about, Jeanne Les

Flambeaux? It seems that scepter belongs to her family. It was stolen. I don't know. Hold on." He looked at me. "What's your cousin's name."

"Johnny Jackson."

"Johnny Jackson," Miguel repeated into the phone. "Yeah. So just hang on to it until we get there. All right. Thanks."

He hung up. "He's still in the air. He wasn't surprised, called your cousin a few choice names."

"He's not a blood relation," I said. "Sosegado is big enough for an airport?"

"Just a little one. Paul chartered a flight."

"You said wait until 'we get there.' You're on vacation."

"I told you I don't really want to be here. I'm ready to go home and get this business straightened out between you and Paul."

I shook my head. "You're willing to keep changing your life for a complete stranger?"

"Paul Gurare is my client. I wouldn't want him charged with receiving stolen property. You can follow me in your car."

"I've had some mechanical problems," I said.

"You're welcome to ride back with me. It's a long drive, but we'll get there by day's end. I'd love the company."

"Show me some ID."

"What?"

"Show me your wallet. I want to make sure you are who you say you are."

Miguel took his wallet from his front pocket and handed it to me. I opened it. He had an Arizona driver's license. "Nice picture," I said. "Miguel Cervantes Madero."

"Gracias."

A Sosegado library card. University of Michigan alumni card. VISA card. Insurance card. I refrained from looking in all of the side pockets. I did take out a business card, then slapped the wallet shut and handed it back to him.

I went to the phone, got Sosegado information, and asked for the business number for Miguel Madero. Information's number matched the one on his card. I hung up.

"OK. I'll come with you. You're sure your client won't get rid of the scepter?"

"I'm sure."

"Do you mind following me to my cousin's place to drop off my dad's car?"

"Not at all."

"Let me call to get directions, and then we're out of here."

We checked out of the Tropicana, and I drove to Miller's restaurant with Miguel right behind me. I asked Miller to take the car in for repairs. He had planned a visit to Scottsdale, so he promised to drop the car off at my parents. I gave him Miguel's card, told him to get a good look at his face and to let the police know who Miguel was with in case I turned up gone.

Then I got into the little red car with Miguel, and we left Las Vegas with Crane chattering all the way.

"This reminds me of the trip I made with Montezuma," Crane said. "He was a speed demon. Always on a time table! Ruled by the stars. I tried to get him to slow down, once by giving him the wrong directions like I did with Cortés, only I liked Monte. Anyway, I'm here to tell you that Monte's revenge began with me. He poisoned my food! I nearly died. Well, I was really sick."

"You're making that up," I said.

"What?" Miguel said.

"Nothing."

We curved down and over Hoover Dam.

"*Oooooeeeee!*" Crane screeched. "This is better than shooting the rapids on the Amazon."

"I didn't know the Amazon had rapids," I said.

"*Ma petite,* your ignorance is charming."

"I don't know anything about the Amazon," Miguel said. "Why?"

"Just thinking out loud," I said.

"You said the scepter was a family heirloom?" Miguel asked.

No signs remained of last night's torrential downpour. Clear bright autumn sunlight bathed the desert.

"Yes," I said. "It's been in my family for generations, along with this skull."

"I've heard about crystal skulls. There aren't many in existence, are there? This one must be very valuable. Don't you worry just carrying it around like that?"

"Why, you gonna steal it?" I asked.

He sighed.

"I brought it because it told me it could help me find the scepter. So far it has not helped at all."

"*Au contraire!* I helped—you didn't listen!"

Miguel laughed. "My mother talks to rocks, too. And chairs. Tables. Food. Especially food. She works at Paul's restaurant. Maybe you'll meet her."

"Is she crazy?"

"No! Why?"

"You said she talks to things."

He laughed again. "She says she often has better conversations with things than she does with people."

"My kind of woman!" Crane said.

"Is Sosegado your hometown?" I asked.

"It's where we live now," he said. "We did live a little closer to the border, but it's gotten dangerous."

"High crime down there with all the drugs?"

Miguel glanced over at me. "High crime because the military has been patrolling the borders. They shot and killed one man herding his goats."

"An illegal?"

"No. An American citizen," he said. "Why? Would it be any less awful if an illegal had been killed?"

"Of course not. My mother is first-generation Mexican immigrant, my father second-generation French."

"Is that the same as saying some of my best friends are immigrants?"

"What a snot you are," I said. "If I'd known you'd be so unpleasant, I'd have taken my chances hitchhiking."

"Oh, yeah, on the road again," Crane said. "Boom! I remember it well."

"Now you're going to tell me you knew Jack Kerouac?" I asked.

"I'm afraid the macho beaten boys of summer were not my thing, *ma petite*. I just try to keep up with the times."

"The beat poets are not exactly timely," I said.

"Whom shall I quote, then? I could tell you about the time I helped Emily Dickinson with a writing block. I mentioned she might want to experiment with capitalization."

"Really? You knew her, too?"

"Who do you think she was addressing when she penned the words, 'I'm nobody, who are you?'"

"Please, Crane. You can't have known everyone."

"Who's Crane?" Miguel asked. "And what's all this about beat poets?"

"You were being so touchy, I decided to talk to Crane, the skull."

"Sorry," he said. "I guess I am overly sensitive. I've done a lot of immigration work. We wouldn't have food on our tables or clothes on our backs without migrant workers."

"I'm not a political person," I said.

"How can you not be?"

"The same way you can not watch the news. What good does it do? I like being uninvolved."

"But it's your world."

I shook my head. "My world is *mi familia.* I don't think much about the broader scheme of things, except to be afraid, watch out for psycho killers, hantaviruses, things like that."

"Why do you watch the news if you don't care about the world?" Miguel asked.

"I need to know what to be afraid of. Now I'll know to avoid Yuma City, Flagstaff, and Tucson for a while because of the WIJ kidnappings. Or maybe not. Actually, those places might be all right now because the psycho has come and gone."

"You're kidding?"

"Sort of," I said. "But I don't really think about the big issues. For the past couple of days I have been trying to get the scepter back before my parents returned from their vacation. It was my responsibility and fault that Johnny got his sorry sack of shit hands on it in the first place. That's what I care about: my family being safe and secure." Or at least I cared about none of them being mad at me. "I'm the fuckup in the family, and I'm tired of it." Look at my mother: she cared about saving the world and that concern got me exposed to nuclear fallout. Or radiation. Whatever. Now I heard voices coming from crystal skulls.

"My family is important to me, too," Miguel said. "My cousin Fernando was shot by the military when he was running in the desert, getting ready for track and field."

"Is he okay?"

"The bullet grazed him. At the last second he heard something and ducked. He has a scar on his cheek. He is a different person now. He doesn't talk much. After he was shot, we moved to Sosegado, him, my mother, and myself. The military isn't in Sosegado."

"When I was in college in Tucson," I said, "the air force dumped toxic waste and contaminated some of the city wells, which then had to be closed. I remember thinking I never wanted to live near a military base again. There were no repercussions for what they did."

"So you do pay attention."

"Yeah. From then on I bought bottled water."

"And that fixed the problem?"

"It did for me."

"You know bottled water is not considered very safe, either. It's not regulated like—"

"Are you going to sit there and be bad news road warrior for the next bizillion hours? I'm not interested. You go and try to save the world. It does no good, but have a ball, anyway."

"Bizillion?" Miguel said. "How many is that?"

"More than a zillion, less than trizillion," Crane said. "Geez."

I laughed and closed my eyes. I needed a rest.

I slept on and off for hours, in that sort of semiconscious state you fall into during a long car ride, coming awake if the car slowed or went over a bump, then falling instantly back to sleep. Once I awakened in a rest stop. I got out and stretched. A magpie stared at me, cocking its head. Then I got back in the car and fell to sleep again before Miguel returned.

I awakened fully on the other side of Phoenix, in the dark, shocked I had slept for so long. Miguel and I changed places, and he fell to sleep.

I turned on the radio, searching the dial for news. ". . . the

Barstow woman is believed to have been missing for some time and may have been the WIJ kidnapper's victim before the Yuma City man. Police say the woman lived alone and was . . ."

Miguel woke up after Tucson. We stopped at a fast food place to use the rest rooms. I bought french fries and a shake. We sat on the edge of the sidewalk, staring into the street-light-blurred night sky.

"Are you afraid of flying?" I asked as I sucked the shake through a straw. "Is that why you drove?"

"No. But I don't fly very often. I don't like going fast."

I laughed.

"I like to stop and smell the cactus bloom," Miguel said.

I smiled. When he wasn't yelling or speechifying, he had a nice voice, with a gentle pleasant rhythm, like my mom sometimes had when she was completely relaxed, when she mixed her Spanish and English words together. She had been born in the United States but her parents spoke their native Spanish exclusively until my mother went to school.

"I'm a city girl myself," I said. "I don't stop to watch anything bloom. Sometimes I stop to watch the sprinklers water the sidewalks."

"What a waste. Do you know how many feet a year the water table drops?"

I looked at him. "I thought I worried a lot. You're worse than I am, except you worry about things you can't do anything about."

"And you can do something about serial killers or hantaviruses?"

"Yes," I said. "I can figure out their modi operandi and steer clear of them."

"Psycho killers or hantaviruses?"

"Both."

"I think you have a better chance of getting poisoned by polluted air or water than getting killed by some psycho."

"Ha! A lot you know. You're obviously not a girl."

He laughed. "Obviously."

"We have more to worry about than you do. Look at all the diseases we get, plus rapists and killers, abusive boyfriends and husbands.

"Those diseases are mostly environmentally caused," Miguel said.

"Look," I said. "You've got your worries; I've got mine. Right now, all I'm really worried about is getting my scepter."

"Yes, my liege!" He bowed, then pushed himself up. "Let's get you on your way."

I thought we would never stop driving. All lights of civilization disappeared, and the night was black. No place on Earth was as primordial looking at night as the desert: there be dragons here. Then a town popped up off the two-lane road that led us to it. No traffic moved on the main street, if that was what it was—it looked like the only street.

Miguel stopped the car in front of a building set off by itself. In blue neon, written in cursive, were the words LA MAGIA. Magic. A false front arched up over the huge picture windows.

"It's near, it's near, m'dear!" Crane shouted.

I dropped the skull in the laundry bag and got out of the car. Miguel went to the front door and unlocked it.

"You have a key?" I said, following him into the restaurant.

"I'm part owner. A tiny part."

The neon sign lit part of the large dining room. On my right a huge recessed display case took up an entire wall. Inside the case was a strange kind of diorama, or museum-like display, soft spotlights over each item. A purple jewel-studded cape was first, the hood and shoulders positioned so it almost appeared as if someone wore it. A tiny sign below read, THE WITCH OF NOB HILL, 1879. Next was a small red leather pouch, with a pipe just over it: MEDICINE BAG AND PIPE OF POWERFUL SIOUX MEDICINE MAN. DATE UNKNOWN. Then a plain-looking chair: SHAKER CHAIR, 1954. A top hat and cane: HOUDINI'S HAT AND WAND, 19—. A Ouija board floated above the hat and cane: OUIJA BOARD, 1970. A twisted stick came next, feathers and beads decorating the sides of it: PERUVIAN SHAMAN, 1948. Then, all by its lonesome, lying across a stool with no sign, was my family's heirloom: the ruby scepter.

"*Viva la France!*" Crane cried. "*Mon* old *ami*. We spent many an hour languishing in our prison together. Never speaking. Words were not needed!"

I sighed. At last.

"Can you get it for me?" I asked.

"No. I don't have the key. Let me see if Paul's in the office."

Miguel walked to the end of the room, past the counter, through to the kitchen. I sat at a deuce next to the scepter and pulled Crane out and set him on the table.

"So, *ma petite,*" Crane said. "Our adventure comes to a close. Life becomes what it was. You return to be hostess with the mostest, and I return to the confines of the safe until the next time *votre père* deigns to let me out."

I put my hands on the top of Crane's head and rested my chin on my fingers.

"I hadn't thought of that," I said. "Maybe I could have Dad build you a display case like this one."

Crane groaned. "Can't I stay *avec vous?*"

"Oh, yeah. I'll end up as some bag lady out on the street because everyone will think I'm crazy, talking to glass. I'd never get a job or a man. My life would be over."

Crane said nothing.

"Look, if you were once alive, that means you're dead now.

Right? So if you're a ghost, shouldn't you follow the light or some nonsense like that? I could help you with that process, if you like. Find a medium or an exorcist."

"You want to get rid of me?"

"That's not what I meant. Wouldn't you rather be at peace instead of haunting this hunk of rock?"

"I bring peace to everyone I meet," Crane said. "I am quite peaceful."

Miguel returned to us. "Paul's home. He waited here, but it got late. He suggested you stay here, and he'll come over in the morning. He'd come in now if you want, but there is a bed in the office if you want to bunk here. Or you can come home with me."

I sighed. "The scepter's here, so I'll stay here. I am tired."

"Do you want something to eat?" He looked tired, too, and he seemed to be favoring his leg again.

"Miguel Madero, road warrior," I said, standing. "Go home to your wife and kiddies—"

He laughed. "My mother and Cousin Fernando."

"Go home to your family, Miguel. I am just fine. I have never depended upon the kindness of strangers before, but you've been a nice guy. Thanks."

"Let me show you the office first."

"I'll find it," I said.

"It's in the back, through the kitchen and to the right, past the rest rooms." He limped to the door. I followed. "I'll see you tomorrow." He leaned over and kissed my forehead as if it were the most natural gesture in the world, as if we had always been friends and this was how we said adios.

After he left, I turned the lock on the door. I picked up Crane and shuffled into the kitchen. The countertop lights let me see enough to find my way around. I set Crane on the cutting board island, then went to the refrigerator and found fixings to make a cheese, avocado, and sprout sandwich, which

I did. I sat at the kitchen counter and looked out the side window into nothing. I heard the front door open and Miguel's voice, "Here's your suitcase and purse."

"Thanks!" I called.

I heard the door lock.

I finished my sandwich, got my suitcase, purse, and Crane, and walked into the back. I opened the door marked OFFICE, switched on the light, and went inside. A desk and chair. File cabinets. A couch bed. A door leading into what I could see was a bathroom. I closed the office door and locked it. Then I changed into a long T-shirt and pulled the cover off the couch bed. Beneath the cover, the bed was made. I switched off the light. With great relief, I slid between the sheets and under the blanket.

"Good night, Crane," I said.

"Good night, *ma petite.* I will take the first watch. No one will get past *moi.* No! No! No!"

"Crane. I'm trying to sleep. I don't need any of your head games."

Crane laughed. I smiled and fell to sleep.

I awakened to dawn light coming through a window over the couch. I got up and went into the bathroom. I urinated, then took a quick shower and got dressed. After I made the bed, I stuffed Crane into the suitcase.

"Pourquoi, pourquoi, ma petite?" Crane said.

"Because this guy obviously collects magical things. What could be more magical than you, my friend?"

"Oh. Well. You have a point, *moi* dear. I will await your return," was Crane's muffled response.

I was famished.

I left the office and went into the kitchen . . .

. . . where in the diffused rose light of early morn stood the most gorgeous man I had ever seen.

He turned from the stove where he was cooking something that smelled exquisite. He was dressed in light gray slacks and a white dress shirt, open at the collar. His hair was short, curly, and black; his skin dark; his eyes cinnamon brown.

He smiled at me and carried the skillet from the stove to the island, where he divided the bright yellow scrambled eggs onto two plates. I walked to the other side of the island. He handed me a plate.

"Fresh eggs, a pinch of cayenne, and a bit of turmeric," he said. "It's all I know how to make. Shall we eat in the dining room?"

I followed him to a deuce already set with silverware and orange juice. Steam rose from a basket of bread.

The man put his plate on the table and extended his right hand. "I am Paul Gurare."

I shook his hand, and my knees trembled. "I'm Jeanne Les Flambeaux."

We sat and began eating silently. The eggs were dry and spicy, the bread soft and buttery. I wondered, since Paul was the cook, would it be his emotions I felt when I finished eating?

I looked forward to that.

I could not stop looking at him.

Was he married? How old? Thirty?

When we finished eating, I felt all aquiver. My feelings or his? He looked too calm, and why would he be all aquiver around me?

For the first time, he looked over at the ruby scepter.

"I am sorry Johnny stole it from you," he said. "Next time I see him, I'll let him know how sorry I am."

"We take it out only twice a year," I said. "For the Day of the Dead festivities, and then in the beginning of May, May Day, or the Feast of the Living, as my father calls it. There's a skull that fits on top of it. I was responsible for putting them both away in our safe. Needless to say, I didn't do a very good job."

"Did he steal the skull, too?"

"No. I have that." So much for secrecy.

"Really? May I see it?"

"Sure. I can show you how they fit together. I'll be right back."

I got up and went to the office, my heart beating in my throat. Geez. I was acting like a thirteen-year-old. I dug out Crane.

"Hello," he said.

"Be good," I said, and carried the skull back to the restaurant. Paul had cleared the table and taken the scepter from the case.

"A scepter, a scepter, my kingdom for a scepter," Crane called.

Paul stood and held out the scepter to me. I took it. Yes! It was in my grasp! I pushed the bottom of Crane onto the top of the scepter. They clicked into place.

"Was it good for you?" Crane asked.

I bit my tongue.

"The scepter has been in my mother's family for generations, given to a family member on an archeological dig in Mayan country, and a priest gave the skull to a member of my father's family—in gratitude for his culinary skills, my ancestor's skills, not the skull's. When my mother and father got together, they discovered the scepter and skull fit together."

"So the story goes," Crane said.

"How extraordinary," Paul said. "Well, I am sorry for your inconvenience."

"And yours," I said. "How much did Johnny owe you?"

"Three thousand," he answered.

"Wow. I don't have that kind of money," I said. "Not that I

would pay off his debt even if I could. He's not really family. He's just an idiot."

Paul smiled. What a beautiful smile. Could he be the one?

"No. You don't owe him or me," Paul said. "I wonder if you could stay in town for a couple of hours until our police chief can talk to you and take our statements, et cetera. I hope he'll only need pictures of the scepter and not the actual object as material evidence."

"I'm not pressing charges," I said. "You didn't know it was stolen."

"But I need Johnny tracked down," he said. "If there's a warrant out on him, maybe I'll be able to get my money once they catch up with him." His voice was quiet: everything would be all right.

Except I felt panic rising. I had been ready to tell my family all, but now that the scepter was safely in my hands, I hoped I could forget about the little mishap.

"I can't afford to lose that money," Paul said. "I wish I could. And Johnny should pay for what he's done to us both."

"Isn't there another way?" I said. "I have two weeks off. Maybe there's something I could do here."

"You could do something worth three thousand smackeroos?" Crane asked. "What are you saying?" I glared at Crane.

"Well," Paul said, smiling, "my waitresses don't get paid quite that much."

"Of course not. I was just hoping—"

"But I have an idea," he said. "Maybe I could borrow your name for two weeks. Les Flambeaux is synonymous with fine cuisine in the Southwest. My chef just quit. If I had you as my chef and I didn't pay you, I might make three thousand extra in two weeks.

"Me?" I laughed. "I can't cook."

"I don't believe you!" he said.

"I can't—"

"I could help," Crane said.

"What?"

"I was an excellent chef," Crane said. "I know many recipes. You could do this, cook for him."

"No. I burn everything."

"Then we would call it Cajun cooking," Paul said. "Your parents are from Louisiana, aren't they?"

"Go ahead," Crane said. "Say yes."

"I—I need to think about this," I said.

"Of course," he said. "I'll go make some calls."

"Crane," I whispered when Paul was gone. "Are you crazy! I burn water."

"That is nothing, *ma petite*," he said. "Your father used to burn air. I taught him everything he knows."

I flopped down onto the nearest chair. "What?" I asked.

"Your father, Jacques. I gave him some of his finest recipes."

"You spoke to my father, too?" I was shocked, aghast, dumbfounded. First I discovered my mother was a former rebel with a cause who exposed her unborn fetus—that would be me—to radiation and then became a gambler without a cause. Now I find out my father talked to a crystal skull and acted like I was crazy when I talked to it, too!

"I've been afraid I was nuts all my life," I said. "I thought I'd end up in a funny farm like Grandma Juarez. How could my father have done that to me?" I held Crane close to my face. "Are you making this all up?"

"I am slayed! I am slew! I am coming apart—don't spare the glue!" Crane sang.

"Tell me the truth."

"The truth is I made your father into the man he is today."

I wanted to scream.

"How could he?" I said. "Why didn't he tell me or my mother? Why didn't you tell me?"

"I just did. Come, *ma petite*. Let us do this. It'll be an adventure."

"Why should I do anything for my family? I should just let Paul keep the scepter."

"And that will prove what?" Crane asked.

"Don't confuse me with the facts!"

I looked around the restaurant, now brightening with daylight. Maybe I could stay. Learn how to do that which my father had pretended all these years was innate in every family member except me. Then I could go home and show them all that I was just as good as they were.

"All right," I said. "I'll stay."

"Viva ma petite!"

Five

Bon Appétit!

When Paul returned to the dining area, I told him I would stay.

"Is there any cheap place in town where I can bunk?" I asked.

"Right here," he said.

"But that's your office."

"I'll do my work when you're in the kitchen."

"I need a television or radio," I said before I could stop myself.

Paul laughed. I smiled.

"Like to keep up with current events, eh?" he said.

"I just figure I'll be alone a lot."

"I doubt it. The men around here will swarm to you like bees to honey, if you'll forgive the cliché."

I actually blushed.

"All right," Paul said. "This will be great. Now, Miguel's mother, Vesta, creates the soups."

Paul and I went into the kitchen. Daylight spilled through the room, and all was clear to me.

"Creates?" I asked. "What a lovely way to think about cooking."

"Vesta does create," Paul said. "She is magic, but she will do only soups and breads. Tangiers can keep cooking our regular dishes and lunch sandwiches. Fernando does prep and washes dishes. We serve lunch from eleven to three and dinner from five to nine."

It seemed a peculiar way to run the kitchen, but what did I know?

"If Vesta makes the soups, Fernando does prep, and Tangiers cooks your menu dishes, what would I do? The dinner specials?"

Paul nodded. "The menu is our bread and butter, but the specials are our meat and potatoes—or our chateaubriand and potatoes!"

"My father says specials are the soul of a restaurant," I said. And my mother was the heart, he always added.

"I'll let you get acclimated," Paul said. "Do you want to start tonight?"

I hesitated, then said, "OK. Just one special. Let me build up to more."

"I know you'll be great," Paul said.

"Because of my name?"

"Because I know magic, and you've got that glow."

"That's just fear and fatigue," I said.

He laughed.

I looked around the kitchen and saw a large range top with two ovens and a microwave next to it, the prep island with sink behind it, and stainless steel countertops in an L against the walls with open shelves of pots and pans above them. Around to the end of the L, the stainless steel became two sinks. One door led outside, another back to the office. Next to that door was the electric dishwasher and stacks of dishes, a refrigerator, walk-in freezer, and the pantry. It all seemed familiar.

And terrifying.

"Do you want to leave the scepter in the display case?" Paul asked. "It has a burglar alarm."

"No. I'd have too much explaining to do if someone we know sees it."

"How about my safe?"

"You wouldn't mind?" I asked.

"Of course not."

We went into the dining room, and I picked up the scepter and crystal skull, who had been remarkably quiet once I had agreed to his scheme. I followed Paul into the office. He opened a cupboard to reveal a small black safe, like my father's. I glanced away while he turned the tumbler. He opened the door, then looked at me.

I snapped the skull off the top of the scepter.

"You don't want both in the safe?"

"No. The skull's going to help me cook."

He nodded. "Whatever fries your eggs."

He put the scepter in the safe and closed the door. I reached over him and twirled the tumbler.

"For good luck," I said.

"You'll be good luck for us," Paul said. "Miguel told me a lot of what has happened in order to get you here. Maybe all the coincidences you've experienced lately were for a reason, and that reason was to get you here to Sosegado and this restaurant. Now, I have to go, but Vesta will be here by ten o'clock. She'll tell you how we get supplies and other details you'll need. Make yourself at home." He reached across his desk, opened the top drawer, and took out a key.

"Here's the key to the castle," he said, pressing it into my palm. "I'll see you later. Thank you."

He left me alone in my new home, the crystal skull in one hand, the key in the other.

"This is stupid," I said. "I can't believe I agreed to this."

"He is cute," Crane said.

"He's gorgeous." I sat on the couch. "So you give my father recipes?"

"At one time," Crane said. "But when he first got me, I—"

"When he first *got* you? I don't understand. You've been in our family forever."

Silence.

I held the skull close to my face. "Answer me, Crane. I've seen pictures of you and my dead relations."

"I don't know what to say, *ma petite*."

"You said when he 'first got me.' Got you from where?"

"From whom," Crane said.

"All right! From whom!" I cried.

"From Winema Juarez, your grandmother."

"She gave you to my father?" I asked.

"Let's just say your father received me from your grandmother."

"Why are you being so coy?" I asked. "I swear, I feel as though I've stepped into the *Twilight Zone* these past few days. Nothing is like it was. I'm learning all this stuff about my family from complete strangers!"

"I am not a stranger!" Crane said.

"Well, Bear Morrison is."

"He's an old family friend. Besides, everyone has family skeletons."

"Apparently our family only has part of one," I said.

Crane giggled.

I smiled.

I leaned over, picked up the phone, and called home.

Belinda answered.

"Hey, Belinda. Is Antoine there?"

"No. Remember, he's on a road trip? Taos was his next stop. Where are you?"

"I'm staying in a little town southwest of Tucson until Mom and Dad get home. Have you heard from them?"

"No. What are you doing in this little town?"

I sighed. Every word out of her mouth always sounded sarcastic.

"I'm cooking. Have Antoine call me if you hear from him. I'm in Sosegado at La Magia restaurant. He can get the number from information. I don't see it on the phone."

"You're cooking?"

"I am a Les Flambeaux, after all." I said. "Just have him call."

"If I talk to him, I'll tell him."

"Belinda." I hesitated.

"Uh-huh."

"Do you remember a Bear Morrison who lived near Las Vegas and went with Mom to anti-nuke rallies?"

"No. But I was too young to tag along during Mom's rebel yell years, and after that, she only took you to Las Vegas. Her own special little baby."

"So you knew she used to go to protests and stuff?" I asked.

"Sure. Then she grew up, I guess, and started gambling. What? You've blocked out her and Dad fighting about those trips?"

"I guess. I don't remember them ever fighting. Did you know Grandma Juarez is alive?"

"Who?"

"Mom's mother."

"I don't know," Belinda said. "Maybe. I've never given her much thought."

"Do you remember her?" I asked.

"Vaguely. Why all these questions? You've never cared about family stuff before."

"What are you talking about?" I asked.

"You've never shown any interest in the family business."

"That's because you all treat me like a half-wit!" I said. "So what if I can't cook? I'm still a human being. I'm still part of this family."

"Yeah, whatever. I've got things to do. Good-bye."

She hung up. I stared at the phone.

"She hung up on me. That little brat. What's she got to be angry about?"

"Well, perhaps—," Crane started.

"That was a rhetorical question."

I took Crane to the kitchen and set him on the shelf above the stove.

"Oh, *bonne amie,* it is so grimy here!"

I got a wet cloth and wiped down the shelf. "I'll buff you every night."

"Oh, oh, oh—*ma chère*—"

"Don't be vulgar," I said, trying to imitate my mother.

I heard the front door unlock, then voices.

A short dark woman with intense black eyes stepped into the kitchen, followed by Miguel.

"Good morning," Miguel said.

"Hi," I said.

"Mom, this is Jeanne Les Flambeaux. Jeanne, this is my mother, Vesta Madero."

"Hello," I said.

The older woman stared at me, her eyes narrowing. "I've told Miguel he is too trusting of strangers. Who are you? Why are you here?"

"Did Paul talk to you?" I asked.

"Me? The big boss talk to me? Not if he knows what's good for him. Miguel, get out of my way." Vesta pushed past Miguel and took down a white apron from a hook near the walk-in.

She faced us as she put on her apron. Miguel smiled at me and shrugged.

"Well, you going to answer me?" Vesta said.

"I came to get something that belonged to me," I said.

"So now you're leaving?" Vesta asked.

"Well, actually, I've agreed to stay on and help out here, to pay off the debt."

"Paul talked you into that?" Miguel asked.

I couldn't remember whose idea it was.

"Mr. Gurare asked me to do the dinner specials for a couple of weeks until he gets a new chef," I said.

Vesta put her hands on her hips. "You? Do you have it in you?"

"I—I—"

"Mom. Don't pick on her."

My face bloomed red. "I'm not a chef," I said. "I tried to explain to Paul."

"You're not a chef?" Vesta asked. "Hmph. Just another pretty thing Paul is dumping on us." She pulled a huge soup pot from beneath the island.

"Madam Madero, give the little gal a chance," Crane said.

Vesta stopped and looked around the kitchen. Her gaze lingered on Crane.

"That's Jeanne's crystal skull," Miguel said. "She talks to it."

I glared at Miguel. Now his mother would think I was crazy as well as incompetent.

Vesta nodded. "So she has some sense." She banged the pot onto the stove. "What was Paul supposed to tell me?"

"He said you would tell me where I could get supplies for my specials. Do you get regular deliveries way out here?"

Vesta blew air out of her mouth. "Yes. We do eat way out here in the desert. We get as much as we can locally. The produce man will be here soon. As far as meat, we have a weekly delivery, which has already come, and an occasional fish run.

Yesterday we got a delivery of snapper you can use tonight if you like."

"Snapper?" Crane said. "Yes, with a little hot sauce and green rice. Sound good?"

"Yes, that sounds fine," I said.

Vesta looked at me. "I'm glad it meets with your approval."

"She was talking to the skull," Miguel said.

"Of course." Vesta rolled her eyes.

A man a few years younger than I sauntered into the kitchen. His black hair was slicked back. A thin gray scar creased his right cheek. This must be Miguel's cousin Fernando, the one who had been shot by the marines.

He looked at the floor as Miguel introduced us. Then he went to the pantry and returned carrying several onions and a bulb of garlic.

Vesta pinched his left shoulder. "See, Nando can read my mind. He knows the base for all my *sopas* is olive oil, onions, and garlic. Stirred together with a bit of heat and just a drop of water, they form a perfect union, eh, Nando?"

"Yes, Aunt Vesta."

"Ah! I hear the truck," Vesta said. "Come, girl who talks to the crystal skull."

Miguel popped a piece of garlic into his mouth, and Fernando began chopping onions very rapidly. I had never seen anyone make a knife move so quickly.

I followed Vesta to the back door, which she flung open. For the first time, I saw the town. In one direction, distant mountains ruffled the horizon. In all other directions was the pale, pale, almost but not quite pink desert. One-story desert buildings slouched along the main street and probably one or two other streets. Saguaros struck poses all up and down the street. Next to us was Madame Wu's American and Chinese

Restaurant. Down and across the street was Mattie's Art Mart. A piñon jay stood on the lip of the garbage Dumpster, watching as a refrigerated truck backed into La Magia's driveway.

After the truck stopped, a tall thin man jumped out of the cab. He went to the back and opened the doors to display his wares of colorful fresh vegetables and fruits.

"What garbage do you have for me this day?" Vesta asked.

"Same ol', same ol'," he said, grinning. "Howdy, I'm Sam. I kind of collect from area growers. Most of it's organic. Good stuff. You the new chef? He goes through them quicker than Elvis went through diet pills."

"Hello. I'm Jeanne Les Flambeaux."

"Oh. I've heard of your family. Wow. You a good cook?"

"Why else would she be here!" Vesta said. "Give her room to breathe."

I moved closer to the produce. I had no idea what to buy. It all looked scrumptious.

Vesta began muttering. "Oh, yes, carrots, you look good. You be part of my soup. Oh, basil. You are lovely. . . ."

Sam smiled and nodded.

"Haven't you ever seen fresh produce, girl?" Vesta said. "Sam hasn't got all day."

"How often do you come?" I asked.

"Usually every second day," he said. "Long as there's something to bring. We're getting to the end. Been going into storage."

I took a deep breath, then plunged in. I put my hands on a bunch of bright orange carrots, a purple turnip, red and green peppers, a few chiles, several zucchini.

Vesta stopped her food monologue long enough to say, "We're feeding a restaurant full of people, not your skinny butt. Tonight, probably twenty specials."

I gathered more vegetables into my arms and carefully dropped them into Sam's proffered box. Then Vesta and Sam argued money.

I went back into the restaurant.

"So you're staying?" Miguel asked.

Fernando now had a large pile of chopped onions in front of him.

"For two weeks. To pay off Johnny's debt. As a favor to Paul."

"Do you want me to show you around town? Where you staying?"

"Here," I answered his last question first. "I better stay and get ready for tonight."

"Dinner isn't until five o'clock," Miguel said.

"Well, I better learn to cook between now and then," I said.

"Go, go," Crane said. "The sauce takes five minutes, the rice thirty. It'll be a cinch."

"OK. But I don't want to be gone for long. Bye, Fernando."

I followed Miguel outside. Sam passed us, carrying the produce into the restaurant.

"Where you going?" Vesta asked.

"To show Jeanne the town."

"I'll see you in five minutes, then," she said.

We went around to the front.

"She was kidding, right?" I asked as we walked down the road together.

He smiled. "This is Madame Wu's. Best Chinese food in town."

"The only Chinese food in town, right?"

"Details, details," Miguel said. "Her family has lived in this area for over a hundred years."

"Wow. The Chinese have been here that long?"

He looked at me.

"Just yanking your chain," I said. "I wanted to hear that immigrant speech again."

"Better watch yourself. I'll sic my mom on you."

"I'll be nice."

Miguel waved to someone going into Mattie's Art Mart. "A lot of the local artists sell their works at the mart," he said. "Sosegado is attempting to be the next Bisbee without having to decapitate a mountain first."

"This is nothing like Bisbee," I said. Or Scottsdale, Tucson, or any other city I had seen. "This looks like some buildings out in the middle of the desert."

"This is the desert," Miguel said. "We don't try to hide that."

As we walked, the buildings got closer together. A bank. Insurance company. Hair salon. Laundromat.

"Would you rather it looked like Phoenix or Tucson?" Miguel asked. "You know, new people have brought so many nonindigenous plants into Tucson, they give nightly pollen reports on the news. Some parts of Tucson look more like suburbs of Detroit than any desert town."

"I was just talking," I said. "I didn't really want to hear another speech."

Miguel frowned. "It's called a conversation. Why do you get offended when I talk to you about important things? What kind of things do you want to talk about?"

I stared, unseeing, into the buildings as we went by. What did I want to talk about? I didn't talk to many people. My family. Only we didn't talk about things. Certainly not about our pasts or futures, or politics, world events.

I didn't talk. I didn't think. What did I do? Why didn't I talk or think?

"You can talk about whatever you want," I said. "I'm sorry

if it seems as though I'm trying to stifle you. I'm not used to having conversations, I guess."

"Why?"

We stopped in front of the bakery, a small stucco building with metal chairs and tables outside.

I shrugged. "I've never felt safe having a voice."

Oops. Did I say that out loud?

"You're safe now," Miguel said. "Mom's got some great baked goods in here. You want something?"

I followed him into the bakery, which was decorated with photographs of various saguaros. Thus the name, Saguaro Café and Bakery.

"Hi, Miguel," the red-haired woman at the counter said.

"Hi, Theresa. This is my friend Jeanne. She's going to be chefing at La Magia for a couple of weeks."

"Good. New blood. I'll stop in. What can I get you?"

"The man who owns this place used to make bagels in New York City," Miguel said. "So the bagels are great. My mom makes some of the other goodies."

I got a hot raisin bagel and cold cider, Miguel a cinnamon roll and coffee. We sat outside. A wren stood on a nearby saguaro. I wondered if she was lusting after our baked goods.

"By the way, I heard that another WIJ woman disappeared," Miguel said. "I remember you said you were interested in that case. From Taos, I think."

Antoine was in Taos. I hoped he was safe.

We ate quietly. I looked around town. A few cars and trucks lumbered past. People walked about. Compared with Scottsdale and Las Vegas, Sosegado was very quiet. Almost as quiet as the goddess temple in Crystal Springs.

"Where's your father?" I asked.

"He died when I was a teenager," Miguel said. "It's been me and my mom for a long time."

"Do you live up to her standards?" I asked.

"I live up to mine," he answered. "Why?"

I shrugged. "I don't know. I'm starting to feel a little peculiar, as if I've been in a dream for a couple of decades and I'm just coming out of it. When I was a kid, my parents thought I was crazy, like my grandma, because I heard voices. I kind of shut down after that, I guess. My family never seemed to expect anything of me, and neither did I. Now I find out that when my mom was pregnant with me, she was exposed to radiation from a nuclear blast. And apparently my father heard voices, too. Well, one voice. But they let me believe something was wrong with me. And I thought my grandmother, the one who was supposed to be crazy, was dead, but she's not. She's living in Mexico. And don't even get me started on food."

I finished the bagel and leaned back in my chair. I felt a rush of—OK, don't fight it, don't fight it. What? Weariness. Whoever made the bagel had been tired. I breathed deeply, and the feeling went away.

"All families are complicated," Miguel said. "Maybe it's just your age."

I rolled my eyes.

"I didn't mean that to sound patronizing. Maybe you've just gotten old enough to step away from your family and take a look at them and yourself."

Paul walked up the street toward us. He smiled and waved.

Miguel stood. "So you conned this poor woman into being your slave for two weeks? I should have been there to protect her rights."

"But you're my lawyer," Paul said, grinning.

"And I don't need protecting," I said.

"I think it's time to talk to the staff about your presence amongst us," Paul said.

"All right," I said. "Thanks for the bagel, Miguel."

"See you later," he said.

As Paul and I walked back to the restaurant, he talked easily about the weather and his hope for a big crowd tonight at the restaurant. I listened quietly, enjoying the sound of his voice. He opened the back door to the restaurant and held it for me to walk in first.

Inside, the kitchen smelled of chiles and rosemary. Vesta stirred a pot on the stove, mumbling like one of *Macbeth*'s witches as the spoon went around and around. Fernando ripped lettuce. A tall blonde stood next to him, slicing tomatoes. All looked up as we entered.

"Hey," Paul said. "I'd like you to meet Jeanne Les Flambeaux."

"We've met," Vesta said. "Now get on with it. Who will do what?"

"Jeanne, this is Fernando, Tangiers, and Vesta. Vesta, why don't you be in charge of the kitchen and Tangiers and Jeanne can wait tables."

"Oh, look at how wide her eyes are!" Vesta said. "She is Les Flambeaux! She wouldn't lower herself to wait tables."

"Of course I'll wait tables," I said. "I was just surprised." It seemed like a crazy way to run a restaurant.

Tangiers shook her head.

"You've done it before, Tangiers," Paul said.

She shook her head again.

"I don't want to be in charge," Vesta said. "Let Tangiers cook. Fernando does his usual, and Miss Fire here and I will wait tables."

"OK. Good thing you don't want to be in charge, Vesta," Paul said. He glanced at his watch. "I'll open her up."

"Do you need my help for lunch?" I asked Vesta as Paul left the kitchen.

Vesta shrugged. "I can do it."

I sighed. The place was disorganized, and Vesta would not

cut me any slack. I had worked in restaurants all my life. I knew what to do.

I went into the dining room. No setup had been started, so I began putting silverware, napkins, and coffee cups on the tables. Paul counted money at the cash register. I looked around behind the counter and tried to memorize where everything was.

When the first customers came in—a couple who sat in a booth—I brought them menus and offered coffee, which they accepted. They smiled and were friendly to me. I had been hostessing for years, but I could not recall if the customers in my parents' restaurant said hello or asked me about my day. If they had, I hadn't noticed. I operated by rote when I was working at the Oui & Sí. It wasn't as if I had to worry about being fired.

I leaned back into the kitchen and said, "Vesta, you've got customers. I gave them a menu and coffee."

"I'm coming," she said. "Tell them to keep their shirts on."

The lunch rush was soon upon us. Vesta leisurely went from table to table. I did not catch much of her conversation, but her customers appeared satisfied with her service and left sizable tips. Paul urged everyone to return tonight for my grand opening.

Miguel came in near the end of the rush with two clients. When the clients finished their meals and got up to go, Paul said, "Come back tonight, and have the meal of your life."

"I wish he'd stop saying that," I told Miguel as I poured coffee into his cup. "I can't cook."

"Then I guess you're in trouble," he said. "I'll come by and see how you're doing later."

"Gee, thanks."

At a quarter to three, Vesta said to me, "Tell Tangiers what you want to eat."

I scanned the menu.

"Try Vesta's soup," Paul said. "It's always wonderful."

I had already experienced a half a day filled with her hostility. I could not imagine what I would feel like after eating her food. Well, actually I could. And I did not relish the idea.

"It'll be great," Paul said.

At three o'clock, Paul locked the door and began to cash out the register.

I went into the kitchen and scooped some of Vesta's soup into a bowl. I got a slice of her bread and joined the others in the dining room, sitting next to Fernando and across from Vesta and Tangiers.

We ate quietly with the sound of coin hitting coins in the background as Paul counted the money. I wished I could turn around and watch him. I had enjoyed us working side by side: him smiling at me, me wiping down tables and pouring coffee. I wondered if my parents ever felt that way when they worked together.

I spooned Vesta's soup into my mouth. Some kind of barley vegetable with a hint of cayenne? Delicious. The bread melted in my mouth.

"This is great," I said.

Vesta nodded.

"She talks to the food," Fernando said quietly. "She says you must always talk to the spirits of the food. Ask their permission."

"Yeah, yeah," Vesta said, as if she had heard it all before.

"What else does she say?" I asked.

Tangiers watched us as she sipped her soup.

"She says cooking is magic," Fernando said. "You take a tomato, for instance. You cut it up, apply heat, add a touch of water, some herbs, sing to it, and you have spaghetti sauce. That's magic."

I smiled. Fernando had an easier time talking when he was repeating someone else's words.

"The tomato is a good example," Vesta said. "The Aztecs offered tomatoes to their gods to ask for healing. So I, too, ask for their healing when I use them."

"I never thought of cooking like that," I said.

"With two great cooks in your family?" Vesta said.

"Five," I said. "My parents, brother, sister, and grandmother. I guess when I think about it, it did seem kind of magical what they did. Magical and mysterious, secret. And I didn't know any of the secret codes."

"It's no secret," Vesta said. "Any idiot can cook, can follow a recipe. But for the ingredients to transform into a wonderful meal, you have to have respect. The magic words come from you. From your own heart."

I waited for her to say I had no heart, or something sarcastic, but she did not.

I drank the rest of my soup.

When I finished, I felt nothing in particular, except contentment from eating a good meal.

Vesta pushed away her bowl and emptied her tips onto the table. I glanced behind us. Paul was not there.

Vesta counted her tips and divided them four ways. Surprised, I did not argue and took my share. We all got up and put our dishes in a bus pan. I went into the kitchen and stood at the stove. I had less than two hours to prepare a meal for twenty-plus strangers.

"I'll be back at four o'clock, in case you need help," Fernando said as he went out the back. Tangiers waved and followed him. I had not heard her utter a single word.

"OK, Crane. What are we making?"

"See if you've got tomatillos," he said.

I opened the refrigerator. "Yes."

"And some chipotle chiles."

"I'm sure. This is Arizona." I closed the refrigerator and went to the pantry and quickly found a jar of chiles.

"All right, *ma petite.* Let's cook."

I retrieved the tomatillos and put them on the island. Then I picked up one and looked at it. "Well, 'little tomato,' will you help me with my debut? Will you help me cook my first meal and not have everyone die of food poisoning? I would appreciate it. Thank you."

"Dry-roast them until they are a little brown," Crane instructed.

"Dry-roast?"

"You know, fry them in a pan with no oil, for about twenty-five minutes."

I peeled and rinsed the tomatillos, one after another, after another. Then I found a huge heavy skillet, put it on the stove, and turned up the heat. I dropped the "little tomatoes" in one by one. Crane began singing some song I did not recognize. I joined in, humming and pushing the tomatillos around the pan with a wooden spatula. As I watched, the tomatillos changed from green to brown, like magic. It was peaceful standing where I was, just me and the tomatillos. And Crane, of course.

"Oh, *ma petite!* You are doing so well! Yes, yes. Now put them in the refrigerator. And while you're in there, grab some limes and cilantro."

I turned off the heat, transferred the tomatillos to a bowl, and put them in the refrigerator.

I brought the limes and cilantro to the island.

"What are we doing now?" I asked.

"Making a marinade for the fish," Crane said.

"I'll get the olive oil."

"Very good, *ma chère.*"

I took the zest out of a few limes, leaving them looking rather bland with their color gone. Then I ripped up the cilantro leaves and dropped them into a bowl and poured olive oil over it all. I took the snapper from the refrigerator and put it in the island sink. I turned on the water, pulled the cellophane off the fish, picked up a fillet, turned on the water and ran the fillet under the stream.

Suddenly the room shifted. Or I did. I felt like I was going to throw up. I dropped the fish and gripped the edge of the island.

I breathed deeply. Everything settled down.

It was that old witch's food. I must be feeling her emotions from eating her food. Pretty sick shit. Some kind of delayed reaction.

I picked up the fish again.

Immediately, the room shifted. I felt as though I was going to fall.

I dropped the fish and sank to the floor.

"Hey! Who left this water running! Don't you know we live in a desert?"

From my position on the floor, I heard the water turn off.

Vesta came around the island to where I was, her hands on her hips. She frowned and leaned down to me.

"What happened?" she asked.

I pushed myself up slowly to a sitting position.

"Something I ate," I said as I stood.

"No," Vesta said. "You only ate my *sopa*. Something else." She was so sure?

"Maybe it's nerves, then," I said.

I picked up the fillet.

A moment later, I was on the floor. I could not recall going from up to down. But there I was. Miguel came in through the back door.

"What happened?" he asked, racing to me. He put his arm around my waist and half carried me to a chair. Vesta brought me a glass of water.

"Mother's milk," she said.

I sipped the water.

"What's wrong?" Miguel asked.

"Hey, Miguel," Paul said, walking into the kitchen. "What's up?"

I squeezed Miguel's hand to keep him silent about my condition. "We're just getting ready for dinner," I said to Paul. "Everything is fine."

"Good," Paul said. "I'll be back for dinner. It'll be great, Jeanne." He smiled and waved. I heard him unlock the front door and leave.

"I—I'm just nervous, I guess," I said to Miguel. "Or I ate something."

"She's a sensitive," Vesta said. She began washing the snapper.

"What?" Miguel and I said at once.

"She's feeling the death of the fish."

"I am not!" I cried. "It's your soup."

Vesta shook her head and held up a fillet.

"Then come wash this, girl who talks to the crystal skull."

Miguel sat next to me and looked at his mother. She patted the fish dry with paper towels, then dropped them in the marinade.

"Mom," Miguel said.

"I have heard of people who are sensitive to the—the emanations of certain items. With some it is rocks, with others it is the dead, with some it is food."

"Does this sound familiar?" Miguel asked me.

I shook my head. "I'm just nervous about cooking."

"Then why did you think it was my soup?"

"Food poisoning," I said.

"No," Vesta said firmly.

I sighed. "Eating has always been difficult for me. After I'd eat, these emotions would just well up in me, and I'd kind of act them out. So I stopped eating in front of other people. I'd always thought I was just a little crazy and food triggered craziness. Recently someone suggested those emotions weren't mine."

"Whoever the someone is is probably correct," Vesta said. "You couldn't have gotten sick from my soup because, first, I am such a kind and loving person that I give off only good vibrations, and secondly, I sing to my soups so that there are no—how shall I say it?—no negative consequences to eating my food."

"Perhaps food for you is the philosopher's stone," Crane said.

"What do you mean?" I asked, putting my head in my hands.

"Alchemists used to believe that if they could obtain a particular substance they would have access to the wisdom of the gods," Crane said. "In other words, with this stone, which really wasn't a stone, the alchemist could turn lead to gold. Of course, if one obtained the wisdom of the universe, would one actually care about changing lead to gold?"

"I don't understand your point," I said.

"My point is that food allows you access to the wisdom or knowledge of the universe," Crane said.

"It makes me crazy."

"Maybe not if you understood what was happening," Vesta said.

I looked up. Oh. Miguel and Vesta had heard my apparently one-sided dialogue with Crane.

"Do you know how to help her?" Miguel asked.

"Me? No!" Vesta said. "I know of a healer in Mexico maybe. You know her. Inez. But for now, I will pray to the fish, and you better talk to your skull and finish dinner."

In a daze, I prepared the rest of the meal. Crane walked me through the salsa first: pureeing the tomatillos with chipoltes, chile sauce, lime juice, and cilantro. I sautéed onions, garlic, and rice for a few minutes, then poured water over it all. As I watched, waiting for it to boil, I mumbled, "Please be good and nourishing."

"Of course it will be nourishing, *ma petite,*" Crane said. "The garlic will keep away the vampires, and rice has always meant happiness, nourishment, and fertility. In some places, rice was thought to have a soul like human beings and was watched over by the great Rice Mother."

"Did you learn this while giving Cortés the wrong directions to the New World?" I asked.

"I don't recall, *ma chère.*"

Fernando arrived. I had him cut the fish into individual servings to be broiled when the time came. Tangiers returned and did her prep work.

Crane told me to blend parsley, chiles, cilantro, and lettuce to a puree, which I added to the rice. I took the rice off the burner, then sliced zucchinis and prepared the steamer.

Near five o'clock, Paul walked into the kitchen, now dressed in a cream-colored suit. I was dazzled out of my daze.

"How's it going?" he asked me.

"Hah," Vesta grunted as she stirred her soup.

"Fine," I answered.

"I'd like to be the first to try your special. What are we calling it?"

"Um. Red snapper with green rice."

"How colorful," Paul said. "Serve two up. One for me and one for Miguel. No soup or salad."

Fernando put two servings into the oven.

"I'm going to splash my face," I said. "I'll be back before it's done."

Fernando nodded. I hurried into the office, locking the

door behind me. I peeled off my clothes, jumped into the shower, stayed two minutes, and hopped out again. I pulled on a shirt and slacks, ran my fingers through my hair, and went back into the kitchen.

Fernando scooped the fish onto the two plates already garnished with slices of lime and sprigs of cilantro. Tangiers had steamed the zucchini, which she now spooned onto the plates. I took the plates to the stove and added rice. Then Fernando ladled the tomatillo sauce over the middle of the fillets. Vesta came and looked at it.

"Very nice presentation," she said.

I carried the plates into the candlelit dining room. Miguel smiled and gratefully did not ask how I was feeling. I set the dishes at their table.

Please, I said silently, give these men the nourishment they need.

I watched as their forks dipped into the salsa-covered fish first, then scooped up the rice, and brought it all up into their mouths. They chewed. Nodded.

Swallowed.

"This is wonderful," Paul said. "Just wonderful!"

Miguel nodded.

"What's the verdict, road warrior?"

"Not bad, WIJ."

I sighed. Yes! I had done it! Well, *we* had done it.

I walked into the kitchen.

"Thanks everyone," I said, including Crane in my glance. "Apparently, it's a hit."

Fernando nodded and went back to slicing limes. Tangiers grinned and gave me a thumbs-up. Vesta took off her apron and went to the sink to wash up.

"Thanks for taking care of the fish," I told her.

She nodded. "Paul ordered chicken breasts for tomorrow."

"OK."

"OK?" She shook her head. "You can't fight this."

"I've ignored it all my life," I said. "I can keep ignoring it."

"And what has that gotten you?" Vesta asked. "You are a skinny little thing with one foot in this world and the other one who knows where."

I stared at her. Who was this woman to speak to me like this? What right had she?

I turned away and went into the dining room.

The evening went by quickly. Although I had only glanced at the menu, I somehow knew it well enough to ask the appropriate questions with each order. I was fast and pleasant. Paul went from table to table, talking with each customer, often stopping to introduce me.

The restaurant patrons seemed to like my dish. I enjoyed watching them eat the first few bites and couldn't help grinning as the apparent pleasure of my food spread across their faces.

We turned the CLOSED sign around at nine o'clock and locked out the final customer at 9:15.

All of us ordered red snapper and green rice. Tangiers and Fernando brought out the plates, and the four of us sat together while Paul counted the money behind us.

The three of us watched Vesta as she mumbled something and then dug into her food.

"What are you looking at? It's delicious. Eat. You—," she said, pointing at me with her fork. "Eat the fish, too. It will be all right."

First I ate a mouthful of rice.

Was this the first real food I had ever made myself?

Even as an adult, I usually reheated someone else's cooking or went out to eat.

I chewed. My mouth filled with luscious flavors.

I took a forkful of salsa and fish. I grinned.

Not bad.

Not bad.

Good, in fact.

And I had made it!

I laughed out loud.

The others looked at me.

"I can't cook," I said. "Everyone knows that."

"Then everyone is wrong," Fernando said.

The four of us giggled until tears ran down our cheeks.

"Good take, guys," Paul said from his place in front of the cash register. "Good job." Then off he went to the office.

"I was exhausted," Fernando said, fingering his scar. "But now I feel like a walk in the desert. Anyone want to come?"

"I need to figure out what I'm going to make tomorrow," I said. "But thanks."

"I've got a date," Vesta said, "with my bed."

Tangiers nodded.

I got my tips and gave them to Vesta. She added hers and divided them four ways.

"We don't do tips like this at our restaurant," I said. "Is this Paul's idea?"

"Hah!" Vesta said. "He has no idea what goes on here most of the time. We decided ourselves. We all work hard. It's nice to have some jingle in our pockets."

I took my share of the tips, said good night, and got Crane from the kitchen.

We passed Paul in the hallway.

"I can't wait to see what you do tomorrow," he said. "Good night!" Then he was gone.

"Good night," I sighed.

"Jeanne's in loooooove!" Crane said.

"Shut up."

"What?" Paul called.

"Nothing!" I answered.

I went into the office and closed the door. A small television was now on the office desk, complete with a remote control.

I smiled. He likes me, he really likes me.

Crane and I stayed up half the night figuring out recipes for the next day. I wrote them out, including the ingredients, arguing with him when some esoteric-sounding herb or spice was needed. I settled on one meat recipe, to use up the chicken breasts, and two meatless ones.

After I got into bed, I switched on the television. CNN talked about the WIJ disappearances, which now appeared to be happening daily in all different parts of the West. Reporters claimed citizens were outraged at the failure of the police to come up with a single clue.

I turned on the timer so the television would switch off in twenty minutes, and then I feel to sleep.

I dreamed I flew over the desert and saw the letters *WIJ* carved into the Earth. Beneath me, Miguel waved.

Six

Les Oeufs et Moi

Someone was knocking at my door.

Bewildered, I sat up.

Where was I?

Oh, yes.

"Jeanne, it's Paul. Sorry to wake you."

"Just a minute," I said.

I got up and pulled on a pair of jeans. Then I opened the door.

"I'm sorry," he said, smiling. He looked perfect, dressed in a cream-colored shirt and pale green slacks. Good enough to eat.

"Jeanne's in loooove!" Crane said.

"I've got some business partners in from out of town," he said. "I told them about you, and they have to leave town right after our meeting. Would you mind making them breakfast, as a favor to me?"

"Jeanne's in loooove!" Crane.

"Well, only eggs. OK?" I said.

"That's great. There's four of them, plus me. You're magic, Jeanne, pure magic," he said, as he walked away.

I closed the door, went to the bathroom, peed, slapped water on my face, and got dressed. Then I picked up Crane and went into the kitchen.

Vesta was already there, her baked goods spread around the countertops and cooling on racks.

"Good morning," I said.

"Good morning, girl who talks to the crystal skull."

"What now, Crane?"

"Get the eggs and some of that leftover rice from yesterday. And a big bowl. Which do you think came first? The egg or the frying pan?"

I did as Crane asked. Then I broke egg after egg into the bowl. I found a whisk and beat them into a frenzy of yellow.

"Add a pinch of cayenne," Crane said.

Sleepily, I went to the spices, got the cayenne, and brought the jar to the eggs. I twisted off the cap and the jar tipped over into the eggs. I quickly pulled the cap out.

"A little cayenne never hurt anyone," Crane said.

"This isn't a little cayenne," I said.

"Just scrape out as much as you can," Crane said. "It'll keep them healthy for weeks."

I tried to get out as much as possible, but when I beat the eggs again, they were slightly red.

Vesta looked into the bowl, said nothing, and took off her apron.

"Use that loaf over there for bread," she said, pointing. "I'll be back."

"Now what?" I asked Crane after she had left.

"Fry the rice until it's hot through; then add the eggs and cook them together.

My eyes watered as I cooked the green rice and eggs. The green, red, and white blended prettily, but I was not sure how it would all taste.

"Please give these people the nourishment they need," I said to the food.

I quickly sliced the bread while the egg-rice combo cooked. I put it in a basket and tossed in lots of butter squares. I poured last night's salsa into a bowl, then carried it and the bread into the dining room, where the five men talked amongst themselves.

I hurried back to the kitchen, stirred the eggs and rice, cut up a couple of oranges and a lime, and put the slices on five plates, along with cilantro sprigs.

I turned off the burner and divided the mixture onto the plates, leaving some in the skillet for me. On a hunch, I took a jar of chiles from the refrigerator and spooned a couple onto each plate. I carried the plates into the dining room in two trips. Then I returned to the kitchen and leaned against the stove.

Soon I heard screams.

Or crying.

"Good lord, man! What is this!"

"Beer! Give me beer!"

"Water!"

I rushed into the dining room, grabbed four beers from the cooler, popped off the tops, and rushed them to the table. The four strangers reached for the beers and chugged them down.

"Damn!" one said, slamming his beer down on the table. "Girl, you must be Texan born and bred. This is damn good chile eggs!"

The others nodded. Paul looked up at me, his eyes tearing. I hurried over to the cooler and got another beer. Paul snatched it from me and guzzled the liquid.

"I'm glad you like it," I said. "Enjoy."

I went back into the kitchen and made myself a plate. I sat

at the counter and ate slowly, pausing to stuff myself with bread and butter so that the eggs would not burn through my stomach. I chewed my food, swallowed it, and felt satisfied. Nobody else's feelings filtered through. This must be why people cooked.

"Thanks, Crane," I said. "I couldn't have done it without you."

"It was nothing," he said.

In the other room, the men laughed and talked.

Miguel came in through the back door, dressed in jeans and a shirt, his hair still wet from a shower. He looked sleepy, like a boy just awakened from his nap. He smiled.

"Hello," I said.

"Hey," he said quietly.

"You look tired."

"Actually, I slept really well, about twelve hours. Must be your cooking. I even had good dreams."

"Is that unusual?"

He shrugged. "Sometimes what I do in real life enters into my dreams. Like if someone has to go to jail and I feel as though I failed him, or if someone is sent back to their country where they might be killed by the government or die for more mundane reasons, like starvation. Then I have nightmares."

"You need a vacation," I said. Suddenly I remembered my dream. "I dreamed I was flying over the desert and you were below waving."

"You dreamed about me?" He grinned.

I slugged his arm. "It's no big deal. I've dreamed about Hitler, but it doesn't mean I want to date him."

"Hitler?"

"Listen," I said. "In the dream you had the letters *WIJ* scratched next to you. Maybe the dream was trying to tell me you are the WIJ kidnapper."

"Yeah, that's it." He rolled his eyes. "Got any of those eggs left?"

"I think I ate the last of it," I said.

He got a plate and went to the stove. "There's plenty," he said, scooping some onto his plate.

"Really?" I could have sworn that pan had been empty.

Miguel sat next to me. I finished my breakfast in silence. Then I sat looking out the window. I could hear the jolly Texans and the sounds of Miguel eating. I glanced at him. I liked Miguel. He talked to me. Treated me like a whole equal person who had a mind and opinions of my own. Not that I *was* a whole person or had a mind and opinions of my own, but he treated me like I did.

"Let's go for a drive into the desert," Miguel said, pushing away his empty plate. "That was great, by the way."

"We are in the desert, Miguel."

"Away from the city."

I laughed. "By no stretch of the imagination is this a city. A town, maybe. A village, perhaps. A crossroads, most likely."

"Semantics."

"That's what a man who is losing an argument says," I said. "Besides, I have to get ready for tonight."

"I didn't know we were arguing," he said. "And it's eight-thirty in the morning. We could be back by eleven o'clock."

"Don't you have a job?"

"Yes, but I want to be out in the desert," he said, "with you."

If I stayed here, maybe I would get to talk to Paul alone.

One of the Texans roared.

No, that was wishful thinking.

"I'm not really a country girl," I said.

"You'll be fine," he said. "I have an appointment at eleven o'clock, so I have to get you back on time."

I nodded. "All right."

"Don't leave me!" Crane cried.

"You'll be all right," I said. "Talk to Vesta. You two should get along just fine."

Miguel looked at me. "The skull?"

"Yes. Are we going or not?"

We passed Vesta returning to the restaurant as we were leaving.

"I'll be back in a couple of hours," I said.

"I'm taking her out to the desert."

"No skin off my knuckles," Vesta said.

Miguel kissed his mother's forehead.

"Get away from me," Vesta said, smiling.

Miguel laughed. "You loved it!"

"Mother harassment. I'll sue! I know a good lawyer."

Miguel and I got in the little red car. The day was brilliant blue, the ground slightly damp, the air pungent with the smell of greasewood.

"I love that smell," Miguel said, driving us away from town with the windows open. "My mother's people say that grease-wood was the first plant in the world and from its magic resin, the Earth Maker shaped the mountains you see all around us."

"Your mother's people?"

"Her mother is Tohono O'odham—what the whites used to call Papago. They are the desert people. I guess I'm a desert people, too."

I stared out into the desert. "It looks all the same to me," I said.

"You're one of those?"

"Those what?"

"Those people who believe the desert is a big Kitty Litter box just waiting for the next fat cat to come shit in it."

"Miguel!"

"Well?"

"I told you before, I've never thought about it. My parents came here from New Orleans. They lived below sea level. Water is in our blood."

"So why are you here if you hate it so much?"

I laughed. "I didn't say I hated it. I said I just don't pay any attention to it. There's a difference. I don't pay any attention to you, but I don't hate you."

Miguel laughed. "Gee, thanks."

"Actually, Johnny and I went to New Orleans a couple of years ago, and I felt like I couldn't breathe. Everything was so moist. I was filled up with water."

"You're a land creature after all," Miguel said.

"I suppose," I said. "But really I don't feel I belong anywhere. You know what I mean? I don't feel connected. I don't feel *here*."

"Never?"

I shook my head. "Sometimes for a second." Like when I was making love with Johnny. But then it passed.

Miguel was silent. We drove for what seemed like a long while. The mountains got closer and farther away. We passed no cars or houses.

"Where are you taking me?" I asked.

"We're almost there," he said.

"You really *love* the desert, don't you? It seems dangerous to me. If I go too far from civilization I feel like I'm in jeopardy. I could die if I got stuck out here."

"You could die anywhere."

"How comforting."

"You could die of hypothermia in a snowstorm on a mountain, drown in water, get trampled by cows."

"Now you're exaggerating," I said. "You wouldn't catch me anywhere near a cow."

"You do have to be more aware in the desert," Miguel said. "Maybe that's why I like it. You can't be any place else. You have to be absolutely aware of your surroundings."

"That's why I don't like it. I don't want to be that aware of anything."

Miguel turned the car onto a dirt road and drove a short distance until we got to the brown shell of a building.

"This used to be a church," Miguel said, shutting off the car.

We got out. Behind the church, low hills stretched into scraggly mountains. A gray curved-bill thrasher stood on a rock, watching us.

"They always look annoyed," I said.

Miguel followed my gaze. "It's just the yellow eyes."

The thrasher cocked its head and then flew away, staying low to the ground. Insects buzzed around us. Above, a vulture flew. Miguel got a pack from his trunk. Then we walked around a thicket of mesquite—with their leathery peapods still clinging onto their spiny branches—and over to the ruins.

Only the rectangular bottom of the church remained. Brittlebush grew up over portions of the ruins, their yellow flowers long gone, their milky green tapered leaves still hanging on.

"I bet this is beautiful in the spring, full of yellow, against the dark brown, and the mountains in the back," I said.

Miguel looked at me. "I thought you didn't know anything about the outdoors?"

"Well, I have lived here all my life," I said. "I must have picked up a few things."

"Come on," Miguel said. "I want to show you something."

"I thought this was the something."

"No. Those are only ruins."

I followed Miguel past the church and up the rocky hills,

my shoes occasionally slipping on loose stones. We climbed the slate gray hillside until it broke off, and we followed a kind of path, then up again, scrambling around the occasional cholla reaching for us and the perched piñon jays screeching at us. I concentrated on the ground and keeping my balance.

"City girl, remember!" I shouted. "Where are you taking me?"

"You're all right."

"Easy for you to say, road warrior."

After a while, we stopped climbing and the hill leveled off. Then Miguel stopped and said, "There it is."

Below us, the desert dipped into a beautiful tableau of scarlet, green, gold, and yellow.

"Are those colors from the leaves on the trees changing?" I asked.

"Yeah, but it's mostly from the scrub, rock, and cactus, except farther on," he said, pointing. "That undulating strip of green and gold hides a stream."

We sat on top of the foothill and gazed about us.

"Across the way, beyond those close mountains, do you see that dark part, like a piece of turret?"

I followed his finger and squinted until I could see past the foothills and distant spiky mountains to the piece of sky he pointed to.

"That's Baboquivari Peak, sacred to the Tohono O'odham."

"That's near Kitt Peak, where the telescopes are," I said. "Isn't it? I went there once in college. They told us that before they built the observatory they asked the Tribal Council to come look through a telescope in Tucson. After the Council looked at the stars through the telescope, they were so impressed that they gave the Long Eyes permission to use their land."

Miguel nodded. "What else do you remember?"

"That I got a headache. It got so bad that I went back to the visitor's center to be alone."

"Maybe the spirits of the place were speaking to you and you weren't listening."

"And maybe I got a headache from bouncing around in a school bus for a couple of hours going up and down and around roads that would make a trip to hell seem like a joyride."

Miguel laughed.

"I took an astronomy class in college," I said, "but the first day the professor started talking about the zenith and the whatsit and I just wanted to look at the stars."

"So what'd you do?"

"I dropped the class," I said.

"And went out and looked at the stars?"

I nodded.

"My mother's ancestors roamed this land and beyond to the really arid part of the Sonoran, past the peak," Miguel said.

"The really arid part? Yeah, this is Miami Beach."

"Some of my ancestors were part of the Sand People, the nomadic Papagos. When the white settlers first came, they hunted down the Sand People as if they were some kind of vermin. The Sand People knew how to live in the desert. They had rain catchments—*tinajas*—all over the desert. Some are still here, but the water is not drinkable. Now it is almost impossible to live here unaided. The aquifers are so low. The cities have sucked too much water out of the desert. There isn't anything left for us."

"It would be a good skill," I said. "To know you could survive on your own."

Miguel nodded. A gila woodpecker landed on a saguaro

below us, becoming a red-and-tan adornment to the giant cactus.

"You love the desert," I said, "but you brought me to a place colored by a river."

"All desert people cherish water," Miguel said. "That is how you can tell the desert people from those who are pretending. A true person of the desert would not plant grass and water it, or water the sidewalk with misplaced sprinkler systems or—"

"I get the picture," I said.

"The word *Arizona* comes from the Tohono O'odham word *Arizonac,* which means 'little spring.' "

"Really?" I said. "I never knew that. I guess I should have listened better in school."

The woodpecker flew away.

"Did you grow up on stories of La Llorona?" Miguel asked.

"Of course," I answered.

"My mom used La Llorona to get me home before dark."

"It wasn't my mom who told stories about her," I said. "It was my sister and brother."

"Every time I crossed a dry wash," Miguel said, "I looked both ways to see if La Llorona was there, weeping and looking for her lost children. She was supposed to be very white, dressed in white, her hair white from grief. 'Don't let her near you,' my mother would say, 'or she'll mistake you for one of her drowned children and snatch you out of this world!' "

"No," I said. "She was dark, with red eyes and long black hair. And it wasn't dry washes, it was right after a rain when the arroyos were full. At those times and at dusk, her power to get you was the greatest. I always pictured her as looking like my mother's mother, the grandmother who was supposed to be crazy. Of course, I didn't really know what she looked like."

"Let's go down to the stream and see if La Llorona is there," Miguel said, standing.

"That looks pretty far away. Isn't it time to get back?"

"No. It's a fifteen-minute walk."

Miguel pulled a plastic jug of water out of his pack and handed it to me. I took a couple of swigs and gave it back to him. He drank some, then returned the water to his pack.

We started down the slope. The incline was not as steep as it had been on the other side, so I was able to occasionally look up. We skirted various cacti, slightly bloated from last night's binge on rainwater. We scattered birds here and there, including several who looked like bobwhite quail, only I recalled they were endangered. Suddenly I remembered wandering in the desert during a rest stop on our way to where? Mexico? Mom and Dad were far away. I heard the *who-who-white* of the quail, then the furious flutter of wings.

The memory flitted away.

What had happened next?

I touched a mesquite pod as I walked around the bush and watched Miguel's back.

What had happened next?

I had gone around a bush where I heard something moaning. It seemed as though the desert itself cried out, the sound undulating up from the ground and through the soles of my tiny boots. Even though I was very young, I knew I was hearing some kind of death rattle.

Then I saw it was not actually the desert who cried but a dog—no, a coyote, like the gray ghosts who sometimes sang in the arroyo behind our apartment building. The coyote had vomited and lay sprawled on the ground, kind of sinking into the sand as if it were already dead and rotting. Its dark yellow eyes looked up at me. It was changing, dissolving. Was it a coyote or a woman? I reached down to touch her . . .

. . . and suddenly I was in the air, my father's arms wrapped around me, turning me from the face of death.

"Why is she sick?" I asked.

"I don't know," my father said as he carried me away.

I squirmed out of his arms and ran toward someone—Who?

"See, it's right up here," Miguel said, pointing to the cottonwoods up ahead.

I had run to a dark-haired woman who held out her arms to me.

"Maam-mah," I called her. "The coyote is dying."

She nodded and sang to me, "Some people leave out poison food for the coyotes."

"Why?"

"They don't like them," she sang. "They do not understand the nature of the coyotes. They are edge dwellers, like us. Some call us coyotes, too, because we are mixed, because they do not understand our nature, either."

"Maam-mah," I cried.

"You're frightening her," my father said.

A teardrop fell onto my dusty new boots.

"She must know these things," the woman sang. She leaned toward me, and her breath smelled like moonlight. "You are my coyote cowgirl today, aren't you? You understand what it is to survive and to thrive."

"Mother," my mother said. "Leave her be."

The day bloomed saguaro flowers. Magenta.

I stopped and looked up at the sky. I could hear Miguel ahead of me. White wisps of clouds decorated the north.

"Miguel, I just had a memory of my grandmother."

He stopped and looked at me.

"I saw a coyote dying and she told me that I was one of the coyotes. Do you know what that means?"

"Sometimes mixed-bloods were called that," he said. "Indian and anything besides Spanish, I think."

"So you're a coyote?" I asked.

"No," he said. "And I'm not one for labels. They're usually used to denigrate and separate."

We reached the cottonwoods. Mesquite also leaned toward the wash, along with scraggly juniper and sycamores on each side, reaching across the divide, trying to join one another.

The stream was barely a trickle. Miguel and I both drank more water from his jug, then sat on separate rocks close to the creek. Most of the round bare rocks were covered in a fine white chalky substance.

"Each stream or river has its own language," Miguel said.

"What's this one saying?"

Miguel turned an ear toward it. "I'm thirsty! I'm thirsty!"

I laughed and looked down the stream. A woman was walking amongst the rocks in the distance. She was barely visible, her gray hair and light-colored clothes blending into the landscape. Only her purple scarf seemed distinct from everything else.

"That's a dangerous place to be," Miguel said. "This river flash floods all the time."

"We're just as close as she is."

"Not quite. It was supposed to rain up north again."

"She's okay," I said. "She's probably La Llorona looking for her children. Better not get too close." I grinned. Miguel rolled his eyes.

The woman seemed to be wandering aimlessly. I looked around. Where had she come from? Miguel took off his pack and began scrounging inside.

When I looked down the dry streambed again, the woman was gone.

Miguel and I ate trail mix and pieces of his mother's bread slathered with honey. When we finished, we checked for snakes and scorpions, then lay back on the ground. I sleepily looked downstream. As my eyes fluttered closed, I thought I saw a coyote fading into the gray white rocks—or was she leaping across the stream, her purple scarf streaming behind her? Coming, coming, coming to whisper me to sleep.

Or awake.

I opened my eyes.

A tortoise stared at me with a half-grin on its face, the skin around its neck loose, giving it the look of an ancient creature, which I supposed it was. I sat up and nudged Miguel next to me. He opened his eyes and sat up, startled.

"What?"

"Look," I said.

"Well, hello, Grandmother, she who wanders the desert with her home on her back."

I smiled. "You know, I almost feel safe here. It's really wonderful. Thanks for bringing me here."

Miguel glanced at his watch.

"Oops. I guess I missed my appointment."

"That means it's past eleven o'clock?"

"Yep. We better get going."

We drank water, then started across the valley and up the hill. I glanced back toward the river. Tortoise, coyote, and wandering woman were all gone, or out of sight. A few minutes later, we were in the car.

Miguel put the key in the ignition and turned it.

The car did not start.

Miguel looked to the left and turned a knob.

He glanced at me. "I left on the lights."

I stared at him.

We were stranded in the middle of the desert.

"Miguel," I said quietly.

"It's all right," he said. "We've got plenty of water. We can walk."

"Walk! How far away are we? It'll take hours. I won't get back in time to do my specials."

We got out of the car. Miguel opened the trunk and stuffed two full jugs of water into his pack. Then he pulled out another backpack and handed it to me.

"Were you planning this?" I asked, slipping on the bright green pack.

"Always be prepared," he said.

"What a Boy Scout."

We walked down the long dusty road out onto the two-lane paved road. Not a car in sight either way.

"This will just confirm Vesta's suspicions of me as a slacker lowlife," I said. "What are we, thirty miles from town?"

"Give or take."

"How many miles a day can a person walk?" I asked.

"It depends upon the person. About twenty, I guess."

"Oh, great. Paul will be so disappointed in me."

Miguel laughed. "Why are you worried about what he thinks? He should be thanking you. He's the one who was in receipt of stolen property."

"He's counting on me," I said. "I'm not used to people expecting good things from me. I kind of like it."

"Do they usually expect bad things?"

"They don't expect anything at all," I said. "What can I say? I've never been very good at connecting with the rest of the human race. Or the animal or plant race. I told you. I don't really feel here here."

"When I went to school back East, I felt that way," he said.

"Foggy. As soon as I got back to the West, everything solidi-fied. I was here here."

I laughed.

We walked silently down the road. Miguel pointed out Baboquivari Peak, which was more visible now. A scrub jay followed us for a while, and a deer crossed the road, stopping to stare at us, looking like it was standing on tiptoes, or in high heels, making it seem off-balance or fragile. Then it was gone, disappearing into the desert camouflage.

Nary a car went by.

Miguel told stories.

I tried to remember recipes.

The mountains, desert, and sky seemed unmoving. I was certain we were going nowhere fast.

"Doesn't anyone live out here?" I asked.

"There's someone a few miles from here," Miguel said, "but they're out of town."

It seemed as though we had walked forever when we finally sat on the side of the road and ate more trail mix, fruit, and Vesta's glorious bread and honey. I drank lots of water. The sun seemed too hot for November, and I felt too weak for any time of the year.

"If this were summer," I said, "I'd be long ago melted."

Miguel smiled. "You're doing OK, city girl. Look at it this way, you came out here today so that you could remember your grandmother."

"I guess. I'm still amazed by that memory. Something about that place must have triggered it."

"It's called Valley of Dreams," Miguel said. "And it's one of my favorite places in the universe." He glanced at me. "You seem different from when I first met you."

"Why? Because I'm not screaming and calling the police?" I asked.

He smiled.

"We've known each other only a few days," I said.

"I know," he said, "but doesn't it seem like a long time? As if we've been friends since we were kids?"

I nodded and chewed on his mother's bread.

"You don't seem as drawn. As scared."

"That's because weird men aren't chasing me," I said.

"But I come to the restaurant as often as I can."

I laughed. "Yeah, I noticed. Momma's boy."

"They say you can judge a man by how he treats his mother," Miguel said.

"I don't believe that little bit of folk wisdom," I said. "Johnny treats his mother like a queen. But going back to what you were saying, I do feel different. Like I'm waking up and really seeing things. I can't explain it. Like I am me again. Or for the first time. Or like I'm alive. Finally. And it all started on the Day of the Dead. Weird."

He nodded. "Yeah. I've been feeling things, too. I don't know if I want to keep lawyering."

We packed away the water and food, then started walking again.

"What would you want to do, then?"

"I like growing things," Miguel said. "I've been a part of this seed diversity program, trying to reintroduce native seeds. So much has been lost to monoculture farming."

"What's monoculture?"

"Well, they find or create hybrids that produce the most yields per season and are drought and disease resistant, and then they plant only that particular type."

"But that sounds good."

"Except there's always a disease that a crop isn't resistant to, no matter how it's been engineered, and that disease could spread and wipe out all of that crop. And if that variety—for instance, if it were corn—was all that was planted, then all the corn would be wiped out."

"So diversity is the key," I said. "And you like getting down and dirty in the earth?"

Miguel smiled. "Yeah, I do."

"Maybe you can do both."

"I just don't see justice happening in the courtroom," he said.

"You've got to have money," I said. "You can't make it as a farmer in the desert, can you?"

"Money isn't everything."

"Only someone with money can say that," I said. "If you're poor, you want the money to buy food and shelter."

"That's true. I just believe you should follow your heart, too."

"My grandmother says to do what your bones tell you, not your heart," I said.

"Your bones?"

"She said she'd seen the raggedy asses my heart had picked, so she figured it was time to listen to my bones."

He laughed. "So what do your bones say?"

"Right now they say they're tired."

The longer we walked, the better I started to feel.

I started pointing out foliage and fauna.

"There's rabbit brush," I said. "Juniper. Cholla. Blue palo verde. Look, that saguaro is using that palo verde for a nurse tree. And over there, that short evergreen, that's ironwood. Isn't it? Don't know that one. Or that. Oh jumping jiminy, it's a jumping cholla." I giggled. A flicker flew over us, flashing its yellows wings and yakking at us, *flick-a*. I laughed.

"Where is all this coming from?" Miguel asked. "I'm impressed."

"Clue zero."

I walked barefoot for a while, but that didn't work. I put on my socks, and that lasted only a few minutes. Eventually, the shoes went on again.

The setting sun colored the world red. Several cars went by, but no one stopped.

Then a shiny blue truck pulled up to us and stopped. The wandering woman from the arroyo sat in the driver's seat.

"Miguel," she said, "how is your mother?" I could not place her accent.

Miguel stared at her for a moment, then shook himself.

"Inez! I'm sorry. She's fine. We're in trouble, though. My car's battery went dead. Can you give us a lift to Sosegado?"

"Of course," she said. "Hop in."

I let Miguel get in first—since they knew each other—and then I sat next to him.

"Inez, this is my friend Jeanne. Jeanne, Inez."

"How do you do?" she asked.

"Better now." I leaned against the door frame as we headed toward Sosegado.

"Was that you in the valley?" Miguel asked. "I didn't recognize you."

"Nor I you," she said. "I am thinking of having a gathering up here, and I'm looking for the right place."

"How's it going?" Miguel asked. "Still trying to save the world?"

I closed my eyes.

"And you, too?" she asked.

"Inez encourages people to find out who they really are," Miguel said, "and to live up to their potential. In a nutshell."

I opened my eyes.

"It is difficult to distill a lifetime of beliefs into a few sentences," Inez said.

"Jeanne is cooking at La Magia. Something Paul conned

her into, taking advantage of her famous name. Her parents own the Oui and Sí. Have you heard of it?"

"I am only a country bumpkin," Inez said.

Within minutes, it seemed, we were at La Magia.

Inez stopped the truck. "Let your mother know I will see her next time if I don't catch her this trip. Tell Paul I'll see him later."

We slid out of the truck.

"You watch out for him," Miguel said to Inez. "He'll rob you blind."

She smiled obliquely and drove away.

"Lucky break," Miguel said. "It's four-thirty. You've got time to make dinner."

"Yeah, right."

We hurried through the back door into La Magia. Everyone stopped and stared at us.

"His car broke down," I said. "We've been trying to get back for hours.

Paul came and took my hands. "Are you all right?"

"I'm fine. I need to figure out what to do. Let me wash up."

I hurried to the office, where I washed up and changed clothes. Then I ran back into the kitchen. Paul was gone. Vesta stirred the soup. Tangiers and Fernando chopped veggies.

"What to do," I said out loud.

"It's about time you got back," Crane cranked. "I've been worried to death."

"Honey, you're way past dead," I said. "Any ideas for dinner?"

Fernando and Tangiers looked up at me, then quickly away.

"Something fast? Uncomplicated? Unsophisticated? I am at a complete loss," Crane said. "Sophisticated elegance is my forte."

I opened the refrigerator.

"I remember something my dad made with just red peppers, onions, and zucchini."

"Ah yes," Crane said. "With pasta and thyme."

"I don't have any time!" I said.

"No, no, *ma petite*. *T-h-y-m-e*. How extraordinary. I never noticed that *thy* and *me* equal *thyme*. Whatever could that signify?"

"That you have way too much time on your . . . mind. Head. Whatever."

I pulled out zucchini and red peppers from the refrigerator.

"Fernando, can you cut these zukes into matchsticks?"

"Julienne, my dear!" Crane shouted. "Julienne!"

"Can you julienne them?" I asked.

Fernando smiled. "Like long matchsticks?"

"Precisely," I said.

"Tangiers, do you have time to cut the red peppers?"

She nodded.

Good.

I dug around the pantry for pasta and found penne.

Perfect.

I put water on to boil, then cut up a few small red onions and several garlic cloves.

The water boiled. I threw in the penne. Next I heated olive oil in a large skillet.

"Onions and garlic first, then red peppers and more garlic, then zucchini," Crane said.

I smiled. That was exactly my plan.

It all looked so colorful and gorgeous, bright red and dark green. Less than ten minutes later, I added thyme and lots of pepper. Vesta drained the penne. I got out two plates. She split the pasta between the plates, and I slid the zucchini and red pepper mixture on top.

I took the plates into the dining room, followed by Fernando carrying a basket of bread.

It was 4:55.

I set the plates in front of Miguel and Paul.

"Wow," Paul said after his first bite. "You are a magical being. You've done it again. What do you call it?"

"Thyme for pasta and red peppers."

Seven

Le Pain et le Poisson

Vesta and I waited tables together again. My thighs and calves started to ache around seven o'clock. Nearly everyone ordered the dinner special.

At the end of night, the four of us sat together eating the thyme pasta while Paul cashed out. When he finished, he left us alone.

"I thought for sure we'd run out," I said.

Fernando nodded. Tangiers smiled.

"What?" I said.

Tangiers looked down at her plate. Fernando shrugged.

"I'm off tomorrow," Vesta said. "You make the soup."

I chewed on the zukes and red pepper. The black pepper and thyme made my mouth tingle.

"OK. If you want," I said.

"That's the way it is," she said.

I nodded. "Thank you all for helping tonight. I'm sorry I was so late. Vesta, did Miguel tell you that a friend of yours brought us back to town. Inez somebody."

"Oh! Good. She is the woman I spoke to you about in Mexico who could help you."

"Miguel took me to the Valley of Dreams," I said, changing the subject. "I hadn't been out in the desert for a long time. I enjoyed it. I had a memory of my grandma. I didn't know I'd ever known her. I saw a poisoned coyote dying, and she told me we were coyotes. In fact, she called me coyote cowgirl."

Fernando touched his scarred cheek and nodded. "It is not an easy way," he said, "being a coyote. Sometimes I know things before they happen, but I can't stop them. I knew those soldiers were there that day, but I went running anyway. I heard the gun. I even saw the bullet. It had writing on it."

"What did it say?" I asked.

"You're dead, sucker," Fernando answered.

"Did it really say that?" I asked.

Vesta sighed. "What a question."

"I'm just trying to understand."

"You don't need to understand, girl who talks to the crystal skull," she said.

I felt all the air go out of me, as though I'd been punched. Vesta stood, picked up our empty plates, and walked away.

Fernando leaned closer to me. "Does the crystal skull really talk to you?"

"As far as I can determine," I said.

He sat back against the booth. "Same with the bullet. Back home, they all called me a gangster, but I wasn't. I was just Fernando. No one knew who that was." His words came out in a singsong, like Miguel's.

"So who is Fernando?" I asked.

"I am Fernando Madero. I live in Sosegado where my aunt Vesta and cousin Miguel came to find peace. That's what *Sosegado* means in Spanish: 'peaceful.' I write songs and sing them to coyotes. I make wishes on falling stars and read the poetry of Jimmy Santiago Baca. I can cut faster than anyone I know—cut vegetables that is. I love the smell right before the monsoons come, when everything in the desert waits in anticipation, and I love the taste of the desert in the middle of the summer when it is so hot my eyelids hurt and I know there is no hope of rain. That is who I am."

Tangiers and I gazed at him. Then she clapped softly. I said, "We are in love."

Fernando smiled shyly. "It is your food. It is a truth serum."

After they had all gone, I locked up. Then I went into the kitchen, took Crane down, and polished his noggin with a tea towel.

"What about tomorrow?" I said. "I've got to make soup."

"That's a cinch," Crane said. "I've got a great pinto bean soup recipe. Soak a mess of beans before you go to bed."

I went into the pantry and found a bag of pinto beans. I poured them into a colander and rinsed them. Then I put them in a pot, filled it with water, and put it in the fridge.

Crane and I went to the office. Paul sat at his desk.

"Oh," I said. "I thought you'd gone. Do you want me to wait?"

"No, come in. This is your room." He stood and came around the desk. "I'm really impressed, Jeanne. Sit." We sat on the bed. "You're doing so well. The staff is rallying around you, and really seem to be blossoming, talking with each other."

"Well, except Tangiers doesn't talk."

He laughed. "That's true! But she's more animated."

"Okay."

"The restaurant's take is double what it was for last Friday and Saturday."

"That's great," I said. "I'm glad it's working out, but I'd

like to ask a favor. I'm really new at this, and I think one special a night is all I can handle. If business goes down, then I'll do more."

He put his hand over mine and squeezed it. "I think you are the greatest."

I looked up at him. He leaned over and kissed me. My knees shook. I parted my lips.

"Not again!" Crane said. "Must I be a witness to your carnal desires again? Johnny was bad enough."

I moved away. Paul smiled. He was so pretty.

"Puh-lease," I whispered.

"It's your funeral," Crane said.

"Please what?" Paul asked.

"Um. I'm pretty tired," I said.

He smiled. "I'll see you tomorrow, then." He kissed my lips lightly. "Good night."

Then he was gone.

I moaned and fell facedown on my bed.

"Crane! I wanted him," I said.

"This guy is slicker than . . . a really slick thing," Crane said.

"Oh, leave him alone. He's just misunderstood."

"Why do you keep having these superficial relationships with men?" Crane asked.

"And women," I corrected. "I have superficial relationships with women, too; I just don't happen to have sex with them."

Crane laughed.

"Hey, I can't deny the obvious," I said.

I switched off the light, peeled down to my underwear, and got beneath the covers. I put Crane on the floor next to me.

"I had a memory about Grandma Juarez," I said. "She didn't seem crazy, but I don't think my parents wanted her around me."

"No. They never did get on. Your grandmother thought the world should be different. She had spent a lot of time in the ruins of former glorious civilizations. She'd seen what happened, how they crumbled. She couldn't stop talking about it."

"You know, Crane," I said. "Everything is so different. My whole life. I'm out on my own. And I don't think I could have done it without your company. I'm glad you talked to me."

"I appreciate your company, too," Crane said. "Now, did I ever tell you about Jeanne d'Arc? You know in the end I really believe she would have lived had she listened to me."

"You're probably the one who told her to put on men's clothes again," I said.

"Men's clothes were so much more practical," Crane said. "It was very cold in that dungeon."

"But that's finally why they took a torch to her."

"For wearing men's clothes? I didn't remember that."

"Yep, that's what happened."

"Well, really, she did not look *that* bad."

I groaned. "Crane, I'm closing my eyes and going to sleep."

"Ah, the little death."

"Crane!"

"Not to worry. I'll watch over you."

"Gee, I feel so much better."

I dreamed I was in the kitchen cooking, surrounded by food. Paul came up behind me and kissed my neck while his fingers reached up my shirt. When I turned around, it was Johnny who held me. Miguel came in the back door and motioned me outside. A red pickup was parked next to the door with the initials *WIJ* on the side. Inside, my brother waved to me.

"Jeanne, *ma petite*. Wake up, *ma chère!*"

I opened my eyes. It was still pitch dark.

"What?" I said.

"The soup. It's time to make the soup."

"It's not even the crack of dawn," I said.

"The soup takes six hours, *ma petite*. Up, up, up!"

Moaning, I dragged my sorry butt out of bed. My legs ached so much I could hardly walk. I shuffled into the kitchen, Crane in hand. Following his instructions, I let the pinto beans drain for a half an hour. Then I took a quick shower and put on clean clothes. Next, I sautéed the beans in olive oil for five minutes, turning them over constantly as I tried not to fall asleep. I filled the pot with water and watched it until it boiled. Then I turned the fire down to let the pot simmer.

"Please give people what they need," I prayed to the soup.

Then I put on a mess of rice for the dinner special. While I waited for the rice to cook, I went to the refrigerator and pulled out the chicken breasts. Now was the time to see if I would have a repeat performance of the fish fiasco. No one was around to see me collapse onto the floor, should that happen again.

I gingerly removed the cellophane and stared at the pink flesh and yellow skin.

"OK, chicken, I'm sorry you're dead, but now I'd like to use you to make a nice meal. What do you say?"

I hesitated, then picked up a breast.

The room shifted. I dropped the chicken. My butt slapped the floor.

Wow.

This was strange.

I tried it again.

This time I fell to the floor and almost threw up.

"OK," I said. "I can take a hint."

I wrapped the chicken again, then put it in the freezer.

When the rice was done, I put it in the refrigerator. Then, in the quiet kitchen, I squeezed oranges into juice, toasted two pieces of Vesta's bread, and sliced a pear. I carried it all outside with Crane tucked under my arm. We watched the sun come up, spreading rose and gold light from one end of town to another. I listened to the noises of the town waking: a dog barking, someone coughing and banging pots, a car driving by. Each sound was distinguishable from the other. Peaceful.

"So what's it all mean?" I asked.

"You're talking about the chicken?" Crane said.

"I guess. And why am I here?" I ate a pear slice. "I'm here because Paul was cute, and I didn't want to go back home where everything would be the same. And you know what else? When I eat, I'm not having those weird bouts of overwhelming emotions. I only feel my own, I guess. It's kind of nice." I paused. "I'm doing something here."

"Cooking?"

"Yes. But it's strange. What we've been creating, Crane, really isn't that special. But people love it. We're packing them in. I like succeeding."

"*Moi aussi.* You and I, *ma petite,* we are destined for great things."

I laughed. "Or maybe just for average things."

After breakfast, I took Crane back inside. Then I gathered my clothes together and went to the Laundromat down the street. I went back to the restaurant a couple of times to check on the soup.

Around nine o'clock, Crane instructed me to add diced onions and minced garlic to the soup. I wasn't sure of the difference between *diced* and *minced,* so I put the onions and a whole bulb of garlic—minus the papery covering—into the food processor, buzzed it a couple of times, and then dumped it all into the soup. An hour later, I added fresh tomatoes and coriander.

The restaurant smelled of garlic.

Fernando and Tangiers came in and started their prep work while I set up the dining room.

Crane sang in French.

Fernando started humming along.

"What song is that?" I asked Fernando.

"I don't know," Fernando said. "It just popped into my head."

I glanced over at Crane. I could have sworn his frozen lip-less grin was even broader than usual.

When Paul returned, he said, "It smells wonderful!" and kissed my hand.

Lunch was so busy that Paul took off his jacket and bused tables and gave coffee refills.

Miguel did not come in.

I was run off my feet.

After lunch, I ate a quick bowl of pinto bean soup. It was exquisite, hearty with beans, delicate with the slight taste of tomatoes and coriander. I felt tired as I sipped the liquid and knew that it was my own well-earned exhaustion I was feeling.

Everyone else left, and I was alone.

Except for Crane, who instructed me on what I should do next. I chopped carrots and tomatoes, sliced green beans, cut red peppers. I minced ginger and stir-fried it in olive oil. When it was golden, I slipped it out of the pan with a slotted spoon. Fernando and Tangiers returned and started their prep. I stir-fried the veggies, carrots first. I watched the colors of the vegetables get brighter. I talked to them, encouraged them to greatness. Crane giggled.

At the precise correct moment, Crane shouted, "Now!" And I said, "Now!" and removed the vegetables from the pan. Then I dumped the cold rice into the pan. When the rice was heated through, I made a little well in the middle of it; into this, I added a few raw scrambled eggs. After they had cooked, I added tomatoes, chile sauce, pepper, salt, lime juice, and the ginger and vegetables. I stirred them all together.

"Voilà!" I said.

It was 4:45 P.M.

I spooned the fried rice onto two plates, garnishing them with slices of lime, and pieces of scallion and cilantro.

I carried the plates into the dining room, where Miguel and Paul now sat.

"Hi," Manual said. "How's it going?"

"Fine," I said, setting the plates in front of the men. *"Bon appétit!"* I hurried back to the office, splashed my face and armpits, and put on a clean camisole and shirt.

I went back into the kitchen.

"Did they like it?" I asked Tangiers and Fernando.

Tangiers gave me a thumbs-up sign.

The restaurant was packed for dinner, and I sorely missed Vesta's presence—literally. My calves throbbed. Paul and I were outnumbered. We just kept going, laughing, and shaking our heads as we passed each other. Paul had to wait tables. Miguel volunteered to bus tables. Paul talked too much to his customers, and I was tempted to tell him to move, move, move. But it was his restaurant. Miguel told lame jokes each time we had a moment to spare. He looked cute in his ponytail, tight jeans, and white apron.

The customers were friendly and polite. I recognized most of them from previous nights. They called me by name. Most ordered soup and salad or the dinner special. I could not imagine I had made enough fried rice, but Tangiers kept filling order after order.

The dining room smelled of garlic and ginger.

We cajoled people out of the restaurant and locked the door at nine-thirty.

Tangiers, Fernando, and I ordered the fried rice. Miguel had soup. Paul counted the money. I lay my head against Tangiers' shoulder as I chewed. She patted my hair. Miguel sighed noisily.

We all laughed.

"Hard work—eh, cuz?" Fernando said. "It's good for you."

"They like your food, Jeanne," Miguel said.

"She's the best," Paul said. He held up a wad of money. "Good job, guys," he said as he left the dining room.

"Greg Stocker said he's going to quit the bank," Miguel said. "He's going to go back East to be closer to his folks. And Martin, he owns the bookstore, told me he's going to ask Gloria to marry him. She's the pharmacist. I didn't even know they dated. All these people tonight kept telling me about these important personal decisions."

"And the soup and rice never ran out," Tangiers said.

We all stopped and looked at her, then kept eating so she wouldn't notice that we had noticed how extraordinary it was to hear her voice.

"It happened yesterday, too," Fernando said, "with the thyme and pasta dish."

Miguel looked from Tangiers to Fernando, and back again. "What do you mean?"

"We always have enough of Jeanne's specials," Fernando said. "Even for us to eat it, too. Now the soup and fried rice are all gone."

Miguel looked at me and blinked.

"Must be a coincidence," I said.

Fernando laughed. "I don't think so."

Tangiers pointed to Fernando's pocket.

"No," Fernando said. "I haven't finished it."

"What?" Miguel asked.

Tangiers raised her eyebrows.

Fernando sighed. Tangiers motioned me out of the booth. I got up. She slid out, went to the kitchen, and then returned with a guitar.

Fernando took it from her and moved over to the closest table. "I told you I wrote songs," Fernando said to me. "Well, I'm writing one now, kind of inspired by you. I haven't finished it. It's called 'Coyote Cowgirl into the Fire.'"

"Into the fire?"

"You've heard of the O'odham, the People," Miguel said. "There were the Desert O'odham, the River People, and the Sand People. It is generally believed that the Sand People are all gone. They lived in the hottest, most arid part of the desert. As far as anyone knows, they probably built no structures; only these sleeping circles made of stone remain. They were nomads living in a place most of us could not survive. In written accounts of the whites, they talk about the Sand People with more disdain than was usual even for them." He paused. "But some believe there were also the Fire People, who lived even closer to the desert than the Sand People."

He looked down at his guitar and began playing. The sound filled the room, and for a moment, I remembered a Christmas in the San Javier Mission church when a man played Christmas carols on his guitar and the sound of the strings vibrating and echoing in the wood chamber reached the pinnacle of the church. Now, candlelight colored Fernando's features gold.

He hummed as he played; then words broke from his lips, as if by accident, and he sang, "The girl talks to the crystal skull and flickers like the shifting Fire People whose blood pulses in her veins." He strummed and sang and talked at the same time, his voice low—listening, too, like a priest taking confession and giving absolution at the same time.

"She sends out loaves and fishes to those hungry for the truth," he sang. "Is she coyote, bear, or bird? / Hey-o, hey-o. I am desert, she says, holding out her hands. / Food pours from her wounds, water from her eyes."

For the first time, Fernando looked up and gazed at me, "When she is empty, will she find her own truth? / Or vanish into the desert of her own making? Coyote Cowgirl into the fire. / Deserted. Desert. O-hey, o-ho."

He played a few more chords, then set the guitar down and looked up at us.

"That's lovely," I said.

"It's more of a poem," he said, "than a song."

"I'm flattered," I said. Should I tell him I didn't even like the desert?

"When we were growing up," Miguel said, "Mom was always telling stories of the Fire People."

"She may have made them up," Fernando said. "None of the rest of the family has ever heard of the Fire People."

"Mom says the Sand and Fire People were like the Australian aborigines," Miguel said. "The Fire People did not live like anyone else. They could become any part of the desert to survive."

"For instance," Fernando said, "if they could find only a teaspoon of water left in the *tinaja,* that amount would not quench the thirst of a single person, let alone an entire family."

"But if they became ants," Miguel said, "they'd have plenty of water."

"The Fire People had to be sensitive to all the nuances of everything around them," Fernando said, "so that they could survive."

"It was from the sun," Miguel said. "Fire transmutes or destroys."

"Vesta believes the Fire People aren't really extinct. It's just that they can no longer live as people. They're still in the desert. Sometimes they get born again as people. Vesta thinks you're one of the Fire People."

"What?" I laughed. "I don't think so. I try to stay out of the sun, and I don't like the desert. But thanks for the song, Fernando. I really enjoyed it."

"You are welcome," he said. He handed me a piece of paper with the words to the song on it.

"Don't you need it?"

"I have it memorized."

I smiled. "Thanks." I slipped the paper into my pocket.

I poured my tips onto the table. Miguel added his. I started to divide the pile four ways, but Miguel put up his hand. "I was just an interloper. It's my contribution."

As I was dividing the money three ways, Paul came back into the room.

"Tomorrow's your day off," he said. "So what are you all still doing here?"

"I've got to clean up," Fernando said. Usually he had everything finished before the last customer was out the door. "We were a little busy tonight."

"Just a little," I said.

We all got up. Tangiers waved good-bye and left. Miguel and I helped Fernando. I was only slightly disappointed when Paul left. I wondered what he had done with his tip money.

When we were finished, the three of us—along with Crane—sat on the back steps.

"I am so tired," I said. "I don't think I've worked that hard in my life."

"Then you've had an easy life," Miguel said.

"Don't start," I said. "I'm too tired to argue with you. I'll have you know I was exposed to the effects of a nuclear blast before I was born. So I am entitled to claim that I've had a rough life." I grinned.

Fernando and Miguel looked over my head at one another.

"What?" I said.

"Doesn't nuclear fission occur on the sun?" Miguel asked.

"Yeah, so?"

"And you claim not to be a Fire Person. Your nuclear blast is proof right there," Fernando said. "Remember, it was the heat that supposedly transformed the Fire People."

"OK. Then what could I change into to make me less tired?" I asked. "A coyote? A rattlesnake?"

"Your pajamas," Miguel said, standing. "We'll let you sleep. You want to go out into the desert tomorrow?"

"Not in your car," I said. "Besides, don't you have a job?"

"You are only going to be here two weeks," Miguel said. "I'd rather take a day off work and spend it with you, and Fernando. And my car is just fine."

"All right. But not too early. I need some rest."

Fernando got up, and the two men disappeared into the darkness, after waving and flashing grins.

"Thanks for the song!" I called.

"Alone at last," Crane said. "Quite a busy day, eh?"

"Are you the reason we never run out of the specials?" I asked.

"Must be your imagination," Crane said. "I've never heard of such a thing."

"Then it's in all our imaginations," I said. "Everyone noticed it. Even Tangiers—she actually spoke!"

I went back into the restaurant, locking the door behind me. I was just about to switch off the light when I noticed Friday's *L.A. Times* on top of the recycle box. At the top, it said: INSIDE: WIJ.

I picked up the newspaper and carried it and Crane into the dining room and sat next to the picture window, under the neon's blue light. I unfolded the paper and turned the pages until I got to the section on WIJ.

THE MYSTERY DEEPENS, the headline read. I skimmed the article. About thirty people were missing, some from other parts of the country. Men and women, some single, some married with children, mostly white and middle class. The only known link were the initials *WIJ* found after each person disappeared.

The opposite page to the article was filled with pictures of the missing: Donna Mason, Richard Serrano, Holly Cannon, Barbara Waker, Trudy Cylind. And on and on. All these people had disappeared, and the police did not know why. Of course, people disappeared or were murdered daily; I supposed the serial nature of these disappearances got the media heads pumped up in anticipation of a story they could milk for weeks.

Perhaps I was being too cynical.

Somebody pounded on the window.

I jumped.

Antoine stood outside, grinning. "Hey seester!" he called.

"Antoine!"

I got up and unlocked the door. Antoine stepped into the restaurant, and we hugged. When we let each other go, Antoine immediately went over to Crane. His eyes widened, then narrowed.

"*Allo, ma petite*'s brother," Crane said.

"You are deeply deranged," Antoine said. "Dad will kill you."

"It's all right," I said. "I'll put him back before Dad and Mom return."

"Why would you take the skull on your vacation?"

"It's not really a vacation," I said, "and the skull asked to come along. Isn't that right?"

"So right!" Crane said.

"Talking to the skull again?" Antoine asked.

"It's a long story," I said. "What brings you here?"

We sat in the booth.

"You got anything to eat?" Antoine asked, not answering my question.

"I think there's one serving left of the dinner special. You want me to pop it into the microwave?"

"Sure, thanks. Any beer?"

"Beer's behind the counter in the cooler," I said as I got up.

I went into the kitchen and got the last helping of fried rice from the refrigerator and stuck it into the microwave. When the rice was hot, I put a slice of lime and a sprig of cilantro on the plate, grabbed a fork, and brought it all into the dining room and set it in front of my brother.

Antoine ate heartily.

When he was finished, he pushed away the plate and said, "Man, that was good. Something so simple. They must have a good cook."

"That would be me," I said.

"Little seester!" he said. "You've finally decided to become one of us. I'm impressed."

"Don't be. The skull gives me the recipes."

"But, *ma petite!*" Crane said. "It is your hands that shape the food. Your intuition that says how little and how much. Don't be so modest."

"The skull gives you recipes?" Antoine said.

"Later. Tell me why you're here?"

"I called home to see if you'd gotten back okay, and Belinda said you were in Sosegado, so I thought I'd stop on my way back home."

"Hah! Belinda was afraid I was cooking, killing, and ruining the family name all in one fell swoop."

Antoine took a swig of his beer. "Something like that."

"The family name is intact. I am doing quite well, thank you very much."

"Because the skull is giving you recipes?" Antoine said.

"Are you sure you want to share your secret?" Crane asked. "Your family is not kind to members they believe are crackers."

"Crane—that's what I call the skull—is afraid you'll want to lock me up. But I've discovered all kinds of things about our family in the last few days. The skull is the one who gave Dad his recipes. I thought he attended some prestigious cooking school in Chicago."

Antoine laughed. "You've always taken this family business stuff way too seriously. So what if Dad fabricated a few things?"

"Like the fact that Grandma Juarez first owned the skull, not a Les Flambeaux?"

"Really?" he asked. "Well, I never believed that cock-and-bull story about the scepter and skull anyway. I don't think anyone did except for you. Belinda and I remember living in an apartment when Dad was working as a short-order cook and Mom was cleaning houses."

"So our entire lives are based on lies?"

"It's America," he said. "You don't have to be authentic, you just have to fake it really well."

"And that doesn't bother you?"

Antoine shrugged. "Lately I've been wondering. I don't know. Right this minute I wonder what I've been doing. I live with Mom and Dad, I date too many women, and I don't even know if I like to cook."

I glanced at his plate. Were they right? Were my dishes

truth potions? I had never known my brother to be intro-spective.

Antoine rubbed his face. "I don't know where that came from. I guess I'm tired. I've been driving all day, and the motel here wouldn't answer my buzzer. There's only one motel in town, Jeanne. That should tell us something."

I laughed. "I'm surprised there's even one. You can sleep in my room. Come on."

I folded up the paper. Antoine glanced at it.

"I was reading about the WIJ disappearances," I said.

"Women in jeopardy?"

I nodded. "You know, I first heard that expression from you. When these women—and men—started turning up missing all over the Southwest, some of them in towns you had just visited, I started to wonder—"

"Par-a-noid. What a thing to believe. I wouldn't hurt a flea. I take spiders outside. I shoo mosquitoes off me!"

We got up. He put his arm across my shoulders and car-ried Crane in his other hand.

"It's the nice ones you have to watch out for," I said.

"No, it's not, Jeanne," he said. "Get that through your flambéed head and maybe you'll stop sleeping with guys like Johnny!" He shuddered. "Yuck."

"I say nothing," Crane said.

The office seemed even smaller with my big brother in it. I gave him the bed, and I slept on the floor beside him. We both knew he would never be able to sleep on the floor, so neither of us argued about it.

In the dark, we said good night to one another.

"You look good," Antoine said. "Different."

"Thanks. I am different."

"Must be the place," he said. "It's good to get away from family."

"Yeah."

"Well, that's all over, little sister. You can run, but you can't hide 'cause I've found you. The family's back."

We giggled, then fell asleep.

Eight

Hermano, Can You Spare Some Thyme?

"Jeanne?"

I opened my eyes. Paul was leaning into the room.

"Oh, sorry. Didn't know you—"

I got up quickly, dressed only in my long T-shirt and underwear.

"He's just my brother," I whispered, glancing at my sleeping sibling. "The motel was closed. I hope you don't mind."

"Of course not."

We went into the hallway.

"I'm sorry to bother you," he said, glancing at my bare legs, "but a business associate of mine is in town. I told him about you, and he'll be gone tomorrow." He shrugged and took my hand. I wondered if I would get another kiss. I wasn't certain I really wanted one.

"Sure," I said, gently taking my hand back. "I can make eggs, or something. I'll be right out."

I dipped back into the room to change clothes and grabbed Crane.

"He's got a lot of nerve asking you to cook on your day off!" Crane said.

"Hey, I'm paying off a debt," I whispered as we went into the kitchen. I set Crane on the island. "Any ideas?"

"Let's be simple but scrumptious," he said.

"French toast?"

"Exactamente."

"I might even know how to do that," I said.

Crane instructed me to beat together eggs, milk, cinnamon, nutmeg, clove, and zest of an orange. I soaked pieces of Vesta's thick spongy bread in the mixture, then took them out and fried them in olive oil. While they cooked, I pushed orange halves down onto the juicer until I filled four glasses with orange juice. I garnished two plates with twisted slices of orange, then flipped the toast out of the frying pan onto the plates. I tapped powdered sugar and cinnamon over the toast and carried the plates out to the dining room along with the maple syrup.

When I brought the orange juice to Paul and his associate, the stranger looked up and grinned, his mouth full. Paul hadn't touched his French toast. I set the glasses on the table and returned to the kitchen. I made Antoine and myself French toast, too. I put the toast and juice on a tray, along with Crane, and carried it all into the office.

Antoine moaned when I set the tray on the desk. "Get up, lazy bones," I said.

I went back into the dining room. The stranger's plate was empty.

"This was magnificent!" the man said.

Paul still hadn't eaten his breakfast. I frowned.

"Excuse me, Paul. Are you finished with the syrup?"

"Sure, go ahead," he said, smiling.

As I took the syrup back to the office, I wondered what was wrong with Paul's breakfast.

I sat on the bed with Antoine, and we ate breakfast silently.

"Gee, Jeanne, this is really superb. I mean it's just French toast, but it's great."

"Vesta made the bread."

When Antoine was finished, he leaned against the wall and patted his stomach.

"So why are you here, sister?" he asked.

"I started off paying a debt," I said. "Now I kind of like being here. The owner seems to need me. He counts on me. Nobody here knows I'm considered incompetent by my family."

Antoine made a noise. "You're the baby, the favored one, why should you do anything?"

"Belinda made some remark similar to that," I said. "What's up with that? I'm not the spoiled one. I'm the one everyone barely tolerates."

"You had different parents than we did," Antoine said. "They were friendly and nice to you. We remember fights over money and Grandma and Mom's trips. It's no big deal. You came after, or at least were too young to remember, I guess. Mom and Dad got after us to succeed. They didn't bug you."

"Maybe they were just tired by the time I was born," I said. "It wasn't because I was considered special."

"I never said you were special," Antoine said. He laughed. "You just never rebelled. Belinda and I did."

"You both still live at home," I said. "That's not very rebellious."

"We moved out before you went to college." He grinned. "Then we came back. We rebelled for a few years."

"I don't think that adult children moving away from home constitutes rebellion."

Antoine laughed. "Yeah, we've definitely got the easy life."

I nodded. "That's for sure. There's a kid working here who was shot by the marines because they thought he looked like a drug smuggler."

"You mean he looked like us?" Antoine said.

"Yep."

"Only not as well dressed," Antoine said.

Crane laughed. "This boy always was amusing."

"They moved up here because they figured it was safer," I said.

"Good luck. Hey, do you think I can fit into that midget shower?"

"I know you aren't used to the hard life," I said, "but I think you can manage a shower."

I took our dishes into the kitchen. Antoine went out to his car for clean clothes, then returned to the office. Paul and his business associate were gone, their dishes cluttering the booth. I bused the table.

Tangiers, Fernando, and Miguel came in through the back door.

"Ready for another desert adventure?" Miguel asked.

"Oh, I forgot," I said. "Ah—"

Antoine walked into the room, big, gorgeous, and freshly showered.

Fernando and Miguel looked startled. Tangiers smiled.

"Everyone, this is my brother, Antoine," I said. "Antoine, this is Tangiers, Fernando, and Miguel. Antoine, Miguel was going to torture us by taking us out into the desert. Would you like to go? We could take Antoine's car. No offense, Miguel."

Miguel smiled. "Great. Let's go!"

We transferred water and backpacks from Miguel's car into Antoine's gas guzzler. Antoine, Miguel, and I sat in the front, Tangiers and Fernando in the back. Miguel directed Antoine onto the same road Miguel and I had taken a few days ago. How different the scenery seemed as we whipped by it in the car.

Antoine parked the car near the ruined church. We got out, put on our packs, and followed Miguel up the same ridge Miguel and I had climbed the other day. Plump white clouds lined up in the middle of the sky. A scrub jay followed us to the top, then flew away to land on a saguaro.

At the top, Antoine pounded his chest and did a Tarzan call. The sound echoed back at us. We started down to the valley floor. This time Miguel took us north. I could not remember ever seeing Antoine out in the wild. He was the same as always, confident and humorous, carrying on conversations with flora and fauna we encountered. Our voices and the sounds of our feet over ground were the only noises, except for an occasional insect buzz or birdcall. The air was crisp and slightly cool. Everyone seemed relaxed and at home. Tangiers blended into the landscape, her blond hair, pale skin, khaki shorts, and cream-colored top nearly camouflaging her. Perhaps she was one of the Fire People.

We took a break at an outcropping up above an arroyo, sitting on a smooth gray and rust-colored rock that had fallen away from the others.

From my pack, I pulled out a sandwich, trail mix, and water.

"Food is courtesy of my mother," Miguel said. "She was going to come but decided a nap would be more fun."

I laughed. "She must have been anticipating a ride in your car."

Antoine watched Miguel and me, one eyebrow raised. I pushed him.

"Shut up," I said.

"I didn't say a word," Antoine said.

"So Fernando," I asked, "do you think there are any Fire People around here?"

Fernando nodded. "Maybe this rock is someone. Who

knows? Vesta would say that maybe a group of Fire People became these rocks—because a jaguar chased them or they were hungry and rocks need little food. And they liked being rocks so much that they forgot how to become O'odham again."

"Fernando is a poet," I said to Antoine, "and a songwriter."

"I am a dishwasher," Fernando said shyly.

"And a poet and songwriter," Miguel said, "who should go to college."

Fernando shrugged.

"You should go to college," I said. "You are very talented."

"If I go to college, will I get a job as a poet?" Fernando asked. "No. I'll get out and be a dishwasher. Did you go to college?"

I nodded.

"And what did you do before you went?" Fernando asked.

I glanced at Antoine. "Don't use me as an example," I said. "I enjoyed college. I learned a great deal about the variety of life. My horizons were broadened and all that crap. Just because I didn't change my life doesn't mean anything to you. Just go to learn." I shrugged. "Or not. Who am I to tell you what to do with your life? It's none of my business."

Miguel glanced at me. "Starting to get involved, huh?"

I bit into my sandwich.

Tangiers began humming the tune Crane had been singing a couple of days ago. A pyrrhuloxia flew over us, whistling, his tail nearly bloodred. I did not remember ever seeing one before, yet I knew its peculiar name. A female followed the male, her crest and tail showing only a hint of red. She squeaked, "Quit, quit, quit," as she flew over us.

"Never," Antoine cried. "I shall never quit!"

When we finished our snacks, Miguel and Fernando took a

walk. Tangiers, Antoine, and I stretched out on the warm rock.

After a while, I said, "I met a man in Nevada who knew Grandma Juarez. He says she's got a Web site."

"A Web site?" Antoine said. "On what? Is she selling something?"

"Apparently she was an archeologist," I said.

"They both were," Antoine said. "Grandma and Grandpa. They were quite well known in their field. Grandpa was killed on one of the digs. I forget where. That's when Grandma started coming up with weird ideas about invaders from space and had her breakdown, or whatever it was, and Mom and Dad committed her to a mental hospital."

"Mom committed her own mother?" I said. "I can't imagine doing that to Mom."

"Mom isn't crazy," Antoine said.

"According to Bear, Grandma wasn't crazy, either."

"I don't remember much about her," Antoine said, "Except that she went away. She used to talk to me about what she did. She could hold a shard in her hands and make it seem magic. When she talked about archeology, it seemed mysterious and fun."

"You took some archeology courses in college, didn't you?"

"I majored in it," he said. "Didn't you pay any attention to me at all?"

"I was thirteen when you went to college," I said. "Give me a break. I barely remember what *I* majored in. So why did you come back to the restaurant instead of getting a job in archeology?"

"Just lazy, I guess," he said. "I did go on some interviews, but I gave up after a while. But I've been thinking about it lately. Maybe doing some amateur work; digs use lots of volunteers. If Grandma Juarez is around and kicking—and sane—maybe I'll give her a call."

Miguel and Fernando returned to the outcropping and badgered us until we got up and resumed our hike. Antoine, Fernando, and Tangiers walked ahead of Miguel and me. We walked toward another wash where the skeleton of the occasional river lay in the form of rocks dusted with white powder.

"So what brings your brother down here?" Miguel asked me, when the others were presumably out of earshot. "I thought you were trying to keep this whole thing a secret, I mean about the scepter being stolen."

"He doesn't know anything about that," I said. "My sister was afraid I was ruining the family name by trying to cook. Antoine came to check up on me."

"He seems to have a lot of affection for you," he said.

"Yeah, we've always gotten along," I said. "But it's not like we know anything about one another or do things together—besides working and living together, of course."

"Is that all?"

"It's different at my family's restaurant," I said. "At La Magia we have fun or at least we seem close. I don't know. I don't even know everyone's name who works at the Oui and Sí; they come and go so often. Or else I wasn't paying attention. Here I feel like I'm coming awake."

"You said that before. Like Sleeping Beauty?" Miguel said.

"Only it wasn't any prince who kissed me awake," I said.

"What was it?"

I shrugged. "Maybe the desert pricked me awake. When I think about it now, I realize that our house was really sad. At least my mother was. My father is jovial, but not really happy. I always felt like things had to be just so. If I didn't act the correct way, then everything would fall apart. And of course,

I never felt as though I acted the right way. My mother seemed so far away. I wanted her to come back, from wherever she had gone."

We reached the wash and walked on the edges of it for a few minutes. I looked up at the ridge once and saw a coyote walking along it. When I glanced up again, the animal was gone, and Fernando was calling to us. Miguel and I hurried toward them.

I started to smell something sickly sweet—a chemical smell.

Fernando, Tangiers, and Antoine stood off to the side of the wash, where a black liquid had stopped flowing and was apparently soaking into the ground.

Miguel jumped in front of us and followed the course of the foul-smelling river with us close at his heels. The wash curved, and the liquid ended where tire tracks started.

"Someone has been dumping," Miguel said. "We need to get away from this stuff. It's probably toxic waste. I need to find a phone."

"I've got one," Antoine said, as we hurried away from the wash.

Antoine reached into his shirt pocket, pulled out his phone, and slapped it open.

After a few moments with the telephone pressed against his ear, Antoine said, "I guess we're too far out. I can't pick up a signal."

We kept walking while Antoine continued to try and get the telephone to work. I looked back once. The liquid was a black gash in the landscape. So much for Miguel's Valley of Dreams.

Once we reached the car, the telephone started to work. Antoine handed it to Miguel. The rest of us sat around the car, eating and drinking silently while Miguel murmured into the phone.

After a few minutes, Miguel handed the phone back to Antoine.

"They're coming in up the other way," Miguel said. "I talked to the sheriff. They want us to go to the hospital."

"What? Why?" Antoine said. "We didn't touch it."

"We may have inhaled something harmful," Miguel said. "They'll send a sample of it to a lab to find out what it is. In the meantime, he said we're probably fine, but just to be sure, we should go to the hospital. Does everyone feel OK?"

I nodded. Tangiers shook her head. Tears spilled down her cheeks. Miguel sat on the ground next to her and put his arm across her shoulders. I took her right hand in mine.

"Are you sick?" Miguel asked.

She shook her head.

"Maybe we better go," I suggested.

Miguel nodded, and we got into the car. Antoine followed Miguel's directions into town to the tiny hospital hanging onto its outskirts.

The doctor had been notified by the sheriff and was waiting for us when we arrived. She and the nurse checked our vital signs and lungs and took blood samples. She found nothing amiss and sent us home.

Antoine drove us back to the restaurant.

"Mom wanted you all to come over after the hike," Miguel said, standing by his little red car. "Fernando, why don't you take them over? I want to go out and make sure the sheriff found the dump."

"Do you want someone to come with you?" I asked.

Miguel shook his head. "No. I'll see you all later." He got in his little red car and drove away.

The four of us stood uncomfortably in the parking lot of La Magia. The day was clear, warm, beautiful, and spoiled. Contaminated.

"Is Miguel's mother the one who provided us with the food in our packs?" Antoine asked.

"Yes," I said.

"Then it would be rude not to thank her," he said. "Shall we go?"

We got into Antoine's car, and Fernando directed us out of town a short way to Vesta's small one-story house that was surrounded by saguaro, cholla, and agave, and cuddled by ochre-colored foothills.

Fernando led us into the house, through to the kitchen and dining area where Vesta sat drinking a cup of coffee. She smiled and stood as we came in. She gave Tangiers a hug, then looked at Antoine.

He held out his hand to her. "I'm Antoine Les Flambeaux," he said. "I'm Jeanne's brother. Thank you so much for the delicious lunch. And thank you for breakfast. Jeanne made French toast from your bread, and it was fabulous. I don't think I've ever tasted such good bread."

Vesta smiled almost shyly as she shook Antoine's hand. I smiled. Antoine could charm the skin off a snake.

"Where is Miguel?" Vesta asked, looking at me. She began giving orders without waiting for an answer. "Let's go outside. We'll eat there. Fernando and Tangiers, take plates out to the table."

"We found something in the Valley of Dreams," I said. "Some kind of toxic dumping, Miguel thinks. He went back out to make certain the sheriff and ranger found it."

"You should have gone with him," Vesta said, stirring a pot on the stove.

"I offered," I said. Why was she always criticizing me? "He wanted to go alone."

"He likes you," Vesta said. "He will be sad now and could have used the company. Grab the salad. Fernando! Get the bread, please." To me, she added, "The dressing is in the fridge."

I took the salad from the counter and the dressing from the refrigerator, then followed Vesta outside as she carried a huge covered black pot to the picnic table and set it down. We sat around the table, and Vesta spooned out paella onto our plates.

"It's vegetarian for Tangiers," Vesta said.

Tangiers smiled and nodded.

The red peppers and green peas looked almost preternaturally bright in amongst the saffron-tinged brown rice. I ate heartily. Vesta and Antoine talked about cooking, comparing recipes. I ate and listened for Miguel's car.

"So you've been eating your sister's cooking," Vesta said at one point. "What do you think?"

"I didn't know she could cook," Antoine said. "Of course, I don't know much about her. She stays to herself."

"Don't talk about me as if I'm not here," I said.

"She's a sensitive," Vesta said.

"Yes, she always was very sensitive," Antoine said. "Mom and Dad thought it was because my mom was exposed to radiation when she was pregnant with Jeanne."

Vesta looked at me.

"You knew that?" I asked. "Why didn't you tell me?"

Antoine shrugged. "I thought you knew. It wasn't a secret."

"No one ever talked about it," I said.

"No one ever talked about Mom's gambling problem, either," Antoine said, "but we all knew."

"I didn't," I said.

"Maybe that is why you are the way you are," Vesta said. "For you, the atomic explosion was like the sun was to the Fire People."

I shook my head. "I may know what some people were feeling when they cooked a meal just by eating it and maybe *possibly* I feel the death throes of a slaughtered animal—"

"And cause people to know the truth after they eat your food," Fernando added.

"What?" Antoine asked.

"*But* I cannot shape-change like you say the Fire People can," I said.

"Miguel and Fernando told you the stories?" Vesta asked. "Good. But it wasn't shape-changing like a man into a wolf. No. It was a way of being and understanding which allowed them to become the other."

"Almost an actual form of empathy," Fernando said, "if you define empathy as vicarious identification with another."

We all looked at him.

He swallowed. "Don't you think?"

"Yes," Vesta said. "I do think. An extreme form of empathy."

I shook my head. "I am not empathic or even compassionate. I really don't pay much attention to the world around me. Ask Miguel. We've talked about this."

"Talked about what?" Miguel asked, walking into the room. He put his hands on my shoulders. Startled, I sat very still.

"She says she is not compassionate or empathic," Fernando said.

Vesta shook her head. "You have been bombarded all your life by forces you did not understand, so of course you withdrew. You had no one to teach you. If I ate a piece of pie and suddenly felt rage, I would be terrified! I'd think I was crazy. Someone should have been there to tell you what was happening."

Miguel squeezed my shoulders, then sat across from me. His mother made him a plate of paella.

"Our grandma Juarez could have helped," Antoine said. "She was crazy, too." He grinned at me, and I stuck out my tongue. "But she went away. She and Jeanne were close."

"I only have one memory of her," I said.

"You said she has a site on the Web," Antoine said. "We should look her up. I brought my laptop. We can do it here."

"No," I said. "I don't want to bore everyone with our family stuff."

Antoine shrugged.

Tangiers nodded. Apparently she liked the idea.

"Well, do whatever you want," I said.

Tangiers and Antoine excused themselves and left the table. Fernando began picking up dishes while Miguel ate.

"That was quick," I said.

"I met the sheriff halfway out," he said. "They already had the hazmat people out there. From looking at it, they think that it's some kind of antifreeze mixed with oil, maybe from some auto service business." He shrugged. "I'd like to go after whoever did this." He rubbed his eyes.

"Maybe you want to become an environmental lawyer," I said.

"Too depressing."

I laughed. "Oh, yeah, immigration law is a heap of fun."

"No, I mean the companies always have so much money and power," he said. "Back East a community wanted to make it mandatory for public disclosure before any agency sprayed pesticides in the area. You know, so parents could keep children and pets inside, et cetera. The chemical companies came into this small town and fought the proposal in court—and the chemical companies won. It's just all fucked."

"Miguel," Vesta said.

"Sorry, Mom."

"What comes around goes around," Vesta said, standing.

"I think it's the other way around," Miguel said.

"Maybe now," she answered.

Vesta went indoors, leaving Miguel and me alone. He put down his fork and stared out at the mountain. He looked miserable, almost childlike in his loss.

"I'm sorry," I said. I reached across the table and grasped his fingers in mine for an instant. Miguel smiled sadly, then finished his dinner.

Fernando played the guitar for Miguel, Vesta, and me while we ate cherry cheesecake and watched the sun paint the hills behind the house in autumn dusk.

When Fernando took a break, I went inside to see how Tangiers and Antoine were doing on the computer.

"It's not under her name," Antoine said as I walked into the living room. "Do you have any ideas?"

I sat on the couch next to him. "I haven't a clue. Bear's the one who told me about her. Did you try utopia, UFO, archeology?" I thought of my recent memory of Grandma and the decaying coyote.

"Try *coyote*," I said.

Tangiers typed in *coyote*.

"She likes this," Antoine said. Tangiers smiled. "Lots of hits on the word *coyote*."

Tangiers scrolled down while we scanned the list.

"There," I said, pointing. I read, "Coyotes. The Noninstitute Institute, Puerto Peñasco, Mexico."

Tangiers clicked on this entry.

"Why *coyote*?" Antoine asked.

"I remembered us being in the desert together, and I saw this coyote die—and kind of fade into the ground. It had been poisoned. I was upset, and Grandma thought I should see it. She said coyotes lived on the edges, just like people like us. And we had to know who we were to survive."

The Coyotes site had no fancy graphics, just a desert scene at the top of the first screen. It seemed to undulate into an ocean, or else it was an optical illusion. Several boxes popped up at the bottom of the screen: The Non-institute Non-doctrine, *Coyotes Newsletter,* Archeological Digs, Upcoming Events, and Index of *Coyotes Newsletter.*

"Must be her," Antoine said.

"Let's read the *Coyotes Newsletter.*"

Tangiers clicked on it.

"Welcome!" I read on the screen. "Today is a beautiful day, looking out into the Sea of Cortés. How many of you are tired of living in the mainstream today? Are the bumps and rough currents too much? Maybe you are not a city dweller. Or a country dweller. Maybe you are an edge dweller like me."

I looked at Antoine. "This is extraordinary. I just remembered her saying stuff like this to me two days ago, and now here it is on the Net."

I continued reading to myself, "Are you weary of fighting the good fight? Tired of trying to change the world? I have seen what happens when a civilization rises. It must, most naturally, fall. That is the way it has to be.

"The United States is a country of roads. You have so many choices on the route you can take. So you just keep going and going. Until you are routeless. Rootless. What kind of community is there anymore? Each day is such a struggle to keep above the fray.

"Let it go.

"Go.

"And then be still.

"Find the edge of your life, and go over it. Find your true community. Your tribe.

"Go the way of the coyotes. They are edge dwellers who survive and adapt. They do not try to change what is.

"We can learn from them.

"Come. Be happy.

"Winema."

"Bingo," Antoine said. "It's Weird Winnie, our blood."

"Actually, that didn't sound so weird," I said.

Tangiers nodded.

"Let's look at the information on archeological digs," Antoine suggested.

"You go ahead."

I was suddenly dead tired. Maybe being around that toxic waste had done something to me. Or maybe just changing my entire life in less than a week had put me off my feed.

"I think I want to go home," I said.

Antoine and Tangiers watched the screen as the archaeology file opened.

"You want to go back to Scottsdale?" Antoine asked without looking at me.

"No, to La Magia," I said, getting up.

"I'll take you home," Miguel said as he came into the room. "Antoine can stay here. The couch folds out."

I could not imagine Antoine agreeing to spend another night on a couch, but he nodded and said, "Sure, thanks," without looking up.

"TV will rot your brain," I said to Antoine.

He ignored me.

I went outside and said good-bye to Fernando and thank you to Vesta. Then Miguel and I got into his little red car and drove away.

When we got to the restaurant, I said, "I'm sorry about your desert."

Miguel smiled. "It's not my desert."

"Do you have to argue about everything?" I asked.

"I'm glad you were there."

"I'm not," I said. I got out out of the car. "See you tomorrow?"

"Sure."

Miguel waited until I unlocked the restaurant and went inside. Then he drove away.

The kitchen vibrated emptiness. I walked into the office and pulled Crane out of my suitcase.

"It's about time," Crane said. "I've been quite alone."

"I figured you'd like some solitary time," I said.

"I've been in solitary confinement for what seems forever," he said, sounding slightly annoyed.

"I'm sorry. I'm tired." And sad. "We'll have breakfast together."

I took off my clothes, turned off the lights, and got under the covers.

"And now you're going to sleep?" Crane said. "Aren't you going to tell me about your day?"

"Can I tell you later? I need rest. I'm human."

"And I'm not!"

"Crane, what's wrong with you?" I asked. "Maybe I need to find you other spirits you can talk to all the time."

"Don't do me any favors," Crane said.

I closed my eyes. Things seemed off again. Nothing was the same.

Maybe in the morning, all would be better.

Nine

Désastre

I awakened to Paul's voice outside the locked door.

"Would you mind making breakfast for me and a business associate?"

"Sure," I said groggily. He had more business associates than anyone I had ever met.

I peed, then splashed my face and washed my hands.

After I put on clean clothes, Crane and I went into the kitchen. I set him on the island, then glanced into the dining room. Paul sat across from Inez, the woman who had picked up Miguel and me in the desert after his car broke down.

She smiled when she saw me.

"Hello," I said. "Nice to see you again.

"And you," she answered. "Any detrimental effects from your long walk?"

"No. My legs were sore for a day, but that was it."

"Good," she said.

"What's for breakfast?" Paul asked.

"We'll see."

I returned to the kitchen. He was rather impatient for a man who was asking me for a favor.

"OK, Crane, what do you say?"

"How about East Indian scrambled eggs?"

"OK."

I got out the eggs, cracked open six, and whisked them in a glass bowl.

"Now add raisins and cinnamon."

"That sounds disgusting," I said.

"No. It's wonderful! *Magnifique! Très* exotic. Add a pinch of cayenne to balance the flavors."

I got raisins from the pantry and cinnamon from the spice shelf and spilled a little of both into the yellow mixture. I stirred them together, and the yellow turned brown.

"Crane. It doesn't look or smell good." In fact, it turned my stomach.

"Pinch of cayenne," Crane said.

I did as he said, then turned on the flame beneath the skillet. When the olive oil was hot, I poured the mixture into the pan and let it sizzle while I heated the bread. Once the eggs were firm, I divided them onto two plates, added bread and butter, and carried them into the dining room.

"Enjoy," I said, looking down at raisins poking up through the brownish scrambled eggs.

I hurried back into the kitchen and started to clean up.

Inez coughed. Or choked.

Crane laughed.

"What the—?" Paul cried.

I went back into the dining room.

"Is this some kind of joke?" Paul asked. His face was red, his eyes watery.

Inez had her hand over her mouth.

"What's wrong?" I asked. "It's East Indian scrambled eggs."

"It's disgusting," Paul said. "I'm so sorry, Inez."

"I'll make you something else," I said. "Just plain eggs?"

Inez shook her head. "No, really. I told Paul I wasn't hungry, but he insisted."

I glanced at him. So why had he dragged her here and me out of bed?

I picked up the plates.

"I'm so sorry," I said. "I guess I got the spices wrong."

Inez smiled weakly. Paul didn't look at me.

I left hurriedly. Vesta was just coming in. She looked at the scrambled eggs and crinkled her nose.

"Looks like the skull steered you wrong this time," Vesta said.

"Looks like," I said as I dumped the food into the garbage.

I grabbed Crane, went into the office, and slammed the door.

"What was that all about?" I asked.

"Well, it sounded good."

"It did not," I said. "It sounded disgusting! I can't believe I listened to you!"

Crane said nothing.

"I'm so embarrassed," I said. "I hope that poor woman doesn't get sick."

"She can take care of herself," Crane said.

"How do you know?" I asked.

"I heard her voice. She sounded like—"

"Oh. That's it. You didn't like her voice, so you sabotaged her breakfast?" I said.

"No, but what about him? What right has he to wake you from a sound sleep—?"

"He has every right if I don't mind. And I don't." Even if I did mind, I was not going to tell Crane. "I've got one big brother; I don't need another."

"Hmph!"

"I'm very disappointed in you," I said.

I got up, went into the bathroom, and slammed the door. I peeled off my clothes and took a shower.

Now I couldn't trust Crane.

I dried off, got dressed again, and went into the kitchen. Vesta kneaded dough. I glanced into the dining room. Inez and Paul were gone, their dirty cups left behind.

"Did you get to see Inez?" I asked.

Vesta nodded.

I toasted a piece of her bread, then sat on a stool eating it.

"It wasn't your fault," Vesta said. "He shouldn't have brought her in. Or any of his other associates."

"What do you mean?" I asked. "I consider it part of our arrangement, to pay off my cousin's debt."

"Your arrangement is to feed people truth food so Paul can pump them for information they wouldn't otherwise give to him?"

"What are you talking about?"

"You haven't noticed he doesn't eat when you cook for him and his guests?" Vesta asked.

"He eats with Miguel."

She made a noise. "Miguel has no secrets Paul needs."

Yesterday Paul hadn't eaten French toast right away.

"Does it work? I mean, do they tell him things that they wouldn't normally say? I don't think I like that. It's not ethical."

Vesta laughed. "Now you're catching on."

I made a face at her back.

She turned around.

I tried to look innocent.

"I've eaten your food," she said. "So have you. Do you think it helps people see the truth?"

I shrugged.

She sighed and turned away. "What truthful food will you make tonight?"

"I don't know. After this morning's debacle, I'm not sure I should be let into a kitchen."

"Don't feel sorry for yourself," Vesta said. "It won't matter what you cook. It will be magic."

"You didn't see Paul and Inez this morning."

"Jeanne," she said, turning enough to look at me. "You must have known cinnamon, raisins, and eggs would not be edible."

I sighed. "I suppose."

"You don't need the skull," Vesta said. "Just make something simple."

"My father always said an idiot could make lasagna."

"Sounds perfect for you," Vesta said.

I looked at her. She smiled. "Thanks a lot," I said.

"You could make it now and bake it this afternoon," she said.

"Why not."

I flipped through a few cookbooks and started remembering my father's recipe. I would leave out the meat and add vegetables instead.

I started by mincing the garlic. Then I sautéed it, added tomatoes and pinches of black pepper and hot pepper flakes. Vesta turned on the radio and sang along to pop tunes. While the tomatoes simmered, I put on water and dropped lasagna noodles into it when it started to boil. I sliced carrots and zucchini, then washed and trimmed spinach. While the vegetables steamed, I grated mozzarella and Parmesan cheese.

When everything was cooked, I layered two long glass dishes first with tomato sauce, then noodles, a few carrots, lots of zucchini slices, spinach, and a layer each of the cheeses—ricotta, mozzarella, and Parmesan. I repeated the layers until I ran out of ingredients.

Vesta came over as I started to cover the dishes with foil.

"Smells good," she said. "And you did it, girl who talks to the crystal skull. Now get out of my way. I've got to make my soup."

Sam drove up to the back of the restaurant, and Vesta and I bought produce from him. Vesta created her soup. Fernando arrived and started prep.

At 10:45 A.M. Tangiers had not come to work. Vesta called her apartment, but no one answered.

Around eleven A.M., Antoine popped into the kitchen.

"Hey, all," he said.

"Hi, brother," I said. "Have you seen Tangiers?"

"Yeah, earlier. Why?"

"She's supposed to be here," I said. "And she's never been late since I've been here."

"Which is what, an entire week?" Antoine asked.

Vesta stirred her brew. "Nothing to do now. I'll cook. You can wait tables by yourself."

"You want to help?" I asked Antoine.

"Not on your life. Can we do something later?" he asked.

"We close at three," I said.

"See you then," he said. He waved good-bye and left.

Paul returned just as we opened. He was friendly, not mentioning my breakfast goof. The dining room quickly filled.

Miguel came in around one o'clock with my brother. Paul sat with them for a time, and I noticed how different the three men were. Antoine was so easy, Miguel relaxed and intense all at the same time, and Paul was—Paul was faux real. Looked good on the outside, but I wasn't sure he had anything on the inside.

Of course, who was I to make judgments? I wasn't certain I had anything on the inside, either. I did know I did not want to know Paul any better than I already did.

After lunch, I wearily ate Vesta's soup, sitting in the

booth opposite Fernando, who looked as tired as I felt. I was not getting up at the crack of dawn again to make Paul's breakfast. He probably would not ask me again, not after this morning's breakfast. Perhaps I should thank Crane after all.

Vesta came out of the kitchen and said, "Paul has left for the night. We're on our own."

"I don't think I can cashier and wait tables by myself," I said.

"I'll try Tangiers again," Fernando said.

Just then, Antoine knocked on the window and motioned to me. I got up and went outside. The day was hot, more like May than November. A storm brewed in the north.

"I'm leaving," Antoine said.

"But you just got here," I said.

"Three days ago."

"Not even forty-eight hours," I said.

He leaned against his car. "I read some more of Granny's stuff. I want to find her. I just don't know if I can cook anymore. I've never had enough guts to do what I really want to do. Grandma Juarez has done what she's wanted all her life."

"Except for that brief stay in the funny farm," I reminded him.

"Yeah, well, I'm going to look for her. Come with me. It'll be fun. Blow this Paul guy off. He's a con."

"What do you mean?" I said. "What do you know about why I'm here?"

"I know you're paying off a debt that isn't yours," he said. "I could have given you money, Jeanne."

"It's more than the money," I said. "This is strange because I don't even believe in this kind of crap, but I feel like I was supposed to come here."

"You've paid off Johnny's debt and then some, girl. Paul told us his business has doubled since you've been here.

You've *done* this place. Come with me. We'll find our long-lost grandmother."

"I can't just desert these people," I said.

"Why not? Who are they to you?"

I looked at the restaurant.

"Right now, they're people who are counting on me. Wait a couple of days."

Antoine shook his head and slapped his car. "I'm ready to go," he said, "before I chicken out. I e-mailed Grandma I was coming. I hope that doesn't send her heading to the hills."

"Can you call me when you get there?"

"Sure." He gave me a bear hug. "See you, Jeanne d'Arc." He let go of me and got into the car. "On the flip side, sister."

He was gone.

I rubbed my face.

Miguel drove up. He got out of his car, walked over to me, and kissed my forehead.

"What was that for?"

"You looked like you could use a little boost of energy," he said.

I laughed. "So you gave me some sugar, huh?"

He grinned. "Guess so. They got the lab tests back. The stuff in the wash is definitely an illegal dump."

"What is it?"

"Well, mostly it's antifreeze. They think they can trace it. At least it has enough of a chemical signature that they can tell what truck it came out of."

"If they find the truck," I said.

He nodded. "Yeah, and provided it's an Arizona company. Anyone could have driven out here from anywhere. But, the doctor says that unless we ate it, touched it, or were really up close and personal breathing the vapors, we're okay."

"Good," I said. "My brother just left for Mexico. He's

going to track down my grandmother. I hope he was a good guest."

"Antoine? He was a kick. And the stories he had to tell about you!"

"What did he say?" I asked.

"I'm not telling," he said.

"You haven't seen Tangiers, have you?" I asked.

"Not since last night, why?"

"She didn't show up for work today," I said. "And we can't get her by phone. On top of that, Paul's decided to skip out. We're kind of shorthanded."

"I can help with dinner," Miguel said. "I don't have any more clients today."

We went into the kitchen. Fernando and Vesta had started dinner prep. Vesta mumbled under her breath as she heated the enchilada sauce. I preheated the oven.

"Miguel can help with dinner," I said.

Vesta made a noise. "Good thing you went to law school."

"Just tell me what to do," Miguel said.

"You and the girl who talks to the crystal skull take care of the dining room. Fernando and I will manage in here. I called in that boy Nathan. He'll do the dishes."

I put the lasagna pans in the oven. Then Miguel and I set up the dining room. He seemed in better spirits today, joking around and teasing me.

"Look, buddy, you stay in line or I'll steal your tips all night," I said.

"And I'll give all your customers caffeinated coffee whether they like it or not."

"Aren't we witty," I said, rolling my eyes.

When we opened the door, the restaurant immediately filled up. Nearly everyone wanted the special. I knew that if this trend continued all night, we would run out of lasagna.

But we didn't. Miguel and I stepped on each other's toes a few times, bumped hips, and I stuck out my tongue at him more than once. Even though we were busy and customers did not get very good attention, everyone seemed to be in a fiesta mood.

A woman grabbed my arm as I passed by, "Two days ago when I had your soup, I decided I really did like my job. Now I'm eating the lasagna to find out what I really think of my husband." She pointed to the man sitting across from her.

"I know she loves me," he said, smiling affectionately, "but I am curious to know whether I really want to run for city council."

Someone behind him said, "Yeah, it's amazing. I thought I hated my boss all these years. Turns out I like her. It's me I can't stand!" He laughed.

I nodded and hurried away. These people all appeared to be intoxicated. Strange. Or maybe it was just me. I was not accustomed to people being open and truthful about their lives.

It was still quite peculiar.

The entire restaurant and its patrons seemed giggly, and the display cases and their magical inhabitants glittered.

A delicious night all around.

Some people even got up and danced.

When the last customer waved good-bye, Miguel twirled me around the room.

"Hallelujah!" I shouted.

The four of us sat exhaustedly in the booth and ate the lasagna. We were so tired, we took turns laughing.

"There's one piece of lasagna left," Fernando said.

"For Nathan?" I asked.

"He's long gone," Vesta said.

"For Tangiers maybe," I said. "After we're finished, could you take me to her place?"

"Sure," Miguel answered.

Vesta pushed away her plate. "This food is simple and delicious."

Fernando nodded.

"If you had been cooking for years, just think what your life would be like now," Miguel said.

Vesta shook her head. "No. Now was the time. Maybe it is this place. These dishes. These days. She is doing now what she should do." She shrugged. "Who knows how long it will last? We should just eat it up while we are able."

We laughed.

Vesta smiled, "No pun intended. Now, go find Tangiers. Tell her she missed a good evening!"

Fernando, Miguel, and I drove to Tangiers's apartment, a walk-up over the garage of someone else's home. The lights were off. Miguel led the way up the gray wooden steps. He knocked on the door. No answer. Fernando leaned over and retrieved a key from beneath the third step from the top. He handed it to Miguel.

"Been here before, Fernando?" Miguel said, fitting the key into the lock—not an easy task in the dark.

"I water her plants when she's gone," Fernando said.

"So she would have told you if she was leaving?" I asked.

"Well, I think so."

Miguel opened the door.

"Tangiers!" he called.

No answer.

"Hello!" Miguel called. He switched on the light, and we went into the apartment.

My mouth fell open. Her walls were covered with murals, most of them realistic desert scenes, a saguaro in the corner, an elf owl staring out from her nest inside the saguaro. A dry wash where a roadrunner dashed. Hills golden red with dusk. An ocotillo reached up and out and everywhere, while a red-tailed hawk flew above it.

Fernando went into what I assumed was the bedroom, Miguel into the small kitchen next to the living room. In a few seconds they came back to me.

"Her bed isn't made," Fernando said. "Maybe that means she slept here."

"Antoine saw her this morning," I said.

"I think some of her clothes are gone," Fernando said.

"I'm going to talk to her landlord," Miguel said.

When he left, I stood staring. "She's extraordinary," I said.

"Come see the bedroom," Fernando said.

I followed him to the tiny bedroom. Mountain and forest scenes covered these walls.

"Why was she working as a short-order cook?" I asked. "She's an artist."

"She liked doing something different from painting," Fernando said, "and she didn't make enough money as an artist."

"She talked to you, huh?"

"She liked my poetry," he said. "So she talked a little. She painted the bathroom, too." He pointed to the open door on the other side of the room.

I walked to the bathroom and switched on the light. The tiny room was painted sea blue with fish, dolphins, and a whale swimming around the walls. I smiled.

And caught sight of my own reflection in the mirror. Across my forehead were the letters *WIJ*. Startled, I blinked. The initials were on the mirror. My heart leaped.

"Fernando," I whispered, pointing.

He looked over my shoulder.

"I'll get Miguel," he said.

I backed out of the bathroom.

Could this be real? Could someone I know have been kidnapped?

Was my brother the last one to see her before it happened? I turned and ran out of the apartment.

Miguel called the police. Fernando and I sat on the bottom steps while Miguel talked with the landlord and the police.

Eventually Miguel went with the chief into Tangiers's apartment. After a few minutes, they came down the steps again.

"I don't see any sign of struggle," the chief told us. "Looks like she packed her bags and left. I'll call the feds. See what those boys say—because of that WIJ thing. She say anything to you folks about leaving town?"

Fernando and I shook our heads.

Fernando cleared his throat, then said, "She was very dependable. I don't think she would have left her plants."

The chief rocked back and forth on his heels. "You never know what gets into people. Maybe she just got tired of slinging hash and headed out to cooler climes. She sure does paint a pretty picture. I'll talk to you later, Miguel."

The chief and his officer got into their cruiser and left. Miguel said good night to the landlord. Then we got into Miguel's car.

"I hope she's all right," Miguel said. "The chief thinks maybe she just wrote WIJ on a lark. He doubts someone really kidnapped her."

I looked out the window into darkness and wondered why I wasn't frightened. Maybe I was too tired. Or numb. Or maybe I did not want to think about what a coincidence it was that my brother left town just as Tangiers disappeared. He had been the first person to say those words to me:

"woman in jeopardy." He had traveled to several of the places where people had disappeared.

No. Wait. I was talking about my brother. Some of the people had been from back East, and Antoine had not left the West in years. It wasn't Antoine.

Miguel pulled the car into La Magia. I put my hand on the door but did not open it.

"Are you all right?" Miguel asked. "Oh. Stupid of me not to think of this. Do you want one of us to stay with you?"

I stared at the restaurant. I was not a baby. I could take care of myself.

"Or you could come to our house," Fernando said.

"Yes, that's a good idea," Miguel said. "You can have my room."

"I'll only come if I can sleep on the sofa, like Antoine did. I don't want to throw anyone out of their bed."

"It's a deal," Miguel said.

When we got to their home, Vesta was asleep. Fernando whispered good night and left Miguel and me alone. Together we made the couch into a bed.

"I should have gotten some clothes," I said.

"I'll get one of my old T-shirts and shorts," Miguel said. He left the room, then returned with a pile of clothes.

"Thanks," I said. "See you in the morning."

I reached for Miguel's hand, and we gently kissed each other good night. The soles of my feet tickled. He smiled shyly and left me alone in the living room. I got under the covers. I liked Miguel. He was a nice man.

I lay awake for a long time. I hoped Tangiers was safe; Antoine had nothing to do with her disappearance. By now, he and my grandmother would have been reunited.

I wondered why he had never called me.

Ten

Sur la Route Again, Again

I dreamed Miguel and I were making love and was rather flummoxed when I awakened to bright sunlight and the sounds of gentle bickering in the kitchen. I got my clothes and went to the bathroom. I washed in the sink, rinsed out my mouth with water, and changed clothes. Then I went into the kitchen. Vesta stood at the stove; the men sat at the kitchen table.

Vesta actually smiled when she saw me. "Good morning."

"Hello," I said.

Miguel smiled, and Fernando yawned. They both ate cereal and toast.

Vesta followed my gaze. "What can I do? They're grown men."

"If that's your bread," I said, "I'll have some, too."

Vesta and I joined the men. I dribbled honey onto the bread and poured orange juice into my glass.

"Will the police call you if they find anything out about Tangiers?" Vesta asked.

"I don't know," Miguel said. "Jeanne probably knows more than they do. She's been following the WIJ cases."

"Just peripherally," I said, "I haven't watched television in days. I don't know what's going on."

"Television will rot your mind," Vesta said.

"That's what my dad says."

"He's a wise man," Vesta said.

"I don't know about that," I said. "The skull used to talk to him, but he never told anyone, not even when they were testing me to see if I was crazy because it talked to me."

"You'll have to ask him about it," Vesta said. "I'm sure he has an explanation."

"Could there be a reason for letting your child believe she might be crazy for a couple of decades?"

"I can't think of one," Vesta said. "But Miguel doesn't know all the things I did when he was a boy."

"Like what?" Miguel asked.

"I don't know," Vesta said. "Like I kicked your father out long before he died because he drank too much."

"I knew that," Miguel said. "I remember that."

"I even remember that, Aunt Vesta," Fernando said.

"OK. So that's not the point!" Vesta said. "Parents are just like you."

The three of us looked at her.

"Stupid and flawed," Vesta said. "Parents can be stupid and flawed. Don't hold it against him forever."

"I only found this out a few days ago," I said, "so I've only been angry a little while."

"All right, then. Just forgive him before forever," she said with exasperation.

The three of us laughed.

"I've got to get to the office," Miguel said, pushing his chair from the table.

"Today you'll be a lawyer?" his mother asked.

"Today I'll be a lawyer," he said.

"Can I catch a ride?" I asked. "I want to shower and

change before lunch. Thanks for the bed and breakfast, Vesta. See you both at lunch."

"Today's my day off," Fernando said. "Nathan's coming in. I'll see you tomorrow."

I waved, and Miguel and I got in the car and drove to La Magia. Paul's car was there.

"Call me if you hear anything about Tangiers," I said.

Miguel nodded, I got out, and he drove off. I went into the restaurant quietly and walked back to the office. It was empty. Crane was going to be angry with me. I'd left him alone for a day. His breakfast fiasco had worked out all right. I had finally cooked a meal by myself, and I had gotten to tango all night with Miguel as we waited tables together.

I closed the door and took my suitcase from beneath the couch bed. I got out clean clothes, then dug around for Crane. He wasn't there. I must have put him under the bed.

Looked there. Wasn't there.

In the bed.

Nope.

I tore the room apart.

"Crane!" I cried. "Tell me where you are!"

No response.

I must have left him in the kitchen.

I raced out of the office. Crane wasn't above the stove or on the island.

Maybe Paul had put him in the display case. I ran into the dining room.

No.

Paul stood at the cash register.

"What's wrong?" he asked.

"The skull is gone," I said.

He looked down at his money.

"I know," he said. "I lost a bet."

"What?"

"I had to trade the skull—and the ruby scepter. I had no choice."

"What!"

He shrugged.

I wanted to eat his heart out.

"You stole from me?" I said. "How could you? Who did you give them to?"

He shook his head. "I can't tell you. Suffice to say the persons I handed them over to said they would return the skull and scepter to their rightful owner."

"I am the rightful owner!" I screamed. "Show me the safe."

"What?"

I pulled his arm. "You open the safe and give me the scepter."

"It's not there," he said.

"Open the safe!"

We went into the office. I watched while Paul dialed the numbers and opened the safe. It was empty.

"What did they promise? A new chef? Another magical toy?"

Paul closed the safe door. "I didn't want to, but I had no choice."

"Bullshit!"

"I guess you'll be leaving us now?"

"And won't you be sorry?" I said. "No more customers lining up at the door."

"I regret that," he said, "but we always knew your stay was temporary. You're welcome to sleep here for a few more days."

He left the room. I breathed deeply, then followed him.

"Were you out all night?" I asked, trying to make my voice sound ordinary.

"Yes. I just got back. I'm starved. Not that I would dream of asking you to make me anything." He opened the refrigerator and gazed inside. "Oh, lasagna. That would hit the spot." He looked at me. "Did you make it?"

Suddenly I knew who that last piece of lasagna was for.

"No. Vesta made it on her day off," I lied. "She had some left, so we used it as one of the specials. Don't tell the health department."

Paul took the lasagna from the refrigerator, lifted off the plastic wrap, and slid it into the microwave. I went back to the office and packed.

Then I closed the door, locked it, and phoned Miguel.

"Paul stole my specter and skull and gave it to someone," I said.

"Who?" Miguel asked.

"I'm about to find out," I said.

"Do you want me to call the police?" Miguel asked.

"He's your client!" I whispered.

"If it's between you and Paul," Miguel said, "I pick you."

"Let's see what I can get out of him first. Talk to you soon."

I hung up and took my suitcase into the dining room. Paul was just finishing the lasagna. I sat across from him.

"I guess this is good-bye," I said.

"Thank you for gracing our place with your presence," he said, smiling.

How had I ever fallen for his fake charm? He was just like Johnny, only better dressed.

"So Paul," I said. "Who has my scepter and skull?"

"I told you," he said. "I had to horse-trade."

"Yes. With whom?"

"Inez." He looked surprised at his answer.

"Vesta's friend Inez from Mexico?" I asked.

"Yes, Vesta knows her."

"Where does she live?"

"I don't know," he said. "She went back to Mexico last night." He looked down at his plate.

"Yes, I made it," I said. "How does it feel to be the screwee?" I stood. "See you around, Johnny-boy."

"You're not comparing me to *him?*"

I was out the door. Miguel drove up in his little red car. I threw my suitcase in the back, then got in the front seat.

"It's Inez," I said. "He gave them to Inez. He doesn't know where she lives."

"Mom does," he said, turning the car around. "Man, I'm sorry, Jeanne. I had no idea he'd ever do anything like that."

"It's not your fault," I said. "I blame him absolutely."

Vesta sat on the porch, staring off at the mountains.

"Vesta," I called as I jumped out of the car. "Paul stole the crystal skull and scepter and gave them to your friend Inez."

"How'd you get him to tell you that? Oh." She nodded. "The last piece of lasagna was for him."

She went into the kitchen, opened up her address book, and wrote Inez's address on a piece of paper.

"I will call her and tell her you are on your way," Vesta said, handing me the paper. "She will keep your skull and scepter safe."

"That's what Miguel said about Paul," I said.

"I am a better judge of character," Vesta said, eyeing her son.

"I didn't mean—"

"She's right," Miguel said.

I looked at the paper. "She lives in Puerto Peñasco. That's where my brother went to look for my grandmother."

"You go with her, Miguel. You need the vacation. She needs the car."

"Oh, I can't ask," I said. "You've got clients."

"I'll take care of it," Miguel said. "I'll be back in an hour."

After he left, Vesta and I looked at each other.

"You'll be shorthanded at the restaurant," I said.

She shrugged. "We will do all right. Say good-bye to Fernando. He is fond of you." She motioned me to go down the hall.

I went and knocked on the closed door. "Fernando, it's Jeanne."

"Oh." He opened the door and smiled. "Hi."

"Fernando, something's happened. I have to go, and I don't know when I'll be back. I wanted to say good-bye. I loved your song." I put my arms around him, and we hugged. "Go to college."

When I let go, Fernando said, "I'll see you again. I liked having you at the restaurant."

"Thanks."

Fernando, Vesta, and I packed a cooler full of sandwiches, water, fruits, snacks, and a thermos of soup. Just as we finished, Miguel drove up. We carried the cooler to the car and put it in the trunk, alongside our suitcases.

"See you in a few days," Vesta said. Then she went back into the house.

I gave Fernando another hug, then got into the little red car.

"On the road again," Miguel said, as he pulled the car out of the driveway.

Only this time, we had no Crane to crack jokes or tell me how he had affected history. We only had us.

We drove in silence for a long while. We rarely passed any cars. The desert stretched away from us, looking hot, desolate, and golden. I knew if we stopped, I would see color and movement, but today we did not stop.

"I'm sorry about Paul," Miguel said. "My mother is right. I should have known. I am his lawyer—*was* his lawyer."

"You've known him longer than you've known me," I said.

"Exactly," he said.

"Don't you own part of the restaurant?"

"Yeah. That is complicated. Did he tell you why he gave the skull and scepter to Inez?"

"It was a gambling debt," I said. "He said he had to trade with her."

"Did you sleep OK?" Miguel asked. "Any nightmares?"

I smiled, remembering my dream. "No. I don't know why. Here I was faced with one of my biggest fears—well, close. I guess I shouldn't be so self-centered. Tangiers has disappeared, not me."

"I did some research at the library about the WIJ case," Miguel said. "They don't really know what's going on. There are no signs of struggle, no bodies found, no ransom notes. They all seemed to have left willingly—or at least without a great deal of fuss. What do you suppose that means?"

"That whoever took them was very charming," I said. "Maybe someone like Paul."

"No. He's too slick. It would have to be someone who seems really harmless, but interesting."

I stared out the window. Someone like my brother? No. I knew Antoine. If he were to kidnap someone, it would be to show her a good time, give her a solid meal. But when we caught up with him, I was going to inquire a little more firmly about his last encounter with Tangiers.

We entered Organ Pipe Cactus National Monument, stopping somewhere midway to eat. We sat beside the car, eating sandwiches and drinking soup. As I stared at the namesake cacti of the monument, I suddenly remembered sitting on the desert floor as a child, looking down at the crystal skull.

"I have seen many things, *ma petite*," Crane said. "And I will tell you all that I can so that you can survive this world, so you will never be in jeopardy."

"Oh, my crystal friend!" Grandmother Juarez said. I looked up at her, but the sun blocked out her face. "We cannot protect her from all danger, but we can help her be more aware." She squatted next to me. "There is no one to teach us anymore. I grew up not understanding the world. But the skull, the crystal skull remembers how the old ones lived."

Then Grandma was gone. Disappeared? And the skull was telling me to close my eyes and cross my legs. To feel the ground beneath me, the air around me. The sun on top of my head, stroking my head, opening, opening.

I floated above the ground, then flew through the sky, up through the atmosphere, zooming into the stars.

Now I looked over at Miguel.

"I just had another memory of my grandmother," I said. "And I was talking to the skull. I thought I only talked to it once. I was flying."

"I used to have flying dreams," Miguel said.

"I wasn't sleeping," I said.

We continued through the monument and over the border. As soon as we were in Mexico, I felt the presence of the other—a sense that all was different. Maybe I was just feeling strange because of the memory. I could still feel the gravel on my butt—and the star ether in my being.

Star ether?

I stared out the car window. A woman dressed in black waved to me, and I waved back. We passed a group of men around a derelict car. They looked like a photograph, or a still-life portrait, unmoving, preternatural in their interest in us.

They knew we did not belong. Would bandits soon surround our car and force us off the road?

I glanced at Miguel. He smiled. He had no irrational fears. No prejudices.

I looked out the window again. No people or cars. Just desert. Comforting, empty desert stretching forever.

If Grandmother and the crystal skull had been teaching me

to live in the world, why hadn't they taught me to go forward fearlessly?

"People didn't always need language," the skull had told me. "It was invented so people could lie to each other. Or to discuss art. One or the other."

I hadn't known what he meant, but I laughed. I was so young. I could see my tiny fingers stroke the head of the skull.

"But language tells you very little," Crane said. "For instance, if you walk past a bird on the ground, it will carry on with its business, but if you stop and crouch, it will fly away. Why?"

I poked my finger in the skull's empty eye socket.

"Because it's scared," I said.

"Your body movements changed. To it, you probably suddenly became a mountain lion."

I poked the skull's other empty eye.

"That bird did not need language," Crane said. "There are many avenues for understanding the world."

"Are you all right?" Miguel asked, interrupting my memories.

"I'm fine," I said. I had a few questions for Crane, too, once I got my hands on him again.

Puerto Peñasco was small and sprawling, with old Spanish colonial buildings mixing with newer, less sturdy-looking buildings digging into the blond desert sand. We drove slowly through town, passing several bakeries, a newsstand, a restaurant or two. Small boys swinging a bucket between them ran to our car and tried to wash our windshields. We kept driving until we got to the beach, where the Gulf of California glimmered next to white sand, an aqua backdrop to a darker blue sky. The sight nearly blinded me—so bright with color it was, or maybe it was the way it all undulated together, as if it were all one being—sky, water, and earth, or many beings, caressing the other, becoming the other.

Miguel stopped the car.

"I need to get directions," he said.

I nodded. After he left, I stepped out of the car and onto the sand. I did not feel well.

Sick to my stomach.

My hands shook.

Maybe I just needed some fresh air. I walked—stumbled— toward the water, my feet pushing against the dry loose hot sand.

It all burned from the fire of the sun. Had this entire beach once been people who could not stand up to the pressures of being human? So they dissolved into sand? Or were transformed by fire into another. The other?

No, too literal, Jeanne. Get a grip.

The sand got firmer. The water gently lapped at my feet. I leaned over and touched it with my fingers. Warm.

I still felt off-balance. I needed to walk. Three or four hours in a stuffy little car had done me in.

I stumbled down the beach. Passed a bonfire, people dancing round it. Music. A firecracker went off. I jumped. Staring at the sand, I kept walking. This was stupid. It would be better to get sick in the car, not out here in front of the world.

I tripped and fell. The sand felt good under my fingers in spite of the cigarette butts and pieces of candy wrappers. I pushed them all away and lay my cheek against the sand.

"I've been expecting you."

I looked up. Inez reached her hand down to me. I grasped it and got unsteadily to my feet.

"You have something that belongs to me," I said.

Inez smiled. "You think so? I believe they belong to me."

I heard Miguel call my name.

"Paul had no right to gamble away my family's possessions!" I said.

"My dear, I believe if you think on it, you will come to realize the skull and scepter are now back with their rightful owner."

Something about her. Voice.

"What?" I still felt ill. "Who are you?"

"Don't you know me, coyote cowgirl?"

That singsong voice. I gazed at her. Suddenly my unsteadiness disappeared.

"Grandma?"

"Hello, little one."

Eleven

Hacienda and Hearth

Miguel ran up to us.

"Inez," he said, catching his breath. "We were looking for you."

"Miguel," I said, "meet my long-lost grandmother, Winema Juarez."

Inez smiled. "Come, we have a great deal to catch up on," she said, touching my arm.

I moved away from her. "Wait a minute," I said. "The only catching up I want to do is to get the ruby scepter and skull. You may be my grandmother, but these items still belong to Mom and Dad."

"Why don't you and Miguel come to my place, and I'll explain the whole thing," she said. "I'm parked up this alley."

She pointed to her truck up by the road.

I grabbed Miguel's hand, and we hurried away. I kept glancing back, half-afraid Inez would disappear and half-afraid she would not.

We got in the little red car, and Miguel drove up the street until we caught up with Inez's truck. Then we followed her.

"You didn't recognize her before? Well, obviously not."

"I haven't seen her in twenty years," I said. "I haven't even seen a picture of her. And her name isn't Inez. It's Winema, as far as I know. Weird Winnie."

We followed the pickup down the highway and out of town, then up a dirt road into the desert. We stopped in front of a hacienda-style building.

I got out of the car. Inez smiled and motioned us to follow her. We walked through an open wrought iron door and into a cool dark hallway of the hacienda. We crossed the hallway, turned, and stepped out into a huge open-air courtyard secluded by the wraparound building. The layout reminded me of the Oui & Sí, only this building was bigger and gracefully older. Water spilled into a fountain that became a swimming pool. Various people walked along the second-story balcony or were seated at tables in the courtyard. Inez took us to a secluded corner, under a palm tree, and we sat at a round wooden table.

A woman hurried up to us.

"Hello, Winema," she said. She looked vaguely familiar to me. Was she another long-lost relative? "Can I get you anything?"

"Donna, this is my granddaughter Jeanne," I said, "and her friend Miguel."

"Hello," I said. "I don't need anything."

Miguel shook his head.

"No, thanks, Donna," Inez said.

"Nice to meet you," she said, and left us alone.

"Is this a restaurant?" I asked.

"What? No. She's just being polite. This is the Non-institute Institute. She lives here."

"So what do I call you?" I asked.

"Grandmother. Grandma. Winema. Inez. Whatever you like," she said.

"Would you two like to talk about this alone?" Miguel asked.

"No," I said. "Tell me why you are Inez in Arizona and Winema in Mexico."

Inez sighed. "I don't want our first meeting in twenty years to be plagued with bad family stories."

"Third meeting," I said. "Please."

"I was Inez in Arizona because I didn't want to risk your parents finding me, and then after so many years, it was just easier to be Inez in Arizona."

"Why were you afraid of my parents?"

"Twenty-five years ago they committed me to a mental hospital against my will," she said.

"Antoine mentioned that, but I didn't really believe it."

"I—I think I'll look around," Miguel said.

"Have Donna take you to your rooms," Inez said. "It'll be dark soon. You'll want to spend the night."

He nodded and quietly left the table.

"Please finish what you were telling me," I said.

"You know your grandfather and I were archeologists," she said. "We spent a good deal of the time away from your mother. Too much. She was resentful, and we never got a chance to reestablish a bond. When your grandpa died, I got very depressed. Your mom and dad committed me to the hospital. I wasn't there long. I just needed a rest. Once I was out, I started getting involved again, and I spent as much time with you kids as possible. Belinda didn't really care, I'm afraid. Antoine was interested in the stories about the digs. You seemed to like being with me. Your grandfather and I had a piece of property in Scottsdale. I wanted to open a shop, sell books and trinkets, tracts about our archeological discoveries."

She smiled. "Weirdo stuff. I never said we came from

UFOs or that aliens built certain ruins—none of the things they accused me of. I was just open to listening to alternative theories. Back then, hardly anyone talked about weirdo stuff. Especially scientists! Your parents wanted to open a restaurant. I said they could have part of whatever building I put up on my property, but they wouldn't do that. They started saying I was crazy. I did get a little depressed again. It is difficult to be so alone in the world. They said I was corrupting you by having you talk to the skull."

"You can't just commit someone," I said.

She shrugged. "Well, they had done it before. They said they'd do it again unless I promised to turn the deed to the property over to them. So before the guys with the white coats could get me, I gave your parents the deed. Then I got out of town."

I stared at her. "My parents did that to you?"

She nodded. "How did they explain my leaving?"

"They didn't. At least not to me. I completely forgot you. I thought you were dead. Then I saw you in the wash at the Valley of Dreams, and that must have triggered some memories. Antoine said they just said you were crazy."

"The skull and scepter were mine," she said. "Your grandpa Juarez and I had them for nearly thirty years before your father got his hands on them."

"Dad says they've been in our family for generations," I said, "just like we supposedly have all these prestigious ancestors who were chefs going back to the Garden of Eden."

Inez laughed. "Your father was a busboy from New Orleans."

"Well, at least the New Orleans part was true. You've been hiding from my parents ever since?"

She shrugged. "Not really. They can't hurt me now, I don't

think. I have nothing they want. I guess the fear became a habit. Every time I go into the States, I went by the name Inez."

"Bear knows you as Weird Winnie."

She laughed. "Yes, he called me and told me about you. When I picked you and Miguel up outside Sosegado that day, I was so surprised—surprised that I was still afraid of my family! But I wanted to see you anyway. When you served me that horrible breakfast, I heard Crane laugh. I couldn't believe it. And I knew if I had the skull, I could lure you down here. This is my territory. I feel safe here." She shrugged again. "Maybe I am a little crazy."

"Bear said you aren't crazy at all," I said. "You just had different ideas about the world."

"I *was* depressed after your grandfather died. But the hospital was so awful, Jeanne. To be caged. I did not want to go back, so I left the U.S. and came back to Mexico. I was born not far from here. Your grandpa was from Spain and settled in New Orleans. The members of my family were Mexican migrant workers and Indians, the O'odham like Vesta. I didn't have anything except the clothes on my back after I left your parents, so I came here to my mother's house."

"If you'd had the scepter, you could have sold the rubies for money," I said.

She smiled. "Those are paste, little one. I'm surprised Paul never took it to a jeweler. They're good paste, so I could have gotten some money, but nothing to build a life on."

"I've been running all over the countryside after something that was worthless?"

"No, not worthless. Not anymore. Someday the ruby scepter might be useful to you or your family." She patted my hand. "Do you want to see my Non-institute?"

"Sure."

We walked side by side across the courtyard. Inez stopped and introduced me to several women and a couple of men. I tried to memorize the faces and names but knew I would forget. We went inside the house.

"Have you read any of our publications?" Inez asked as we walked down the cool hallway into a large open room with sliding glass doors that looked out onto the desert. The doors were open, and sunlight filtered in to us. Inez stepped outside onto a stone patio.

"I read one," I said. "Part of a newsletter."

She nodded. "I learned many things from my travels. Mostly I learned that civilizations come and go. No matter how prosperous a civilization is, what they create dies out. Civilizations erode and collapse. It is inevitable. Ours is collapsing now. So many of us are exhausting ourselves trying to save it." She shook her head. "Your mother ended up exposing herself to radiation. I was declared a crazy lady. Nothing changed. Exhausted or injured from trying to save the world, we inevitably return to our homes to find only a few like-minded people—so we feel more and more isolated. We can't change the world, and we've lost community. I decided to create my own community." She turned from the desert and looked at the room we had just walked through. "This is where we meditate, do yoga, have workshops. We have other common rooms. Each community member has his or her own room or shares a room. We all share in the work and responsibilities. I'm trying to make a safe place for people who are feeling tired and lost."

"How do you support this project?" I asked.

"Those who join have their own funds."

"Join? Like a cult."

Inez laughed. "No, like a club, I suppose. Actually, anyone is welcome. There is no doctrine. No row to hoe. No barge to tote. I've just seen how exhausted good people have become. That must have happened before every collapse, don't you think? Everyone got tired. You are welcome to stay as long as you like."

She led me out of the room, down a hallway, and into another room.

"This is my office," she said.

I looked around. "Gee, Grandma, this looks like a pretty conventional office for a Non-institute Institute."

She sat at her desk, and I sat across from her.

"What can I say? I'm not as wild as everyone believes."

"I remembered something about you today," I said. "Before a few days ago, I didn't remember anything about you or Crane before the last day the skull talked to me— which I thought was the first time."

Inez watched me.

"When my parents realized I heard the skull talking, they freaked out, my mom called the doctor, and they did lots of tests to make certain I wasn't crazy—like you."

Inez laughed.

"You know what I mean," I said. "Then today I remembered talking to Crane before that. He was instructing me on how to get along in the world. What do you know about Crane?"

"Your grandpa and I were given the skull and scepter when we were newlyweds on an expedition in Guatemala," she said. "We were out in a wilderness I cannot even describe to you. When we breathed, we breathed in life—killing it along the way, of course. It was an extraordinary place, vibrating, and we came upon these ruins, huge stone faces peering at us through jungle vines—we still called it jungle back then. Of course, the native people knew all about the ruins. They asked us not to desecrate them by excavating. We owed a lot of money. If we didn't make a find, our careers could have been ruined. But we had to do as the community asked. It was their ruined city, their spirits and deities who lived there. After we agreed not to excavate, they showed us around the ruins. Tendrils curved around the rocks, gradually crushing them through the years, along with earthquakes, rain, et cetera. They told us that the Fire People used to live in the ruins."

"The Fire People? Vesta talks about the Fire People living in the desert. She says they're like shape-changers."

Inez nodded. "Yes, we've talked about this. There are People of the Fire everywhere, called by many different names. They all have the power to transform, to transmute. These Fire People in Guatemala were transmutators, too. They breathed fire—and were tremendously courageous and helped those who needed courage, or so the people who lived near them claimed. And Jeanne, in some of the smaller carved faces were the most exquisite rubies you have ever seen."

"I've never seen a ruby," I said. "Remember? The ones on the scepter are fake."

"The villagers believed the spirits of the place lived in these stones," Inez said, "the spirits of the place, spirits of those who had died, and of those spirits who had not been born yet. When the rubies were placed in the eyes of the stone faces, the people believed they could then communicate with the spirits. After this communication, whatever spirit had spoken with them would then be released to go on its way. Anyway, when we left, the villagers offered us rubies and the crystal skull. We refused the rubies—at least I did— because the villagers were so poor. They needed them more than we did. They never told us where they got the skull from. It was very different from the stone carvings in the jungle. We brought the skull back with us. Your grandfather had the scepter especially made, with the paste rubies, as a present for me."

"When did the skull start talking to you?" I asked.

"Not until after your grandfather died," she said. "About the time you were born, actually. At first I thought it was your grandfather, but it wasn't. I never figured out who he was or where he came from. He knew so much about so many things, especially past civilizations."

"You mean in addition to the stuff he makes up," I said.

Inez laughed. "Yes! I have missed his sense of humor all these years," she said. "I had hoped Crane could help you. In our present-day society, we don't have many traditions that help us live in this world. We learn math and science and how to be polite, but we know nothing about communication besides language, nothing about intuition except fear. Before they deteriorated or were destroyed, some civilizations or clans or tribes or family units—or whatever you want to call them—relied heavily on intuition, and children were taught how to access these gifts, just as you were taught how to access your abilities in math in school. I wanted you to learn to use all your abilities. I had always felt rather lost in the world, as if it were all a mystery or puzzle. People perplexed me. I wanted life to be easier for you."

"Why did I forget everything you and Crane taught me for all these years?" I asked.

"I don't know. You were barely five when I left. Maybe you were just too young."

We sat silently for a few minutes. I felt relaxed, safe.

"How were you able to create the Non-institute Institute if you came back to Mexico with no money?" I asked.

"As I said, I came back to my mother's house. She had died many years earlier, but your grandpa and I had kept the property. A cousin of mine lived in the house with her family. Many of Grandpa Juarez's things were there because we had lived there off and on for years. I discovered a secret hiding place under the floorboards, left over from when my family were bandits, no doubt."

"Bandits?"

Inez laughed. "Or left over from when my family was hiding things from the bandits, who knows? Anyway, there was a strongbox inside the hole. I pulled it out, opened it up, and found a letter from your grandfather, saying he had saved this for a rainy day and I would know whether it was a rainy day or not, for me or for Alita. The letter sat on top of a cloth all bunched up. I carefully unwrapped it." Inez opened her top drawer and picked something up. "And what I found was a couple of handfuls of these." She held out her hand and opened it. On her palm was a quarter-sized bloodred rock.

"Go ahead," she said. "You can touch it."

I picked it up. It felt heavy for its size, and warm.

"Some were cut, others were not," Inez said. "But I knew then I would not be out in the streets. They were all genuine rubies."

I placed the ruby on Grandma's palm again. She folded her fingers over it and put it back in her drawer.

"I'm glad he saved those for you," I said. "I'd be even angrier with my parents if I thought you'd been in poverty on top of everything else."

Inez smiled. "Holding a ruby is supposed to quell one's anger," she said. "Anyway, your parents did me a favor, I suppose. I lost my family in the States, but I found my life here. Come. Let me show you to your room."

We left the room, went down the hall, then up narrow stairs onto the second-story balcony.

"I almost forgot," I said. "Is Antoine here?"

"Yes," she answered. "But I think he's down at the beach with some of the others."

As we walked, I looked at the fountain and pool and suddenly longed to be down by the water, relaxing, forgetting that anything in my life or the world had ever gone wrong.

Inez opened a door to a corner room. Inside was a medium-size off-white room—the walls, bedspread, sofa, chairs, all white with a bit of peach-colored accenting. The wall opposite the door was nearly all window with a view of the gulf.

"This is lovely," I said.

"I'm glad you like it," she said. "Why don't you get comfortable? Come down whenever you want to eat." She smiled and walked out the door.

"Thank you, Grandma Winnie," I said.

I closed the door and looked around. My suitcase was in the closet. I pulled off my clothes and took a shower. Then I put on clean underwear and a camisole and slipped under the covers. I groaned in ecstasy. I had not slept on a bed in nearly a week. Had not gotten a full sleep in over a week. My body sank comfortably into place, and I closed my eyes. At last.

When I awakened, it was night. I slipped on a white cotton dress and went out onto the balcony, which was now illuminated by soft recessed lights. I heard murmurs coming from below, but I could see no one.

I went downstairs and walked around until I found a common room where a couple of dozen people were gathered around my grandmother. I stood to the side listening for a few minutes as she talked about ruins in the Yucatán she had explored with my grandfather. Antoine sat near her. I caught his eye and waved. He grinned.

I was hungry. I wandered around the building until I found the kitchen. Several people washing dishes said hello. I made myself a sandwich, then continued exploring the hacienda. So many rooms, many of them empty, some with boxes piled in corners.

I ended up in the courtyard. I took off my shoes and sat at the edge of the pool. Maybe when everyone had gone to bed I would take off all my clothes and slip into the cool warm water and let it seep into my every crevice.

"Hello."

I looked up.

"Miguel. Sit with me." I grabbed his hand and pulled him down. He took off his shoes and socks and dangled his legs in the pool.

"You missed a helluva dinner," he said.

"I needed the sleep," I said. "What have you been up to?"

"Walking. They've done a good job of not disturbing the surrounding habitats. I saw all kinds of desert critters."

"Did you talk to my grandmother?" I asked.

"Just a little," he said. "She gave me some issues of the newsletter. I skimmed a few. You want to go to the beach? I told some people I'd take them down."

I shrugged. "I'm easy."

Miguel rounded up his new acquaintances. Then the four of us drove to town. The other two went to the Lost Dolphin for a late dinner. Miguel and I walked along the beach. Every hundred feet or so, a huge bonfire roared. People danced, drank, and sang. Miguel and I smiled at each other as we went by the fire. Farther up on the beach we walked by several people sleeping. We found a spot between fires and close to the water and stared out at a star-dotted sky that fell into the dark mass of water.

"I like it here," I said. "I think I could stay. I think Grandma's got the right idea. Why fight the inevitable? Just relax. Be happy."

Miguel made a noise.

"What? You don't like my grandmother?"

"That's not what I said. I find it hard to believe that it is acceptable to just drop everything and sit on the beach for the rest of your life."

"There is no beach at the hacienda," I said.

"OK. To sit around the pool."

"They're doing more than that," I said. "They're trying to make a community."

"A community of rich white people—or at least middle-class white people."

"You are such a snob," I said. "My grandmother is not a quote-unquote white person. Does everyone have to be poor and struggling to be allowed to relax and have a good time? Why do you insist that we must suffer all the time?"

He looked at me. I could scarcely see his features in the darkness. "Is that how you see me?" he asked.

I sighed. "I don't know. I was enjoying myself, and I don't think I should feel guilty about that. What good does it do to worry about things all of the time?"

"This from the woman who watches the news so she can know what to be afraid of?"

"I haven't seen or read the news in days," I said, "and I've been feeling much better."

"In spite of toxic wastes and missing coworkers?" Miguel said.

"And getting stranded in the middle of the desert," I said. "My grandmother told me some things about my family that aren't very . . . flattering. I always thought I wasn't good enough for my family. Now I don't know if they're good enough for me." I shuddered. "I can't believe I said that. You know I started this whole crazy thing so that my family wouldn't lose these great historical family jewels, and now I find out they stole them from my grandmother in the first place and have been lying all these years about the family's past. I'm not who I thought I was and neither are they. And as crummy as Paul was to me, he was right about one thing, I think. All that has happened this last week, all the strange coincidences, have brought me to this place. Maybe to my grandmother."

"Maybe to me," Miguel said.

I took his hand. "I don't think the universe is arranging things for your benefit."

"But for yours?"

"Absolutely."

I laughed and started running down the dark beach, the bitter smell of burned wood tickling my nose, the soft wet sand trembling slightly under my feet, and the sound of Miguel's laughter in my ears as he tried to catch up with me.

Later, we picked up the two women at the Lost Dolphin and drove back to the hacienda. The house was quiet, most of the lights out. We walked into the main living room where Winema sat with Antoine.

"I'll let you be with your family," Miguel said.

"No, stay," I said, grabbing his hand.

He kissed my lips quickly. "Good night." And the darkness enveloped him.

I went into the living room.

Antoine stood and gave me a bear hug. "Hiya, sis," he said. "Been having fun?"

I nodded. Winema squeezed my hand, and I sat next to her.

"So what have you two been up to?" I asked.

"He's been nagging me about my old digs," Winema said. "He almost makes me want to go on another."

"Has she told you about Mom and Dad?" I asked.

Antoine looked at Winema. "No. What?"

Winema patted my leg. "All that happened a long time ago. It no longer concerns me."

"It concerns you enough that they still scare you."

"Jeanne, that is not my world anymore. And I'm tired. I'll see you both in the morning."

She smiled and got up.

"I didn't mean to run you off," I said.

"You didn't, darling. See you tomorrow."

After she left, Antoine said, "So? What?"

"Mom and Dad were going to commit her again," I said. "They said they'd do it if she didn't turn over the deed to the property where the restaurant is now."

Antoine leaned back against the couch. "Wow. Well, she did seem strange back then."

"Compared to what?" I asked. "Mom was out protesting the bomb. She must have been around lots of different kinds of people. Why was Grandma suddenly crazy?"

"I remember she talked to the dead, or at least she claimed she did," Antoine said. "She talked to the skull and encouraged you to do it, too. Maybe they were worried about her influence on you."

"They could have asked her to leave," I said. "They didn't have to threaten to commit her. They stole her land, the skull, and the scepter. They aren't real rubies, by the way."

Antoine laughed. "I kind of figured that out. I told you you took all that stuff way too seriously."

"I don't know if I ever want to speak to them again," I said.

"Oh, don't get all holier than thou," Antoine said. "They're still family."

"So is Grandma," I said. "But I guess her philosophy is to let it all go. Be happy. I'll try to try it. Hey, do you know anything about Tangiers's disappearance."

"Can we talk about this later? I'm wiped."

"Antoine, it's a simple question."

He stood and pulled me up. "Go to bed. We'll talk tomorrow."

"Antoine!"

He gently pushed me away. I went to my darkened room. After I closed the curtains, I turned on a light near my bed. Sitting on my nightstand was my old crystal friend.

"Hiya, Crane."

"Hello, *ma petite*."

I picked him up and plopped myself down on the bed.

"I've been worried about you. Why didn't you tell me Inez was my grandmother when you first heard her voice? That was a dirty trick having me make that disgusting breakfast."

Crane laughed. "Yes! It was mean of me, but she had left me behind to rot in that safe all these years."

"Why didn't you tell me what my parents had done to her?"

"I didn't know the details, *ma petite*," Crane said. "I only knew she was gone. She had asked me to teach you how to use your innate knowledge, and I tried to do that, but we got interrupted."

"Until this week I only remembered the time Dad and Mom were taking a picture of us, and you told me which way to turn you. I wonder why I forgot?"

"Who knows, *ma petite?* You were young. The last thing I had been teaching you was how to know what people were communicating without them talking. You know, from their touch, or from things they had touched. Some people are naturally sensitive to other people's feelings. You were one of those people, I believed. I encouraged you in that direction. You seemed to be able to pick up other people's feelings from food."

"I still don't understand why I forgot it all."

"You were very young," Crane said, "and after your grandmother left and I was put away, you had no one to help you continue with what we had started. It seems to me your family was trying to hide a great deal. They didn't need some little thing being able to tell what they were really feeling."

"On some level I knew their truths," I said. "They gurgled up in me every time I ate. And now for some reason when I cook, whoever eats my food knows their own truths. What strange creatures we are, to exhaust so much energy in hiding who and what we are until we can't remember."

"I tried talking to you every year when your father took me out of the safe," Crane said. "But after they sent you to the doctors to see if you were crazy, you didn't hear me. Just like Sleeping Beauty, I suppose. They pricked you with their needles, and you fell to sleep."

"And then when I touched you again, I woke up. So that's who you are! My Prince Charming!" I giggled. "I always thought he'd have more meat on his bones."

Crane groaned.

"Who are you, Crane?"

The skull was quiet for a few moments. Then, sounding tired, he said, "I must tell you, *ma chère,* I don't remember who I am. Maybe I was Joan of Arc. Or Cortés. Or Montezuma. Or maybe I only knew them. Or didn't. Maybe I was one of the Fire People. Or maybe none of what I've said is true. Or—"

"OK, Crane. I get the point. I'm going to sleep," I said, pulling off my clothes. "Scream if anyone tries to take you again.

"OK. Sweet dreams."

I dreamed I was a golden child sitting on golden sand with Crane cradled on my palms as the sun came up. A ray from the sun, red and gold, shot straight into Crane's eye—or maybe it came from Crane and went to the sun. Then slowly, Crane began to turn into cool flames that changed into sand running through my fingers until he was all gone, and I was completely alone in the world.

Twelve

C'est la Vie

I awakened feeling stiff and sore. Apparently my body liked hard and lumpy couches better than soft luxurious beds.

I got dressed, then looked around for Crane—he was gone again. I hurried out onto the balcony, then downstairs. I went into the courtyard, where people walked to and from a buffet table. Inez waved me over to her table by the pool. I sat between her and Donna.

"Do you have Crane?" I asked.

"Yes," Inez said. "I want him to teach intuitive skills, like what he started teaching you when you were a child."

"I think he did a better job teaching me to cook," I said. "He gave Dad all his recipes, you know, and me, too. All of the meals worked out except the cinnamon eggs."

Inez laughed. "Yes, I won't soon forget that taste."

I saw Miguel at the buffet table.

"I'll be right back," I said, and went to the buffet where Miguel was loading up his plate with fruit, eggs, beans, and salsa.

"Hiya, road warrior," I said. "How'd you sleep?"

"OK."

He looked a little weary.

"Are you all right?" I asked.

He shrugged. "Maybe I'm homesick." He smiled. "Or just slow to awaken."

"Do you want to do something today?" I asked, scooping eggs, beans, and guacamole onto a plate.

"Sure," he said. "I've decided to take your advice. I don't like the idea that I seem like a drudge. I am going to try and relax."

"You're not a drudge, Miguel," I said. "I like your company, argumentative as you may be." I grinned. "But maybe a vacation is a good idea. We can lounge around the pool together."

We started walking to Inez's table.

"Have you ever really lounged around a pool?" he asked.

"Sure."

"Did you like it?" he asked.

I laughed. "I guess. I never really thought about it."

We sat with Inez and Donna and began eating.

"So how did you happen to come here, Donna?" I asked between mouthfuls.

"I read Winema's newsletters on the Internet," Donna said. "I had been feeling so exhausted. Then I read about the Non-institute Non-doctrine—the way Winema said we could stop worrying, just let go. The world is exactly the way it is supposed to be. I could stop trying to change myself or the world. So I just picked up and left. I've never been sorry."

As I ate, I began feeling a rush of guilt and sadness. I breathed deeply, and the feelings dropped away. I wondered who had made breakfast.

"How long have you been here?" Miguel asked.

"About two months," Donna said.

"I just started asking people to come join me in the last few months," Winema said. "It's only been in the past few years that I decided to start an actual community. I've been tired and lonely and assumed others must feel the same way. I tried all those years to let people know what I had learned excavating collapsed civilizations. I thought if I could tell people what had happened just before the civilization ended, then we could learn from that. Often they ended because of stresses from natural disasters created from overpopulation and depletion of natural resources. Then all the other stuff would happen: human sacrifice, murder, war, et cetera. So if we stop overpopulation and resource depletion we can stop all the other consequences of that, right?" She shook her head. "No one listened to me or anyone else. We're going to hell in a handbasket. I have bowed to the inevitable. I have listened to the universe. We who try to change the world are struggling for naught. We are put here to be happy—to be a world in joy!"

"How do you know your struggles didn't make a difference?" Miguel asked.

"Because things keep getting worse," Winema said.

"I look at it differently," Miguel said. "I believe I make a difference every day. Every day that I am kind and loving I have changed the world. When I help an individual, I've made a difference in that person's life. By being there for my family and helping out in my community, I'm making things better."

Winema shook her head. "It's not enough. It doesn't change anything on a broader scale. But I agree, you can help your community, so that's what we're doing here, creating a new community—with none of the old problems. We have no history together, so we can start with a clean slate."

"Speaking of clean slates," I said, "Grandmother, how did

you get Paul to give you the skull and scepter? Did you beat him at cards?"

"No. I discovered something about him. I told him I'd tell the police if he didn't return the skull and scepter to me."

Miguel put down his fork. "What did he do?"

"Miguel is Paul's attorney," I said.

"*Was.* What did he do?" Miguel asked.

"He's been contracting with some Texas company to dispose of their toxic wastes. I'm not exactly sure how. His brother or cousin got permits and has the company. Apparently it's very costly to dispose of toxic wastes properly. Lots of regulations—as well there should be. Again, I don't know the details, but they've been disposing of part of their loads in the desert."

Miguel and I looked at each other.

"In the Valley of Dreams?" I asked.

"Yes."

"How did you find out?" I asked.

Winema shrugged. "I know people who know people."

"Really?" Miguel said. "How? Do you have evidence?"

She nodded. "He had some land I wanted to buy. I knew his reputation. I hired an investigator—someone who dug a little deeper than the average Joe. Paul Gurare has his fingers in way too many pies."

Miguel stared at her. "Did you buy the land?"

"No. As it turns out, there wasn't enough water. But I haggled for the skull and scepter. He was reluctant to let you go, Jeanne. He was making a great deal of money off you."

"So you gave him the evidence in exchange for the skull and scepter?" Miguel said.

"No. I told him I'd keep the file, and if he did anything like that again, I would contact the proper authorities."

"And you think that will work?" Miguel asked. His hands were still, his jaw tight.

"Actually, no," Winema said. "I intended to send the information to the police once I got back here. Which has only been barely a day."

Miguel picked up his fork again. "If you like, I'll take the file into the sheriff myself today."

"That would be nice," Winema said. "I'm sorry you're leaving so soon."

"I guess I'm not the vacation type," Miguel said.

"This isn't about being on vacation," Donna said. "It's about creating a new world starting right here and now."

"The trouble with that," Miguel said, "is that the old world is still out there. Excuse me. I'll go get my things and then come back down for the file. If that's all right, Winema?"

Winema nodded. I excused myself and followed Miguel up to his room.

"Do you have to go now?" I asked.

"Yes," he answered, shoving yesterday's clothes into his bag. "You can ride back with Antoine, can't you?"

"Don't worry about me," I said. "I thought you were going to take a vacation."

"I have to let the sheriff know," Miguel said. "I can't let Paul keep dumping shit in the desert."

"Will a day or two make a difference?" I asked.

He stopped and looked at me.

"OK. So a day or two will make a difference. I'll just miss you."

"Come with me."

I shook my head. "No. I want to stay with my grandmother."

We went downstairs together. Winema met us at the door and handed Miguel a large manila envelope.

"My investigator's name and number is in there, too," she said. "Say hello to Vesta."

"Thanks," Miguel said.

"I hope it goes well for you," she said. She smiled and left us alone.

Miguel and I went into the sunshine. At his little red car, I put my arms around him, and we embraced. He kissed my forehead. I kissed his lips.

"I hope you'll be very happy," he said softly.

"You sound like this is good-bye forever," I said.

"You're coming back to Sosegado?" he asked.

"Why not? I have friends there."

"Yes, you do." He moved back away from me.

My stomach fluttered. "I don't want you to go," I said.

He took my hand and raised it to his mouth. He kissed the back of my hand, then turned it around and kissed the inside of it.

"I need to take care of this myself," Miguel said.

"I know," I said. "I may have only known you a week—"

"But it feels like forever," Miguel said. He kissed my lips quickly. "Remember this, woman who talks to the crystal skull. I like you. I could say I love you, which I do, but that's easy. It's easy to love, isn't it? You can do that in an instant. I did. As soon as you grabbed your purse out of my hands. But to really like someone is more difficult. I like you."

I laughed. "I like you, too. Because you argue with me. No one does that but you. Well, now you and Vesta."

We hugged each other again.

"I know you think all these stories about the Fire People are just stories," Miguel said, "and maybe they are. But what if you are one of the People of the Fire? That means you can be anything you want. Your grandmother, too. Your ancestors didn't leave the desert when the going got rough. Just like we shouldn't leave this planet—or our communities— just because we've screwed up. We need to change. And look, you can really do that. Perhaps even literally."

"What would you like me to change into? Someone taller? Thinner? A blonde?"

Miguel shook his head. "You know that's not what I mean. Change into yourself, then stick around. Be here now." He sighed. "I'll call you in a few days."

He let me go, got in his car, and drove away. Through the dust Miguel raised, I saw the Gulf of California, today dark blue, stretching out until it reached Baja California. When the dust settled, I turned and went back into the hacienda.

I spent most of the morning lounging near the pool. People came and talked with me occasionally, or brought me something to drink. Apparently as Winema's granddaughter, I was exempt from work, at least for now.

Winema gave a talk about an excavation of a Mayan ruin in Guatemala. Antoine sat at my grandmother's feet, this huge man looking like an eager boy again. I walked alone in the desert, then returned for lunch.

I sat with Donna. After I ate squash and bean soup, I felt almost sick with sadness. I breathed deeply, letting it pass, and asked Donna who had made lunch.

"Holly. Why?"

"She's very sad," I said.

"Is she?" Donna said. "She always seems so happy. She left behind two teenaged children and a husband. I suppose she misses them."

"She just left them?"

Donna nodded. "Most everyone has left loved ones behind. We had to."

"What do you mean you had to? You mean Winema required it before you could come?"

"No! I mean all of us had to give up the trappings of our former lives. How else could we start again?"

"I guess," I said. "Excuse me, Donna."

I got up from the table and went to look for my grandmother. I found her in her office, sitting at her computer. Crane sat on a pile of papers. I sat across from Winema.

"*Ma petite,* nice to see you," Crane said.

"Hello," Winema said. "I'm just finishing up the next newsletter."

"Grandma," I said, "did you know some of these people left behind families?"

"Of course. We all have families, Jeanne. If we start a new life, we leave loved ones behind."

"But some of them have children," I said.

Winema smiled. "I did not ask them to do this. They did it of their own free will."

We were silent for a moment.

"Are you enjoying your stay?" Winema asked.

"It's very nice here. I feel relaxed."

"I'm glad."

I heard Antoine's laughter. He walked by the door with Tangiers on his arm.

"Tangiers!" I cried, standing abruptly.

Antoine and Tangiers backed up the door.

"Jeanne," she said. "How nice to see you." She gave me a hug.

"Where have you been?" I asked. "We were scared to death for you. We thought you had been kidnapped or worse. I was even afraid Antoine had kidnapped you."

"Are you still on that kick?" Antoine asked. "How could you believe such things about me? Tangiers read the *Coyotes Newsletter*s that night at Vesta's house and decided to come here with me."

"Well, you could tell a person!" I cried.

"What difference does it make to you?" Tangiers asked. "I've known you for a week. For an instant. It's my life. Here

I can paint and be free from all that I've been struggling with out there. Here, we can make the world that we want." She smiled. "Your grandmother is a brilliant woman. You should listen to her. I've just gotten back from two days in the desert. A kind of personal vision quest. I need to rest and eat. We'll talk later."

"See you, Jeanne d'Arc," my brother said.

I stood staring at them as they walked away. Then I turned to my grandmother.

"This is all very weird," I said. "She didn't used to talk."

"She didn't have anyone to talk with before," Winema said. She picked up Crane, grasped the pile of paper beneath him, and held the paper out to me. "Here are most of the *Coyotes Newsletter*s. See what you think. I've got a class. Or shall I say, an unclass." She laughed. "See you later."

"What do you think of all this?" I asked Crane after Winema left.

"I don't think. I haven't the brains for it."

I groaned.

I started leafing through the printouts of *Coyotes Newsletter*. Some were nearly ten years old. They contained mostly odd bits of archeological data, news about the destruction of the rain forest, the ozone layer, questions about how life started on the planet, questions about possible alien invasion. My grandmother's interests were eclectic, if nothing else.

Then, about three years ago, she began talking more about being an edge dweller. She wrote about feeling alone and abandoned in a world she did not understand.

"Why can't others see what we see?" she wrote. "How can they continue to rush us closer to the apocalypse, to the collapse of all we know?

"Because they cannot help themselves. It is the way of the

world. It is the natural progression: birth, growth, fruition, dissolution, and death. Why fight it? Let us participate in this process fully—but in a way of our own choosing."

Later she talked about buying land and starting a community.

"We must pick and choose, each of us, what to leave behind and what to take with us. I left my family. They do not know where I am. They chose to think of me as insane because I did not believe what they believed. Without my husband, I became a nobody, unprotected in the world. The family as it is today is unbalanced. We live in a world of tiny fiefdoms called family units. Within this dysfunctional unit, we learn so-called family values: how the power structure works, who rules the world, who manipulates others, who is most important. I was a widow with bizarre opinions. I was dangerous and therefore became a woman in jeopardy. *No longer.* I reject that structure and way of being. I left it all with only the clothes on my back. I became a woman in joy!"

And there was more: directions on how to get to the Noninstitute Institute; ways to cover your tracks if you didn't want to be found; ideas on sending items to the institute ahead of time so no one would suspect you were preparing to leave.

"What is this?" I said aloud.

Crane was silent.

Winema began signing the newsletters: Winema Inez Juarez.

My heart pounded in my ears.

I flipped forward a couple of newsletters.

Her column ended: *W*inema *I*nez *J*uarez. *W*omen *i*n *J*oy. *W*orld *i*n *J*oy. WIJ.

WIJ.

My grandmother was WIJ? She was responsible for the

disappearances of all those people? It was because of her that I and probably thousands of other people had been afraid of being murdered or kidnapped?

My grandmother was WIJ.

I jumped up and ran to the conference room. My grandmother stood at the front of the semicircle of people, talking and gesturing. My brother sat near the door. I pulled him out into the hall.

"What?" he asked. "I wanted to hear that."

I yanked him down the hall.

"Have you read Grandmother's *Coyotes Newsletters*?"

"Yeah, most of them. Why?"

"Did you notice how she signs them?" I asked.

"Gee, I don't know. Winema Juarez?"

We walked into her office.

"WIJ. She signs them WIJ."

"So?"

"Antoine! She writes about dropping out of society. Tangiers wrote *WIJ* on the mirror before she left. All those missing people, the ones supposedly kidnapped, wrote the initials *WIJ* somewhere before they dropped out of sight. There is a nationwide manhunt for the WIJ kidnapper, and it turns out it's our grandmother!"

"Jeanne. Relax. She hasn't kidnapped anyone."

"I thought I recognized some of the people when I got here. Wait. The *L.A. Times*. There was an article about WIJ with a bunch of photographs of the missing people. Use Grandmother's computer and get on the Internet and look at last Friday's paper."

"All right. All right."

He went around the desk and sat on Grandmother's chair. I stood at his shoulder as he worked. After a minute or so, he had the article on the screen.

"There are photographs. Go to them."

"Hang on. Jeez."

"Look. Ohmigod. There's Donna. Donna Mason. Holly Cannon—she made lunch today. Richard Serrano. I met him by the pool. Trudy Cylind. I can't believe this! Antoine, these people are all here. And they've got friends and family who think they've been kidnapped or murdered. Print this off."

A few seconds later, I grabbed the pages from the printer and hurried out of the room, Antoine right behind me.

"What are you doing?" he asked.

I ran into the conference room.

"Are you people crazy?" I shouted.

"Jeanne," Winema said.

"Grandmother, do you know what these people have done? They've left families behind who don't know where they are. Don't you read the papers? Watch TV? Half the nation's police force is looking for these people."

"We've done nothing wrong," someone said.

"We had to make sacrifices," another intoned.

"Grandmother. The police are looking for the WIJ kidnapper. They believe these people have been taken against their will."

"I don't understand," Winema said.

"My family knows where I am," one woman said.

"I don't have family," Donna said.

"But Holly does. And Robert Serrano. Trudy. They just signed your initials and left."

"Not her initials," Robert said. "World in Joy."

"Woman in joy," someone else said.

"Women in jeopardy no longer," Donna said.

"World in juxtaposition."

"Waltzes in July," someone said.

"This isn't funny," I said. "You've put your families in jeopardy."

"We had to start a new and better world. A more functional place to ride out the storm."

"The end justifies the means, is that what you're saying?" I asked. "Grandmother, not every family was like ours. You don't know what it was like when you left. My life shattered. How many lives have all of you left in ruins as you waltzed out on your families?"

"It was easier this way," Holly said.

"For whom?" I asked.

They all stared at me. One woman started weeping quietly.

"We just thought there were answers here," someone said. "That it wouldn't be so scary here."

A woman came to the door.

"Antoine, there's a phone call for you," she said. "They said it's important."

Antoine left. I handed Winema the newspaper article, then followed my brother back to the office.

"You made some excellent points," Crane said.

"Isn't this a kick," I said to Crane as my brother talked quietly into the phone. "I've been worried someone was about to kidnap or murder me, and it's only my grandmother starting a cult."

"It's not a cult," my grandmother said, coming into the room. "I told you that."

Antoine waved us away. We stepped into the hallway.

"I didn't know anything about this WIJ thing," Winema said, holding up the article. "Part of the new Non-doctrine is leaving the old world behind."

"Which part?" I asked. "This hacienda? Electricity? Flush toilets? Aren't those all things from the past? I agreed with everything you had to say in the newsletters. I don't like thinking about the future. I don't want to struggle to save something that isn't worth saving. A lot of it is shit. But

Grandmother, it's so easy to walk away from everything. You're right. These people are all tired. It's great to have a rest. But the people you're preaching to have responsibilities! It's easier to forge new relationships than work on the old, huh? And when the new relationships get hard, do they drop them, too, and start again? Miguel was right, Grandma. We have the ability to transform, shape-change. So let's do it. Don't waste your talents running away."

"Yes, I have talent. And for once, people are listening to me. They've come to me for the answers."

"And do you have them?"

She looked away from me. "I don't know. I was tired of being ignored. I was lonely. I didn't know—"

"Or care how they got here, did you? As long as they came."

"That's not fair."

"You've obviously got money now and position," I said. "Why not offer your services to people to help them work in their own communities, with their own families, without getting burned out? You can offer them temporary respite."

Winema laughed. "I know nothing about getting along with families."

"But you were an organizer," I said. "Hire people. Make your non-institute a real thing—to help people be a part of the world, not drop-out of it."

"But it's all collapsing. It is foolish to struggle against the dying of the light."

"How do you know it's collapsing? Maybe it's just coming to fruition and needs a kick in the butt. If it is dying, what's wrong with being foolish?"

We looked at each other. I could not believe all of that had come pouring out of my mouth.

"Amazing what truths you can realize after a week of eating your own cooking, eh, *ma petite?*" Crane said.

Antoine hung up the phone.

"That was Belinda," he said. "Mom and Dad came home early. It seems they are about to lose the restaurant."

Thirteen

Casa Les Flambeaux

"What are you talking about?" I asked Antoine.

"I didn't get many details," Antoine said. "Belinda didn't know much. Except the business is in trouble. She wanted me to come home."

"You? Did she ask for me?" I asked.

"They want us both home," he said.

"You don't have to go," Winema said.

"I'm going," Antoine said, "but I'll be back. Jeanne?"

"Of course I'm going," I said.

"I'll meet you at the car in ten minutes," Antoine said as he walked away.

"I wish you wouldn't go," Winema said. "We're kindred spirits."

"If that's true, why did you stay away for so long? Why didn't you write to me?"

"I know. I'm sorry. I was frightened. You can't imagine what it's like to be afraid of being locked up against your will."

"Yes, I can. I was afraid all my life that I'd hear voices, and they'd lock me up or send me away."

My grandmother hugged me.

"Think about at least notifying the police," I said.

"And what if their families try to kidnap them and lock them up?" Winema said. "It has to be their decision."

I sighed.

Winema went into her office and picked up Crane.

"Would you like to take him with you?" Winema asked.

"He's yours," I said. "I thought you wanted him to help teach."

"I did," Winema said.

"But no one can hear me," Crane said.

"Where do you want to go, Crane?" I asked.

"I don't want to be locked up in a safe again," he said.

"If you want to come with me," I said, "you are welcome. I'll keep you out of the safe."

"Yes, I want to come with you," Crane said. "It is for you that I exist."

"What do you mean?" I asked.

"I don't really know," he said.

"It's been nice being around someone who hears him besides me," I said. "I don't feel so odd."

"There's nothing wrong with being odd," Winema said.

I smiled. "But, Grandma, isn't that why you ran away from home and convinced all these other people to run away from home? You were all tired of feeling odd?"

"No. Just tired and lonely."

Winema went around her desk, leaned over, and opened the bottom drawer. When she stood straight again, she held the ruby scepter.

"Take this, too," she said. "As my gift."

"Thanks," I said, taking it. "I don't mean to be rude, but isn't it worthless?"

Winema shook her head. "It was mine, and now it's my gift to your family. Maybe it will help."

"Dad will be surprised these rubies are no rubies."

"He already knows," Winema said.

I rolled my eyes. "Yes, I should have guessed that."

I took Crane and the scepter upstairs and packed. When I was finished, I stepped out on the balcony and looked down at the pool and fountain. I had only just arrived and now I had to leave. It all looked so inviting. To spend a lifetime walking along the beach might not be so bad.

Antoine waved at me from below. "Let's go, little sister."

I went downstairs and outside where Winema and Antoine waited for me.

Winema kissed and hugged me. "Remember, Jeanne, it's what is inside that counts."

I frowned. That remark seemed to come out of nowhere.

"It was nice seeing you again," I said.

"I love you both," she said.

Antoine and I got in his car, and he drove us away from the hacienda. I looked back once and waved.

"We come from strange people," Antoine said.

"I thought you liked her," I said.

"I do," Antoine said. "Strange is not a bad thing, sister."

"Do you think it was right, having those people run away from their families?"

He shrugged. "I don't think she thought about people actually doing that. She was just trying to draw other lost souls to her. She didn't realize people could have families and still feel lost and alone. Maybe your tirade gave them all something to think about."

"I doubt it."

After an hour and a half or so, we crossed the border, back into the land of the familiar, only now it seemed to vibrate with the other, too. Perhaps it was me who was the other. I was the odd one, the strange one. Ready for my own transmutation. Antoine turned up the radio. The sky was clear, the sun heading for the horizon. We passed no other cars as we drove through the monument.

Suddenly, the car shimmied slightly and we heard the *slap, slap, slap* of a tire gone bad. Antoine pulled off to the side of the road. My luck with cars lately just went on and on.

Maybe Grandmother was right: we were all routeless.

"Do you have a real spare?" I asked. "Or one of those fifty-mile jobs."

"It's real, but I won't guarantee the air."

We got out of the car. I stretched. In every direction was desert and mountains.

"Hey, Crane, you want to see the desert?" I called.

"*Oooooooeeeee!*" came the muffled reply.

I unzipped my suitcase, reached inside it, and pulled out Crane. Antoine popped open the trunk.

"This will only take a few minutes," Antoine said. "Don't be long."

"Yesssir."

Cradling Crane against my breasts, I stepped off the road and into the desert. Watching my footfalls carefully, I walked around the organ cactus and prickly pear. The setting sun turned the landscape golden red and stretched shadows into other exaggerated shadows.

I walked to an outcropping of sandy-colored rocks, climbed up, and sat on one, facing the sun and the ruddy sky. The rays of the sun seemed to be reaching for us. I put my fingers in Crane's eyes, just as I had as a child. The sun moved, or I did, and suddenly a diamond flash of light or flame pierced my eyes. Startled, I cried out and fell, Crane slipping from my hands.

Then everything changed. Stars rained on my head, tiny bits of flame. Then blackness. I opened my eyes and the desert was different, light. Was it dawn? I looked around for Crane but could not find him. A saguaro sneezed, then lowered its arms and reached for me. I held out my hand, and the saguaro became a person. All around me, that which had been one thing was now another. The ocotillo held octopus tentacles to the sky one second, in the next two boys wrestled on the ground.

"Who are you?" I asked Saguaro Woman.

She bent to the Earth and scooped up a handful of sand. The sun reflected off each grain for a moment, until she let it fall to the ground again. "We are the People," she said.

I looked up, and a man walked toward me. His hair was long and dark, his eyes black crystal. He smiled and waved. I had seen his smile in my mirror. I went to meet him. When we were close, we each raised a hand and stroked the other's cheek. Then we embraced.

"Ahhhh," I sighed.

This was what it was like to belong in the arms of another. Only he was not other. We were the same.

We sat on the ground. The Ocotillo Twins ran after the Elf Owl Man who became a Mountain Lion who sent the twins scrambling away.

"Imagine this, *ma petite,*" the man with my smile said.

I looked down at a round cake with red frosting.

"This is all of us," he said. "All the ingredients shifted and stirred, then baked. You can't separate one grain from the other. It's all of a piece." He broke off a small section and popped it into his mouth. "See. The rest still remains."

I laughed and scooped off a piece and ate it.

"If we eat it all," I said, "none of it remains."

The man laughed. "That's true. But you, you are still a part of this world no matter what happens."

The cake dissolved into sand.

The man and I held hands and walked around the desert.

The ground shook.

We embraced again.

The wind howled. The world became all light. Flame.

Then darkness. Dawn.

My arms were empty.

I screamed.

Around me, sand had melted into glass. Nothing remained of the man with my smile, the Ocotillo Twins, Saguaro Woman, or any of the People.

I bent down and touched glass.

And opened my eyes. My fingers grasped Crane in the desert at dusk.

"What happened?" I asked.

"Jeanne!" Antoine called.

I stood and momentarily glanced around the darkening desert. Then I hurried back to my big brother.

"Have I been gone long?" I asked.

"No, why?"

"Nothing."

"Then let's go home."

I held Crane in my lap and closed my eyes as Antoine drove down the desert road. Strange how in a flash, life could change again. And again.

I fell to sleep.

We arrived home late. Antoine and I quietly stumbled into the house and went to our respective rooms. I set Crane on my nightstand, took off my clothes, and got under the covers. All felt familiar. Except for me. I was not the same person who had left here in a panic less then ten days ago.

I breathed deeply.

"Good night, Crane."

"Good night, *ma petite.*"

"Don't worry. I won't let them put you away again."

"I know, *ma soeur*."

I quickly fell to sleep again.

When I awakened, it was morning. I rubbed Crane's forehead, then took a shower. After I dressed, I set Crane on my windowsill.

"Enjoy the view," I said.

Mom and Nana were making breakfast when I came downstairs. My father, Belinda, and Antoine sat at the kitchen table, reading the paper.

I kissed Nana as she flipped pancakes.

"Hello, Jeanne. Did you have a good vacation?"

"Yes, Nana. Hi, Mom." I kissed my mother's soft cool cheek. She smelled vaguely of lipstick.

"Hello, Jeanne," Alita said. "It's nice to see you."

I tried to catch her eye as she scrambled eggs, but she was focused on the yellow mess in the pan.

"Can I do anything?" I asked.

My mother shook her head.

I went to the table and kissed my father.

"Hello, little one," he said. "I hope you had a relaxing time."

Antoine winked at me as I sat next to him.

"Hi, Belinda," I said.

She grunted. Life as usual at the Les Flambeaux household. No mention of why we had all come scrambling home. Or why we were having this Sunday-like breakfast on a weekday.

Nana brought pancakes and sausage to the table; my mom carried over the eggs.

"A coronary breakfast," Antoine said. "Come to Poppa."

"It doesn't hurt to eat like this once in a while," Alita said. She looked around the table. "It's nice to have us all here together."

I silently ate my eggs and toast. Belinda stopped eating and watched me.

"Since when did you join the land of the living?" Belinda asked.

"Belinda, eat your own breakfast," Jacques said. "Quit sticking your nose into other people's business."

"I'm not two years old," Belinda said. "I wish you wouldn't talk to me as if I were."

"Then stop acting like it," Jacques said.

"Jacques, put the paper down and eat with us," Alita said.

My father snapped the paper shut. My sister gave me a dirty look. I wanted to laugh—and be sick.

"How old are you?" I asked my sister.

Antoine laughed.

"Oh, so now she eats and talks," Belinda said.

"Why don't you like me?" I asked.

"Don't be silly," Alita said. "Your sister likes you."

"Mom, I can speak for myself," Belinda said. "Why do you baby her? You've always taken her side."

"You do sound like a two-year-old," Antoine said.

"Two-year-olds aren't this articulate!" Belinda said.

"Actually, you were quite chatty as a child," Nana said.

I laughed nervously.

"Shut up," Belinda said.

Suddenly, I felt angry and shameful. I looked at my eggs and breathed deeply. These were not my feelings. I glanced at my mother. They were her feelings. I breathed deeply again, and the feelings floated away.

"We have always treated you all the same," Alita said.

"Could we just eat?" Jacques said.

"Antoine, take some sausages. They're getting cold," Nana said.

"Jeanne's always been your perfect child," Belinda said.

"Don't be childish," Jacques said. "You were all perfect."

"None were perfect, Jacques," Nana said.

I laughed.

"Got that right," Antoine said.

"You should ask Jeanne what she's been doing while you were out of town," Belinda said.

"I was cooking at a restaurant in Sosegado," I said. "It's no secret."

"Cooking?" my father said. "Really?"

"Yes, really, Dad."

"She was good," Antoine said. "Simple stuff. She's been holding out on us."

"I had a little help," I said.

Antoine gave me a look. I stared back at him. I would stop, if they stopped.

"Oh? Who?" Jacques asked.

"Crane," I answered.

Jacques stopped chewing but did not look up at me.

"Who's Crane?" Belinda asked.

I bit into a piece of toast.

"Dad knows him," I said. I could not believe I was saying these things. I had never been the daughter with an attitude or the rebel without a cause.

"I don't remember anyone called Crane," Jacques said.

"He has great recipes," I said. "Grandma knew him."

"I don't know any Crane," Nana said. "Anyone want more orange juice?"

"Grandma Winema," I said.

Everyone looked at me.

"So what are we going to do about the restaurant?" Antoine asked.

The attention shifted away from me.

My father shrugged. "It's our business. We'll take care of it."

My mother stared at her plate.

"But Dad, we all work there," Belinda said. "If the restaurant is going down the tubes, we have a right to know."

"We've had some setbacks," Jacques said. "Your mother and I will take care of it."

"We've been doing so well," Belinda said. "What could have happened?"

"You all spend too much money!" Nana said. "We can cut down on expenses."

"Sure we can," Antoine said. "Will that help?"

Jacques glanced at Alita, who still looked at her plate.

"We don't know what will happen," Jacques said. "You needn't worry."

"Worry? Dad, you're scaring me," Belinda said. "This is our lives."

"Maybe we should get other lives," I said. "More honest ones."

"Jeanne!" my mother said.

"I'll start," I said. "I've had an interesting ten days. First, Johnny stole the scepter."

"What?" Jacques said.

"Yep. I was in such terror that you'd all find out how I had failed this family once again—this wonderful capable honest family full of overachievers. So I chased Johnny down to Las Vegas, then Crystal Springs. I didn't get the scepter, but I met Bear Morrison. I learned from him some interesting things about my birth. He said—"

"Jeanne," Jacques said. "We're eating. This is no time—"

"For what? The truth. The truth is that I was exposed to radiation while Mom was protesting nuclear bomb testing."

Alita looked up at me. Her eyes filled with tears.

Instantly, my anger evaporated. "It wasn't your fault," I said. "I just wondered why it's been this big secret all these years. Why didn't someone tell me?"

"This explains why she's so weird," Belinda said.

"I'm not weird," I said. "Grandma Winema hears the crystal skull talk, too."

"Well, the apple doesn't drop far from the tree," Belinda said.

"You came from the same tree," Antoine said. "And Jeanne, I told you it wasn't a big secret. I knew."

"Well, I didn't," Belinda said.

"Dad heard the skull, too," I said.

Jacques pushed away his plate. "Now I have indigestion, and your mother is crying!"

"You eat too fast," Nana said.

"I followed the scepter to Sosegado," I said. "And the crystal skull helped me cook."

"That must have been something to see," Belinda said.

"Dad, the skull talked to you, too. How could you let everyone think I was crazy?"

"Jacques?" my mother said.

"It was Winema's influence," Jacques said.

"Don't badmouth Grandma," I said.

"She deserted this family," Nana said.

"After Mom and Dad threatened to commit her," I said. "Tell them how you got the deed to the land where the restaurant is now."

"But she was crazy," Alita said.

"She is your mother!" I cried.

"Who was never there," Alita said, "and when she was, she talked to rocks and saw UFOs and had you acting strange, too. I had already lost—" She stopped and wiped her eyes. "I didn't want to lose you."

"You weren't afraid of losing me," Belinda said. "All our lives you pushed Antoine and me to go, go, go. To be these great chefs, to make our ancestors proud. But not her. What did she have to do? She breathed the air, and you were ecstatic."

"We loved you all," Alita said. "Can we talk about something else?"

"You sound like a broken record, Mom," Belinda said. "Where have you been for the last twenty-five years? Where did you go?"

"I've been right here, raising you children," she said.

"No, Mom," Belinda said. "You packed your bags and left long ago."

"Leave her alone," Antoine said.

"No. She's right," Alita said. "I have failed this family. It's my fault we're in trouble."

"Alita," Jacques said. "Enough of this. We've got work to do if we're going to open the restaurant on Tuesday."

"We should talk about this," I said. "Don't you want to know where the scepter and skull are? Don't you want to tell Belinda we really don't have any illustrious ancestors? Can't we just have a normal family discussion?"

"This is a normal family discussion," Antoine said. "Deny and ignore all unpleasantness. It's the American way. The least we could do, *familia,* is let Jeanne cook for us." He winked at me. "And learn the *truth* about her cooking."

I stared at him. What was he saying?

If they wouldn't tell us the truth willingly, we'd trick it out of them via my cooking.

"Yes," I said. "That's a good idea. I want you to see what I can do in the kitchen."

"I'll bring the antacids," Belinda said.

"That would be lovely," Jacques said, obviously relieved that we were onto another topic. "After we open the restaurant new week?"

"No," I said. "Tonight, at the restaurant."

"There's no food there," Alita said. "We won't get deliveries again until Monday."

"I'll go shopping," I said.

My father cleared his throat.

"Yes, Dad. I am capable of shopping for food. I promise

not to poison any of you." I picked up my plate and pushed away from the table. "Let's say five o'clock. In the courtyard."

"It's a little chilly, sweetheart," Alita said.

"We can wear sweaters," I said as I put my plate in the sink. "I'll see you all later."

As I passed the table, my father grabbed my hand.

"Where are the skull and scepter?" he asked quietly.

"I have them," I said. "I'll take them back to the apartment, but I promised Crane you wouldn't lock him in the safe again. See ya."

I hurried up to my bedroom.

"I heard most of that," Crane said. "It's so pathetic, it's funny."

"Yeah, no wonder eating made me sick. These people are tense!"

"You're one of those people."

"Yes, but I never knew that everyone else had bottled up all their emotions. Yuck. You heard about dinner?"

"Yes, *chère*. I hope you understand the consequences of what you're about to do."

"Of course I don't. But I'm tired of secrets. I want to know who I am."

"You need them to spill their guts for you to figure out who are you are?"

"I need them for the truth. And they won't give it to me."

"Do you want the truth or do you want to humiliate them?"

I remembered my mother's tears.

"Winema was right," I said. "Families are too hard. But I can save years of tension with one meal. Don't you think that would be better for everyone?"

"The ends justifying the means?"

I sighed. "Don't confuse me with the facts. You want to come or not?"

"Weren't you supposed to call Miguel?"

I looked at the telephone next to my bed. What would I say? You love me, but I'm a coldhearted woman who can't connect with anything or anyone. A woman in jeopardy of being alone forever.

Speaking of WIJ, I wondered if my grandmother had called the police. I would have to watch the news. Or read the paper.

Later.

Now I had a meal to create.

I stuffed Crane into my suitcase, zipped it up again, and went downstairs with it.

"I'll see you tonight!" I called as I left.

Antoine followed me out to my car.

"You need any help?" he asked.

"Yes, you can help with prep and wait tables."

"Oh! You slay me! How low can I go?"

"Be there or be square, bro."

I got in my wonderfully familiar car and drove away from my parents' house.

Fourteen

Vérité & Verdad

The Oui & Sí was stuffy with disuse. I set Crane on the counter, then opened the windows and the doors into the courtyard.

I scanned cookbooks for recipes and made a list of ingredients.

"I'll be back," I told Crane as I set him on a windowsill.

I got into my car and drove to Ruby's Ranch Market. Once there, I picked out organic red and green peppers, green chile peppers, corn on the cob, a bunch of cilantro, a small head of green cabbage, limes, leeks, acorn squash, Granny Smith apples, jicama, onions, and garlic. As I drove back to the restaurant, I breathed deeply the smell of a garden.

After I put away the groceries, I ate lunch. Crane babbled on about some journey into the wilderness with Montezuma. I wondered what Miguel, Vesta, and Fernando were doing.

Crane and I went up to the apartment. Everything was just as I had left it. My bed was unmade. The black leather couch in my father's office still had a dent in it where I had sat in disbelief after discovering the theft of the scepter.

"The horror, the horror," Crane said.

"I'm sorry," I said. "Does being in here make you uncomfortable?"

"Oh, no. I have great memories of being left alone in the dark for months at a time."

"I get your point."

We went into my bedroom, and I unpacked my suitcase. When I was finished, I held the scepter in my hand.

"I can't believe all that I did to get this back, only to find out it's worthless."

"Didn't Winema say it could be useful to the family?"

"How? I could pretend it is the scepter of kings and queens. Weren't scepters some kind of phallic symbol? Always next to an orb that represented Mother Earth? I guess you're the orb."

"I hardly think I qualify," Crane said.

"If I remember my history, the scepters used to be made out of reed and were ritually broken at the end of the monarch's reign."

"And the orb? What happened to it?"

"Nothing. One shouldn't mess with Momma Earth. Later, of course, a cross was put on the orb. It was the church's oh-so-subtle way of saying the church ruled the Earth."

"Notice I have no cross," Crane said. "I am ruled by no one. Not even myself."

"Tell me the truth, Crane. Do you want to spend the rest of your existence in a crystal skull?"

"Perhaps this is who and what I am."

"Maybe."

I washed a load of clothes, then went down to the kitchen. Time was awasting.

I peeled, seeded, and chopped the acorn squash into tiny pieces. I sang to it while I cut. The orange flesh of it reminded me of the color of a harvest moon.

Crane howled.

I laughed.

"Table queen squash," Crane said. "That's another name for it. Shall we bow down to it?"

"I don't think that's physically possible for you," I said. "So I will bow for both of us."

Next I peeled and chopped the apples.

"Ahh, the apple," Crane said. "Little do you know, *ma chère.*"

"What?" I asked. "You were Johnny Appleseed?"

"If those are magic apples, they could give all of you immortality after you consume them tonight. Would you trade truth for immortality?"

I laughed. "I don't think I have that choice."

"But what if you did? What would you choose?"

"Truth. But ask me again when I'm eighty."

After I cut up the leeks and garlic, I sautéed the squash and apples in olive oil, then added the leeks and garlic. While they cooked, I sliced kernels from the corn cobs. I added water and some of the corn to the mixture and let it simmer.

"I'll call it Truth or Immortality Squash and Corn Soup," I said.

Belinda arrived, carrying a paper sack.

"Did you think of dessert?" she asked.

"No. Would you like to make some?"

"No, but I will," she said, pulling cantaloupes, peaches, and eggs from the bag.

"Thank you, sister," I said.

"Hey, seeesters!" Antoine came into the kitchen. "I am here to be of service."

"All right, then. Shred this cabbage. Then cut these peppers and chiles. Then julienne the jicama."

"Julienne the jicama. Yes, yes. I will help create this mess!" Antoine sang.

"He's off key," Crane said. "I remember eating jicama— which we called *xīcamatl*—on the banks of the Amazon."

"Really? Or are you making this up?"

"I am always truthful."

"OK. So what were you? A man? Woman? Tree."

"You're so fussy about details. I'll tell you I watched pink dolphins swim in the muddy waters of the Amazon while I chewed on jicama."

Belinda stared at me. Antoine chuckled.

"She's talking to the skull," he said.

"Uh-huh." Belinda began cracking eggs into a bowl. "I'll make peach-stuffed melons with meringue, OK?"

"Sounds great," I said.

Belinda glanced at me, then away.

"The peach!" Crane cried, startling me. "Another fruit of immortality. In China, it's called the Tree of the Fairy Fruit. The fruit of Venus! And guess what, *ma petite,* the peach symbolizes truth."

"I don't want symbols. I want the actual truth."

"*Owooooh!*" Crane howled.

Antoine did likewise.

"Can't come from the town of Cantalup, which means 'wolf howl' in Italian, without howling."

"You're speaking of the cantaloupes now?" I said. "You're just full of trivia tonight, aren't you?"

"This is creepy," Belinda said. "It's like cooking with a madwoman."

"You're the one who's always pissed off," I said. "I'm actually having a good time."

"OK. Insane. Ready for the funny farm. Crackers!" Belinda said.

I roasted chile peppers and red peppers while Antoine

chopped. When he was finished, I put all the chopped good-ies in a bowl. I added chopped scallions and cilantro. I threw in sliced pickled jalapeño peppers and minced garlic for good measure. Antoine squeezed lime juice over it, and I ground black pepper into it.

"Looks good," Antoine said.

Belinda leaned over to look. "Very colorful," she said.

"I'll go set up the table," Antoine said.

I dumped a can of tomato puree into a pot to simmer. I chopped a red onion and several garlic cloves and added them to the puree. Then I pulled the skins from the roasted peppers and seeded and chopped them. I stirred the peppers into the pot, then measured out cumin, oregano, chili pow-der, and cayenne. Belinda raised an eyebrow as she watched.

"Hey, I'm new at this," I said.

"I had to use measuring cups and spoons when I started, too," Belinda said.

Then I stirred in canned pinto beans.

"Sorry about the can," I said.

"It'll taste fine," Belinda said.

I added the rest of the sliced corn.

"All done," Antoine said.

"Do you want me to make the pasta?" Belinda asked.

"Let's wait until just before we start," I said.

The three of us sat at the counter, staring at Crane.

"We've got almost a half an hour," Antoine said. "What should we do?"

"I should grate some cheese and chop more cilantro," I said.

"Why do I have the feeling that this is more than an ordi-nary meal?" Belinda asked.

She got up, went to the freezer, and pulled out a box of Neapolitan ice cream. Antoine got three large spoons and handed them all around. We jabbed the ice cream with our spoons at the same time. Laughing, we played a kind of sword spoons until we each came up with a scoop of ice cream.

Silently, we sucked on our spoons.

"No ice cream lore to share with us?" I asked Crane.

"Not a word," he said.

"It was invented by Americans," Belinda said.

"No, Catherine de Medici invented it," Antoine said.

"Who cares?" I said. "It's exquisite."

"Hello, children," my father said behind us, causing the three of us to jump, then laugh.

"Care for some ice cream, Pops?" Antoine offered.

"Maybe later." Jacques smiled as he went up the stairs to the apartment.

I heard Mom and Nana in the courtyard.

"I'll make coffee," Antoine said.

"I'll boil water for the pasta," Belinda said, closing the ice cream and putting it away.

I sprinkled a tiny bit of nutmeg into the soup. Then I grated cheese and added it to the bean-and-pepper sauce. I minced cilantro, then heated flour tortillas in the oven.

Butterflies tickled my stomach. I was cooking for my family!

And I was about to manipulate them into saying things they did not want to say.

"Why don't you get Mom, Dad, and Nana to sit," I said.

"Mom! Dad!" Antoine called up the stairs. "It's soup."

"Gee, thanks," I said.

Nana walked into the kitchen. "This all smells delicious," she said. "Can I help?"

"Um, could you carry out the coleslaw? Antoine, could you take out the soup?"

Alita and Jacques came down the stairs.

"Please," I said. "Go sit."

Belinda poured the water out of the shell pasta, then put the pasta in a serving bowl.

"Thanks," I said. "I'll be right out."

I had chastised all those WIJ people at my grandmother's for the "ends justifying the means." Now here I was, doing the same.

And Paul. Paul had used my cooking to get his business associates to tell the truth.

I did not want to emulate him.

I carried the pasta sauce into the courtyard. The table was alight with candles. One flickered as I came out. A tiny stream of black smoke rose into the dark sky.

The table was beautiful: white tablecloth, gold silverware, crystal goblets Antoine now filled with red wine. Nana's fine china awaited our food. I set down the sauce.

"Wait for me. I'll be right back," I said.

I hurried into the kitchen.

Soon, my father and mother would have to confess all their sins.

I would know all the answers to all my questions.

I would be just like Paul. Just like the WIJ people who left their families in ruins.

I ran upstairs and got the scepter. I returned to the kitchen and carried the skull and scepter into the courtyard. My family was seated around the table, looking at me expectantly.

I set Crane and the scepter in the middle of the table. The fake rubies seemed to deepen in color, looking even bloodier than usual.

I cleared my throat and sat down. Antoine began ladling soup into the bowls. He finished with his bowl, then sat with us. My father picked up his spoon, lowered it into the soup, and brought it up to his mouth.

"Wait," I said.

They all stopped and looked at me.

"I can't do this," I said.

"What? You did poison it?" Belinda asked.

I shook my head. "No. But there is a kind of side benefit to eating my food."

They stared at me.

"Yes?" Nana asked.

"People have to tell the truth after they eat her food," Antoine said. "Or at least they learn their own truths."

"I thought maybe I could get you to finally tell the truth," I said. "It seems like everything is a sham. I've been living in a fog for twenty-five years, and you've raised us on lies. I wanted to hear the truth, but I don't want to force you."

I waited for all of them to tell me how ridiculous I sounded. Truth food, come on!

Instead, my father looked at my mother. She picked up her spoon and began eating my soup. One by one, each family member started eating. In silence, we ate the soup and colorful coleslaw, along with the bean-and-pepper pasta dish. Silverware clicked against china. Light sparkled off crystal. Stars began coming out above us, yet the night remained comfortably warm.

"This is delicious," Alita said. "Extraordinarily so."

"Antoine and Belinda helped," I said.

"Yeah, she can be bossy if she wants to be," Belinda said.

This was a compliment. Belinda had no patience for wilting flowers.

Antoine was the first to tell the truth.

"We visited Grandmother Winema in Mexico," he said. "I had forgotten so much about her. She is wacky." He laughed. "But I like her. I've gotten interested in archeology again. I'm thinking of spending some time with her and then going on some digs."

I waited for Dad's protests, but he remained quiet.

"She told us how she happened to leave us," I said.

"She never was part of this family," Nana said. "She always had her head buried in the past. You couldn't get her to commit to the here and now. When your grandpa Juarez died, she had a rough time. She was suicidal. We were afraid she'd hurt herself. We had to get her help."

"I never understood her," Alita said. "She thought differently than I did. We never had a normal household. I don't know how she ever had the time to actually birth me. But she did make me believe that we had a responsibility to this world, to make it better. So I went to peace demonstrations. I protested the bomb. I never went when I was pregnant, but then I did, when I was pregnant with Jeanne, just once. I can't remember why now. I didn't know it, Jeanne, but we were downwind to the test." She wiped tears from her eyes. "I knew immediately something was wrong. It was as if when the bomb exploded, I felt the pain of everyone who had died in Nagasaki and Hiroshima and beyond that. The very Earth seemed shattered. Like an electric shock treatment. It was as if with each bomb blast, the planet was given an electric shock. A terrible one. Wiping out part of the planet's brain. With each bomb blast, something was lost. But I didn't know what. The ability to clean the air? Regulate viruses and bacteria? Repair the ozone? All this happened in a millisecond." She began sobbing.

"We were protective of Jeanne," Jacques said, "after she was born because we almost lost her. We were grateful she was alive. Then Grandma Winema seemed to be teaching you strange things, and you'd get that faraway look. I know now she was teaching you meditation and things like that. She wanted you to stay connected to this world, but back then she just scared us. And angered me. She wanted to put a UFO shop or something where the restaurant was. I thought that was nuts! I was trying to feed my family. The land seemed like our only hope." My father looked at me. "It was wrong what we did. We shouldn't have threatened to commit her. We just wanted to save our family."

"Don't use us as an excuse," Belinda said. "We were doing OK. You just wanted a valuable piece of real estate to do with as you pleased."

Jacques took a sip of wine. His hand shook slightly. "I suppose you're right," he said. "I was tired of being poor."

Belinda shook her head. "I've hated Grandma all these years for leaving us. And you drove her away. And what did Jeanne say at breakfast about our illustrious ancestors? Do we have any?"

Jacques breathed deeply. "None that I know of. I was a short-order cook. Dad worked in a gas station when he wasn't dead drunk."

"Jacques!" Nana said.

"It's true," he said. "My real name is Jack Flame. I don't even know if I'm French."

"I'm French," Nana said. "There's nothing wrong with pulling yourself up out of the mud."

"It is wrong if you lie and cheat to get out," Jacques said.

"I never believed that crap, anyway," Antoine said.

"I can forgive all that," I said, "but, Daddy, how could you have let everyone think I was crazy? The skull talked to you, too."

Jacques cleared his throat. "Yes, it did."

"Jacques!" my mother said.

"It started soon after Jeanne was born," he said. "I thought I was going crazy. When I said I wanted to be a chef, he started helping me with recipes. I guess I just pretended it was my imagination until you said you heard it. That scared me. My little girl. I thought you might disappear, too. It wasn't rational. I thought we'd lose you, too."

"You keep saying that! Lose me, too? Disappear, too. What do you mean?"

"Nothing," Jacques said. "It was just that your mother had started gambling heavily," Jacques said. "She was always gone. I felt as though I had lost her, and I didn't want you to go, too."

I frowned.

"After you told us the skull talked to you," Alita said. "I gave up gambling. I had lapses every once in a while. But I stopped. And then I started again this past year. I don't know why. I just started feeling lost. They still bomb the desert, did you know that?" She looked at my father. "I gambled away everything. We are going to lose the restaurant because I have gotten us so far into debt."

The world became infinitely silent.

"So you see, we lied and tricked and stole for nothing," Alita said.

"We still have our family," my father said. "We'll work it out."

Alita shook her head. "We lost our family the second I put those children in jeopardy out in the Nevada desert."

"Children?" I said. "I thought Antoine and Belinda stayed at home."

"They did," my mother said. She looked at my father, then across the table at me, her eyes shiny with tears. For the first time in a long while, she was in her eyes. "Your father and I never told anyone, but I was pregnant with twins."

Gasps fluttered the candlelight.

"Your brother died just after birth," Alita said. "You screamed when his little heart stopped."

I remembered my vision. The man with my smile. I could still feel his hand on my cheek, and mine on his. I had slept in his arms in my mother's womb. His body was the first I had ever touched. And the first who ever touched me.

He was who I had longed for all my life.

"I had taken a gamble on your lives without really knowing it," Alita said. "And I lost."

"And you think gambling in Las Vegas is going to make up for that?" Antoine asked gently.

"I don't know what I think."

"The doctors said the explosion had nothing to do with his death," my father said, patting Alita's hand.

"So I had a baby brother," Antoine said.

"You all did," Jacques said. "He was born after Jeanne."

Tears streamed down my cheeks. We sat silently for a long time.

Finally my grandmother said, "This was good, Jeanne, but the soup could have used some salt."

"Maybe a little cream, too?" Belinda suggested.

"And sour cream in the pasta dish," Antoine said.

I laughed. No one at La Magia had ever criticized my food—except for the cinnamon eggs. And suddenly I knew it was gone. My reign as the truthful chef was over.

"I'm sorry it took your food to get us to tell the truth," Jacques said.

"Actually, I don't think it was the food," I said.

"Does he have a grave?" Belinda asked. "And a name?"

"We called him Jean," Jacques said. "Or John. We can take you to the cemetery."

"I'll go put in dessert," Belinda said.

Antoine began picking up dirty dishes.

"He was a beautiful baby," Alita said. "He looked just like you. For a while, we thought we'd lose both of you. All of us in the delivery room could see how shattered you were. You kept reaching—" Her voice broke. "You kept reaching your arms—spastic as they were. And I could not calm you. It wasn't me you wanted."

Jacques wiped his eyes and stared into space.

Minutes later, Antoine and Belinda brought the melons straight from the oven, the meringue golden brown.

"So what are we going to do about the restaurant?" Antoine said.

"We?" Jacques said. "You're going to be an archeologist. And what about you, Belinda?"

"Me? Well, Denton and I are engaged."

"What?" Jacques said. "Congratulations!"

"Who's Denton?" I asked.

Antoine nudged me.

"Oh, the nice-looking guy with the glasses I met at Fourth of July?"

Belinda nodded.

"Congratulations, darling," Alita said.

"Besides that, I like cooking," she said. "I like managing. I'd like to manage the restaurant someday."

"I'd like to take a trip to France," Nana said.

"I want to travel," Alita said. "Plant a garden. Make love on the beach."

"Mom!" Belinda said.

"That's OK with me," Jacques said. "I can always work as a short-order cook again."

"Those were fun times," Antoine said. "We lived in an apartment, and you'd bring home these delicious huge juicy hamburgers."

"With greasy fries," Belinda said.

Mom crinkled her nose.

Dad looked around. "I will miss this place."

"Break the scepter," Crane said.

I glanced at my father, but he didn't appear to have heard Crane.

"Why?" I whispered. "Are we ending the monarchy?"

"Just do it."

"Is this like the cinnamon eggs?" I asked.

"No," Crane said. "I promise."

I picked up the scepter. "Grandmother Winema gave the scepter and skull to me," I said to the family. "Even though they were hers."

"We should thank her," Jacques said.

"Break it," Crane said.

I moved to the statue of Saint Brigid behind my father. I raised the scepter and brought it down hard on her gray concrete feet.

The scepter shattered. And something dark poured from the hollow inside. I knelt to the ground. Ruby-colored stones shone in the light. I picked up the rocks, one at a time, and piled them on the table.

My father picked up one and held it toward the light. Then he handed it to my mother.

"Rubies," she whispered. "Real rubies. My mother used to talk about the rubies the villagers offered her and my father, along with the skull. But she told me she hadn't taken them."

"Your father took them and hid them," I said. "Winema found them when she left here. I guess she figured we—the family—might need them now."

I picked up Crane and kissed his glassy forehead. "Thank you."

"It was nothing."

Fifteen

Mon Cher

I dreamed my brother and I ran through the desert together, hand in hand. When we stopped, I gazed at the man with my smile.

"You belong here," he whispered.

Then bright light engulfed us. In a flash, it was over. I was alone, and only the bones of my brother remained, sculpted into clear glass by the heat of the blast.

"Come back," I whispered.

I looked down, and the skull sat at my feet. I picked him up and stared into his ruby eyes.

I awakened crying. And cradled Crane in my lap.

I ate an early breakfast of fruit.

Then Jacques drove the family to the cemetery. This was Scottsdale, so the grounds were green, nearly all signs of desertification driven out. Shivering in the early morning, we walked amongst the tombstones until we came to a grave with the tiny tombstone that read, JEAN LES FLAMBEAUX, SON AND BROTHER.

My mother knelt and laid two red roses in front of the tombstone.

"It's really nice here," she said. "I just come here and sit sometimes."

But he's not here, I wanted to say. *He's not here!*

My father put his arm around my waist. We stood together for a moment. Nana touched the top of the headstone and whispered something. Antoine and Belinda went back to the car, arm in arm. Alita and Nana followed. Then my father.

I glanced around at the well-manicured grounds.

My brother was not here.

On the way home, I rode with my mother and father.

"I called my banker," Jacques said. "Your grandmother's gift will save the restaurant. I called her and offered her the restaurant. She said to give it to you."

"To me!" I said. "I don't want it." I looked out the window. "I don't know what I want."

"We'll invest what's left and then let you each decide what to do with your share," Jacques said.

"But the whole family wanted you to have some extra," Alita said.

"Oh, no. I don't want Belinda to be resentful for another twenty years."

"It was partially her idea," Jacques said.

"I guess the truth serum has worn off," I said.

They laughed. My mother turned around and handed me a ruby-red pouch. Inside were several rubies, including two cut rubies shaped somewhat like eyes.

I closed the pouch. "Thank you," I said.

"What would you like to do now?" Jacques asked. "Everyone else told us their wish."

"I think I'd like to take a trip," I said.

When we got home, I packed my suitcase again, slipping Crane into the soft middle.

I hugged and kissed everyone good-bye, even Belinda, who bussed my cheek. My mother took my chin in her hand. "Look, Jacques," she said. "She's in her eyes."

I smiled. "You, too, Mom." I hugged her. "It wasn't your fault. It was good you were out there trying to make things better. We all want to change the world."

"Didn't John Lennon say that?" Antoine said.

I let my mother go, and Antoine slapped my butt. "Call us when you get to where you're going."

My father kissed me. "Thanks for dinner."

I laughed.

"Be careful," Nana said.

"You're all crazy," I said. "See you soon."

Once in the car, I set Crane on the windowsill. Singing most of the way, we headed down the highway toward Las Vegas. I drove too fast, but I wanted to make Crystal Springs before dark.

It didn't work. I got tired and had to stop to eat and get gas.

I waved to the lights of Las Vegas, and Crane shouted to Lady Liberty as we drove by the city and onto the road into the desert. The sun had set, and the world was dark. When I got to Crystal Springs, I had to drive around for a while before I found the dirt driveway to the temple.

I turned off the car and sat in the darkness for a few minutes. Then I picked up the flashlight and Crane, and I got out of the car. I shined the light on the temple, said hello to the darkness and the figures inside, then clumsily followed the path down and away from the temple to a small wooden building. I knocked on the door.

No answer. I tried the door, and it opened easily. Inside was one small room—two if I counted the toilet and tiny shower as a separate room.

The place was not much bigger than Paul's office. A cot at

one end, refrigerator, sink, and desk at the other. I set Crane on the desk and read the square cardboard note: "Make yourself at home. Blessings, Bear."

"Well, here we are, Crane," I said, opening the refrigerator. I took out bottled water, raspberry jam, almond butter, and bread. I drank the water and made a sandwich out of the others.

"Why are we here?" Crane asked.

"You said before that you wanted to stay here," I said.

"That was then," Crane said.

"Well, sleep on it," I said between mouthfuls.

"Easy for you to say."

I heard few sounds as I tried to sleep—distant traffic, an occasional insect, Crane singing.

I dreamed I walked outside near the temple. The pads on my paws pressed against the hard ground, still warm with day. The air smelled of darkness, and I lifted my head and howled. The other coyotes answered.

I slept until just before dawn. When I awakened, my hands and feet had bits of desert sand on them.

I picked up Crane and went out into the chilly gray morning. The temple looked gray for a moment, too. I stepped inside. Everything was as it had been: Sekhmet, *Madre del Mundo,* Virgin of Guadalupe.

I sat cross-legged on the cool floor with Crane between my legs. I pulled the pouch from my pants pocket and shook out the two ruby eyes.

The gray sharpened into pink. Scrub became gold and rose. Sekhmet got a bit of gold on her black skin. Crane became red with dawn.

"Crane, do you remember who you are?"

"What do you mean, *ma petite?*"

"Do you remember when you first became a part of this skull?" I asked.

"Wasn't I always?"

"Do you really think so?" I asked.

He sighed. "I don't know, *ma petite*. I don't know."

The desert started getting lighter: gold, red, and pink. A jay squawked; a coyote hurried through the desert in the near distance.

"Do you want to know the truth about yourself?" I asked.

"Yes, but I can't eat your food."

"I think I can help."

I slipped one ruby eye into each of Crane's empty sockets.

Suddenly everything shifted as it had before down in the Organ Pipe Cactus Monument. The sun streaked across the desert and pierced Crane's ruby eyes.

The coyote looked up, stopped, and was a man, sitting, watching us. The jay flowed into a woman running. The brush shimmered, shook, and then burst into flames.

My brother held his hand down for me. I took it and stood. We looked into each other's eyes.

"You left me," I whispered.

"In a flash," he said. "I could not bear the unbearable one more time. But then I guess I couldn't leave all the way. I forgot who I was."

"But you knew so much. The recipes, Cortés, Joan of Arc, Montezuma."

He laughed. Crane's laugh. He sounded like Antoine. I had not noticed that before.

"You don't remember before this lifetime?" he asked.

"I live in the present," I said.

He laughed. "Obviously, *ma petite*."

We embraced. I wanted to sink into he who was my brother, he who had shared my mother's quiet womb for all those months.

"Don't go," I whispered. "You're the only one I love."

"Oh, *ma chère*," he said. "That's not true."

"Where will you go now?" I asked.

"Who knows."

"Is any of it true?" I asked.

"What?"

"Montezuma, the Fire People, Jeanne d'Arc, the food."

"Does it matter?" he asked.

"This matters," I said, holding him tightly.

"I will never leave you, coyote cowgirl," he whispered.

"And I will never leave you."

We slowly let each other go.

"Eat hearty," he said.

Then he turned and walked away, his black hair flowing behind him. He was so beautiful. I watched until he was a raven. Then dust. Then sun rays. The burning bushes shook off their fire. The jay became a bird.

I reached down to the crystal skull and plucked out its eyes. The world shifted again.

"Crane?" I whispered.

Silence.

My brother was gone.

A tiny dust tornado whirled past the temple.

Was that him?

Maybe. But dust tornadoes didn't tell bad jokes. Or sing off-key.

I set the crystal skull on Sekhmet's lap.

"Thanks," I whispered.

I put the rubies in my pocket and kissed *Madre del Mundo*'s forehead. Then I left the temple in the desert and drove away.

I drove in silence all day. No radio. No Crane. Past Las Vegas, Scottsdale, and Tucson, stopping along the way for food and gas.

In Sosegado, I parked the car out in front of La Magia. It looked as though they were in the middle of dinner rush.

I switched on the radio as I watched the people walking to

and fro inside La Magia. A sign hung across the front of the restaurant: UNDER NEW MANAGEMENT.

". . . Police now say persons involved in the so-called WIJ kidnappings have all been accounted for. No charges have been filed. . . ." I switched off the radio.

"Good for you, Grandma."

I got out of the car and walked to the phone booth next door at Madame Wu's. I called my house. Antoine answered.

"Hey," I said.

"Hey, yourself. Did you hear about Grandma Winema? I guess you made an impression on her, after all."

"I guess," I said.

"I called her," he said. "She's thinking of doing what you suggest. Help train people to be a part of this world, without losing hope and getting burned out. She sounds excited. She even said she'd be willing to see Mom and Dad. Maybe in neutral territory."

"Like in Sosegado."

"She did mention that."

"That's where I am."

"You going to stay awhile?" he asked.

"I don't know. We'll see. This is where I am right now. Bye, big brother."

"Don't be a stranger," he said. "Well, no stranger than usual."

I laughed and hung up the telephone.

The little red car drove up to the restaurant. Miguel got out. The neon light blued his face. My stomach fluttered.

"Miguel," I whispered.

Somehow he heard.

He turned to me and smiled. I grinned. My chest hurt. He was not my brother. He was not that part of me I had been missing. But I did love him.

I hurried to him, and we hugged. I felt his chest press

against mine, his thighs against mine, our arms wrapped around the other. I laughed. Yes. This was all right.

We kissed.

"What took you so long?" Miguel asked.

"Not so long," I said. "I've got a lot to tell you. Tangiers is safe, by the way. She's in Mexico."

"Really?" he asked. We walked arm in arm to the back door of the restaurant. "I have a few tales myself. Paul is in jail. He *was* in jail, actually. He didn't have money for bail at first."

I glanced at the "new management" sign.

"At first?" I said. "He got the money? Who's the new owner?"

We stepped into the busy kitchen. Vesta stood at the stove, Fernando at the island, and Nathan by the dishwasher. A sweet young girl handed Vesta an order.

"Whew. It's awfully busy," the teenage girl said.

"Spare me the young!" Vesta cried.

"Meet the new owner," Miguel said, looking at his mother.

"Congratulations, Vesta," I said.

Fernando looked up and grinned. I hugged his waist.

"Hiya, sugar," I said.

"Oh, so it's you!" Vesta said. "Don't just stand there! We've got people to feed. This little girl here doesn't know tea from coffee, enchiladas from burritos."

The girl opened her mouth but said nothing. I smiled.

"Vesta, don't be so hard on her," I said. "I'll help you out. But just tonight."

"Yeah, sure. Put on an apron and get going."

I turned to Miguel and kissed him hard on his luscious lips.

"I love you," I said. "See you later."

"I love you, too," he said. "I'll be out front. Momma, you behave."

He smiled and weaved around us and went into the dining room.

I went to the island sink and washed my hands.

"So what's been happening?" I asked.

"It seems now that when people eat food Fernando has touched, it makes them declare their heart's desires," Vesta said. "You know, love stuff. It's been so syrupy in here listening to people talk about love that I've been sticking to the floor."

Fernando grinned, and I laughed.

"How about you, girl who is in her eyes," Vesta said. "Everything all right?"

I picked up a piece of chopped red pepper, fresh from Fernando's knife and fingers, and popped it into my mouth.

"I am quite content," I said, grinning.

I was a woman in joy.

Appendix

Recipes from La Magia
by Jeanne Les Flambeaux
à la Crane

CRANE: *Cooking is not a science,* ma petite! *You ask for amounts, ingredients! Hah! Use your intuition! Use the seasons of the year! It all depends if you like something, say, very hot, or if you are not so adventurous, like Hernán Cortés. If he had only taken off that* stupide *armor, maybe he would not have been so ill-mannered. . . .*

JEANNE: I will try to give you the correct ingredients, but I agree with Crane on this—and Vesta. Cooking is about feeling. And taste. I use very little salt or cheese. If it isn't flavorful to you, you can always add salt, cayenne, cheese. In most of the recipes where I call for eggs, you can substitute scrambled tofu if you want it to be vegan. I use fresh organic ingredients, except for the occasional canned tomatoes or beans. If I use canned, the contents are organic with no additives. These recipes generally serve about four, depending upon your appetites. Have fun; eat hearty! Maybe you'll find the truth, too.

CRANE: *Ah,* ma petite! *What is truth?* La vérité? *I had a conversation with Jeanne d'Arc on this very issue, but her voices kept interrupting me, so I wasn't able to make my point.*

Green Rice

5	large leaves tender green lettuce (any lettuce except iceberg)
2	garlic cloves
3	chile peppers, roasted
¼	cup minced onion
1	small bunch cilantro leaves
½	bunch fresh tender parsley (if not tender, eliminate the parsley and use more cilantro, more lettuce, or both)
3½	cups water
2	cups brown rice
3	tablespoons olive oil

Puree everything except the rice and olive oil. Heat the oil in a large pan, and add the rice. Cook until the mixture is translucent, stirring often. (If you don't want to sauté, just put the rice in the pan, and add the puree.) Either way you do it, bring rice and liquid to a boil, cook for a minute, reduce the heat to low, and cover and simmer until done, about 20 to 35 minutes, until the water is gone but the rice is not sticking to the pan. Garnish with cilantro and lime.

Serve with raw or lightly steamed sliced zucchini, refried beans, and a mixed green salad with tomatoes or red cabbage for color. Green rice is a great side dish, especially when served with enchiladas.

(Don't forget presentation! It must look good enough to kiss. It's all about l'amour! Especially with food.)

Green Rice Redux and Eggs with Salsa

8 eggs

Pinch of cayenne

¼ cup olive oil (use enough to coat the rice but not so much it comes out oily)

4 cups leftover Green Rice (page 274)

4 chile peppers (your choice of what kind of pepper)

Salsa

Whisk the eggs in a medium bowl. Add a pinch of cayenne (or a lot if you like it *hot*). Heat up the oil in a large skillet over medium heat. Toss in the rice, and heat it. Then make a hole in the middle of the rice. Pour the eggs into the rice. Cook them for a bit. As they start to set, mix them together with the rice.

Divide among 4 plates, and serve with chile peppers, salsa, Vesta's Bread (pages 277–78), and lots of orange juice (or beer).

(Green is the best color, ma chérie. The color of la vida! Also the color of dead and molding things, true enough. Still, think of it as Nature's color, and munch away.)

Thyme for Pasta, Red Peppers, and Zukes

2 tablespoons olive oil (again, use enough to sauté the food and not burn it, but not so much it comes out oily)

½ small red onion, chopped

1 large red bell pepper, minced

3 large garlic cloves, minced or pressed

2 medium zucchini, cut into matchsticks

Freshly ground black pepper

1 tablespoon fresh thyme (or 1 teaspoon dried)

Enough pasta for 4 people (spaghetti-style works best, either wheat or rice)

Heat olive oil in a large skillet. On medium heat, sauté the onion until it softens. (You need to stir this dish nearly constantly.) Add red peppers and half the garlic. Sauté until the red peppers just begin to soften. Then add the zucchini. Add the rest of the garlic. (Add salt if you really *must.*) Cook for about 5 to 7 minutes. Make certain the veggies are not mushy. Zukes should be green. Add gads of fresh pepper and the thyme. Remove from the heat.

Cook the pasta, but don't let it get too done. (*That's* al dente *moi dearest,* al dente.) Toss pasta with the red peppers and zucchini in individuals bowls. Serve with a mixed green salad or sliced peeled cucumbers.

Pinto Bean Soup

3   cups dried pinto beans (rinse these well and soak them overnight in water)
3   tablespoons olive oil
1   garlic bulb (at least 10 cloves), minced or pressed
3   medium onions, coarsely chopped
1   (28-ounce) can ground peeled tomatoes (no preservatives or any additives, except salt) *(Yes,* moi petite *the canned love apples are better than the fresh tomatoes in this recipe! Believe it or not.)*
½   teaspoon coriander or several sprigs fresh chopped cilantro

Let the pinto beans drain for 30 minutes before cooking. Heat the oil in a large pot. When a drop of water will sizzle in the pot, add the pinto beans. Keep them moving constantly as you sauté them for 4 to 5 minutes. If they start to stick or burn, add a bit more oil. Add water, about double the level of the beans. Cook for 4 hours. (Add more water if needed, depending upon how watery or thick you like your soups.) After the 4 hours, add the garlic and onion. Cook for another hour. Add the tomatoes and coriander. Cook for another hour.

You can always add Monterey Jack cheese and salsa to this soup if it feels too plain to you. Serve with Vesta's Bread (pages 277–78).

Très Simple Petit Déjeuner

5 or 6 oranges per person
Vesta's Bread (pages 277–78)
1   washed pear per person

Squeeze the orange juice. *(You can do it,* mon ami! *It is good for your arms! I taught King Louis how. I can teach you, too.)* Lightly toast a slice of Vesta's Bread. Thinly slice the pears.

Spiral the pear slices on the plates. *(Presentation is everything, remember! You can dress up the Emperor-with-no-clothes, but you can't undress him.* What does that mean, Crane? *Oh,* ma petite! *It is a Zen thing. Which I invented, you know. Or at least I influenced Miss Zen in her thinking. . . .)*

Vesta's Bread

Take any yeasted bread recipe, and prepare the dough. As you knead the dough, think about what makes you happy. Make general wishes for all who will eat it: wish them happiness, love, good health, prosperity. Even if you don't think this will make any difference, it is more fun than thinking about doing the laundry or paying the bills while you're kneading the dough!

Eggs, Cold as Rice, and Vegetables

4 garlic cloves, minced or pressed
½ tablespoon minced fresh ginger
2 tablespoons olive oil (experiment with this amount—you don't want the food oily or burnt)
   Combine several of the following vegetables to make 2½ to 3 cups: diced carrots, minced red peppers, green peas, sliced snow peas, or sliced zucchini.
4 cups cooked rice (preferably cold)
4 eggs, beaten
1 cup fresh skinned, seeded, and chopped tomatoes
Juice of ½ lime

In a wok, sauté garlic and ginger in the olive oil. When golden, take them out and reserve them for later. Stir-fry the veggies until just cooked. (Start with the carrots; end with the zukes.) Remove the veggies. Heat the rice. Make a hole in the middle. Pour in the eggs. After they begin to set, stir them in with the rice. Add the tomatoes, and the sautéed garlic and ginger, and stir. Then return the vegetables to the pan. (If you want it hot, add chile sauce or salsa.) Drizzle with lime juice.

(Does it seem we are obsessed with eggs? They are tidy bits of creation, aren't they? Round. Shiny and smooth. Perfection. All the secrets of the world inside. But wait, you wanted to hear about eggs, not about my brilliance, eh?)

La Toast Française

2 eggs (more if you like it richer)
1 cup milk (more if you start to run out)
½ teaspoon vanilla extract
¼ to ½ teaspoon cinnamon
Pinch of grated nutmeg
Pinch of ground clove
Zest of 1 small orange
8 slices of thick stale (but not hard) bread or fresh bread
1 tablespoon olive oil
Powdered white sugar.

Beat together the eggs, milk, vanilla, cinnamon, nutmeg, clove, and orange zest. Soak the bread in the mixture, coating both sides. Cook the bread in the olive oil, letting one side brown (and harden slightly) before turning it over to do the other side. Once on the plate, dust the up-side with powdered white sugar, and sprinkle with more cinnamon. (Leave off the sugar if you wish.)

This dish was originally called German Toast. During one of the large wars when anything German was *verboten*, restaurateurs began calling it French Toast, and *voilà!* What is German for *voilà?*

Lasagna Primavera

3 cloves garlic, minced or pressed
1 medium or large chopped onion
1 teaspoon olive oil
2 (28-ounce) cans crushed peeled tomatoes
Dash of freshly ground black pepper
Pinch of hot pepper flakes
12 to 14 lasagna noodles

1 medium zucchini, thinly sliced
1 bunch spinach, cleaned and stems removed
½ pound mozzarella cheese, grated
½ pound ricotta cheese
¼ pound Parmesan cheese, grated (plus more for topping)

Sauté the garlic and onion in the olive oil until the onion starts to soften. Add the tomatoes, black pepper and hot pepper flakes. Let the sauce simmer. Cook the lasagna noodles. Steam the zucchini for 5 minutes at the most. (No mushy vegetables for us!) Take the zucchini slices out of the steamer. Steam the spinach for a minute or two.

In a deep dish, start with a layer of the sauce, then a layer of lasagna noodles, a layer of spinach leaves, layer of zucchini slices, and a layer of each of the three cheeses. Keep layering until you run out of ingredients. Finish with a layer of noodles, and top with a dusting of Parmesan cheese.

Bake for 1 hour at 350° F.

Serve this lasagna with Vesta's bread and a mixed green salad.

If you want a little crunch in your lasagna, steam sliced carrots—but not for too long—and add those to your vegetable layer.

The Truth-Telling Feast

Truth or Immortality
Squash and Corn Soup

1 pound acorn or butternut squash, peeled, seeded, and finely
   chopped (about 3 cups)
3 tart apples, peeled, cored, and finely chopped

2   tablespoons olive oil
3   medium leeks, sliced
1   clove garlic, minced or pressed
1½ cups frozen corn, or the corn from 1 cob
4   cups broth (or water)
4 to 6 scallions, minced

Sauté the squash and apples in the olive oil for about 5 minutes. Add the leeks and garlic, and sauté for 5 minutes. Add the corn and broth. Simmer the soup for about 20 minutes. Garnish it with the minced scallions.

(The lovely squash has been in the Americas for at least six thousand years! That's even older than moi, *I believe. It is said that if you eat squash, you can see the Invisibles as well as the Visibles. Try it. You might even see me. Or am I a Visible? A Visible but an Inaudible? Or an Audible? I'm suddenly at a loss for words. The horror, The horror!)*

Colorful Coleslaw

½   teaspoon honey
3   tablespoons fresh lime juice
⅓   green cabbage shredded, (about 3 cups)
¼   red cabbage, shredded (must be fresh and tender—leave out if it isn't)
½   red pepper, diced
½   yellow pepper, diced (or add more red pepper if yellow is not available)
1   anaheim chile pepper, diced
1   jalapeño pepper (omit if you like a milder slaw)
½   cup jicama (or daikon radish), julienned
2   scallions, chopped
1 or 2 cloves of garlic, minced or pressed
Salt and freshly ground pepper

Dissolve about ½ teaspoon of the honey into the lime juice. Combine all the veggies in a large bowl. Toss with the honey mixture. Add salt and black pepper, to taste. Add more lime and honey, to taste.

(What can I say about cabbage that has not already been said? Of course, it was not said by moi! *In Greece* B.C.E., *if you stole cabbage, you could get the death sentence. Luckily, I was never caught. . . .)*

Pasta Sauce

1   pasilla chile pepper (hot) or 1 anaheim chile pepper (mild) roasted and chopped

2   large red bell peppers, roasted and chopped

1   cup canned tomato puree or crushed peeled tomatoes

1   medium red onion, chopped

3   garlic cloves, minced or pressed

2   teaspoons ground cumin

2   tablespoons fresh oregano (or 2 teaspoons dried)

1 to 2 teaspoons chili powder

Pinch of cayenne

1   tablespoon lemon juice

1½ cups kidney beans (cooked or canned)

Corn kernels from one ear of corn

Serve over pasta or brown rice

Roast the chile peppers and red peppers: The best way to roast peppers is to preheat the oven to 500° F. Cut the peppers into pie pieces; remove their seeds and stems. Put them on a lightly oiled baking sheet with the skins up. Put them in the oven, close to the heating element. The skin will begin to blister. When most of the skin is blistered (but the pepper isn't burnt), remove the peppers, put them in a bowl, and cover the bowl. The slices will steam up. After about 15 minutes, dip your fingers in cold water, and then peel the skins off the peppers.

Heat the tomato puree. Let it simmer. Add the onion and garlic. After the onion has softened, stir in the roasted peppers. Stir in the cumin, oregano, chili powder, cayenne, and lemon juice. Add the beans and corn. Prepare the pasta. Spoon the sauce over pasta.

(I cannot tell you everything I know about beans in mixed company—the living and the undead. But I can say beans will help you in the area of l'amour. *The Romans believed their dead lived in beans. Maybe* lived *is the wrong word. Perhaps they resided in the beans? At midnight, the Romans had bean-throwing ceremonies for their ancestors. They really knew how to live it up, those Roman patriarchs, didn't they?)*

Howling Good Lemon Meringue Melon

2   cantaloupes, cut in half crosswise and seeded
About ⅓ cup strawberries, blueberries, or huckleberries (or some of each)
2 peaches, peeled and sliced
1   cup plain or lemon yogurt (omit if you want it to be dairy-free)
2 large eggs, whites only
2   tablespoons honey, liquid
Dash of cream of tartar
2   teaspoons vanilla extract

Preheat the oven to 450° F. Slice off the bottoms of the cantaloupes so that they will rest flat. Take out some of the melon to widen the bowl. Cut up these melon parts. Combine the cut-up melon with the berries, peaches, and yogurt in a medium bowl. Divide this mixture into the 4 melon halves.

Whip the egg whites and honey together until it begins to stiffen. Add the cream of tartar, and beat some more. Fold in the vanilla. Spoon the egg whites over the filled melon cavities. Bake for 3 to 5 minutes, until browned.

(Beware of this feast, or any truth-telling food. The truth isn't always what we want, moi dear, is it? But you are different, aren't you? You can take it. Eyes wide open. Greet the day. C'est la vie!)